SCENT OF A MATE
The Gallize Series

978-1-940651-06-4

Cover Design and Interior Format
© KILLION
THE
GROUP INC.

SCENT OF A MATE

DIANNA LOVE

PRAISE FOR THE LEAGUE OF GALLIZE SHIFTERS SERIES

GRAY WOLF MATE

"Gray Wolf Mate is a brilliant start to this epic new series." ~Clare & Lou's Mad About Books

"Dianna Love once again gives us another wonderful series for us to savor and follow." ~ The Reading Cafe

"Gray Wolf Mate is the first in an exciting new shifter series by the fantastic Dianna Love. There are shifters and then there are Gallize Shifters." ~ In My Humble Opinion

MATING A GRIZZLY

"A remarkable story with characters that knock heads and hips and holds you hostage until the last page.!! Loved it!!" ~ Amazon reviewer

"The League Of Gallize Shifters is definitely original in many areas, and I was totally intrigued during every compelling incident." ~ Always Reviewing

"Mating A Grizzly is a smart shifter romance that had me thinking about it long after the last page." ~ In My Humble Opinion

STALKING HIS MATE

"This story is an emotional thriller that will keep you wondering what will happen next. And the author surprises you at every junction." ~Amazon reviewer

DEDICATION

Thank you Judy Carney for your enthusiasm, the amazing work you perform each time, and always being willing to help in any way.

PRONUNCIATION GUIDE

Baatar –*BAH tar*
Cadell – *kah DELL*
Gallize – *gah LEEZ*
Ganbaatar *(or Gan)* – *GAN bah tar*
Gemelo – *heh MEL o*
Isleen – *IZ leen*
Jazlyn – *JAZZ len*
Siofra - *sheef RAH*
Teàrlach - CH-EH-R-lack

CHAPTER 1

———————

Near Balsam Grove, North Carolina

TITANIUM HANDCUFFS HAD A CLEAR advantage over steel cuffs when dealing with a nonhuman. For one, they possessed the highest strength-to-weight ratio between the two metals.

More than that, titanium contained a dangerous shifter better than any other known metal.

Scarlett had used those cuffs more than once to manacle a shifter perpetrator, but she couldn't dig up any appreciation for the pair locked on *her* wrists at the moment.

The damned hyena was lucky she hadn't ripped his face off when he cuffed her, but that would have defeated the purpose of getting caught.

Every time her captor yanked the eight-foot length of thick chain attached to the cuffs, he gouged a new wound into her wrists. How much farther did they have to go?

She lifted her gaze, searching through trees not yet changing to fall colors in early September, and spotted his destination.

A fifty-foot-long commercial trailer used for over-the-road hauling stood thirty yards away in the North Carolina forest. Someone with no artistic talent had painted LAUGHING DOG FREIGHT LINES over the dirty white side with rust eating up the back corner. The Pagan Nomads mixed pack of shifters hadn't hunted the Great Smoky Mountains National Park in over two years. Why now?

The grungy predator with a dark buzz cut, thick neck, and wide forehead muttered to himself. He slowed, looked over his shoulder, and made a gruff groan, then continued on.

What? Did he think she'd left him?

Not yet. Not until she got what she came for.

He made a disgusting snort that sounded amused, probably looking forward to shoving her in that trailer and bolting the door.

That could not happen.

Someone would bleed.

Of course, that threat would carry more weight if her wrists weren't bound. She'd put herself in dangerous situations more times than she cared to admit, but she'd face a *rabid* hyena shifter any day over being locked in a box … or cage.

She slowed her steps, mentally prepared to pay a price for provoking a hyena shifter with the personality of a wild hog left hungry for a week. His size advantage over her wouldn't be an issue if not for titanium stifling her ability to shift.

Six-and-a-half feet of malevolent halitosis.

Hal for short.

He had the strange pack tattoo of fangs with a P and N initials in runic letters on the back of his hand. The Pagan Nomads made a living by trafficking shifters, mostly females.

Time to test Hal's patience. She took another step and stopped.

The chain tightened and slid through his loose grasp.

He snarled and twisted around, letting out a high-pitched cackle. People mistook the giggling hyena sound for laughter, when it normally meant the opposite. That had been a warning.

Baring his blood-stained fangs, he said, "Don't fuck with me, bitch. You may be used to men drooling over that pretty face and hot tits, but I'm immune to your kind."

Easy to be immune when the pig had so little chance of getting a female willingly.

Channeling Jazlyn, a friend of hers who liked to quote Confucius and sometimes had more guts than sanity, Scarlett gave this guy a blank look and muttered, "The superior man, when resting in safety, does not forget that danger may come."

Her cougar chuffed a laugh and sent Scarlett a telepathic message. *Hyena idiot.*

The idiot turned his back again.

He didn't see her as a threat.

Scarlett flashed a razor smile, then back to her blank face.

She remained still, inhaling the scent of pine and clean air she normally associated with a run through these mountains.

Hal tossed a mean look over his shoulder, eyes a sickly yellow glow. Hate bled through his emotions. Balling up the chain in his big fist, he snatched it hard and almost yanked her off her feet. But she leaned back at the last second and stayed upright, almost yanking him off his own feet with that move.

He dropped his ugly head down and did his best to intimidate her with crazy eyes under a thick brow.

Not working.

But that little exercise did tell her she could catch him off guard without too much effort.

Hyenas were thought to be fairly intelligent, but Pagan Nomads didn't send out Rhodes Scholars to capture female shifters, just the strongest predators in their organization.

Licking his lips and still squinting as if he tried to digest her words, he said, "Keep that smart mouth shut or I'll make you regret ever learning how to talk."

No longer amused, her cougar snarled a demand to be freed so she could smack him around.

Scarlett replied silently, *No, Chica.*

Why? the cranky cat grumbled. *Kill hyena. One less moron.*

True, but Chica easily lost sight of their goal when her hackles got raised. Much as Scarlett would like to perform a service to humanity by eliminating this tumor on the world's ass, she had a bigger goal.

Lives depended on her. Getting mauled while in cuffs would destroy any chance of succeeding.

She'd explained to Chica more than once that killing an annoyance was careless when the situation called for patience.

Patience wasn't Chica's strong suit.

Or Scarlett's.

Hal grumbled louder and snatched the chain for no obvious reason. Scarlett leaped forward to keep her balance and growled at the dick move.

Chica argued, *Turn hyena into rock.*

No! Scarlett snapped at her animal for suggesting she expose an ability she'd kept secret since her teen years. *You want to end up in a cage?*

That silenced Chica, who knew better than to suggest Scarlett expose herself as not just another cougar shifter. She switched the topic to get her cat back on track.

We have to find out if this guy has all three female shifters first. Her animal grumbled in discontent.

Even if she intended to shift, Scarlett couldn't do it while wearing these damn cuffs with zero wiggle room. Her cougar's paws were even larger than her human wrists. No shifter with any sense tried to change while contained in nonbreakable material.

On top of which, the hyena shifter would call up his animal faster and catch her in a vulnerable position.

Scarlett hurried her steps, catching up to Hal, which created slack for her damaged wrists. Bastard whipped the chain over his shoulder, which tightened it again, and jerked her hands up at an awkward angle. She gritted her teeth as fresh blood oozed around the titanium, which impeded her natural healing.

Slop Breath stopped abruptly.

She almost ran into him.

Eww. She sucked in too much of his rank smell. She held her breath as she backed up where the air smelled better then breathed again.

Turning slowly, his eyes narrowed until she wondered if he thought they shot lasers at her. He bared his teeth. "You insulted me."

She had to think back on what he referenced. Oh, the Confucius quote. She gave him points for figuring it out before tomorrow.

Just to screw with him, Scarlett feigned surprise, but was careful to not lie. Even an imbecilic shifter should be able to smell a lie.

"What? You don't know that famous quote?" She frowned hard to appear truly confused. "I said '*superior* men.' Didn't you hear that part?"

His eyebrows raised in response before bewilderment dulled the glow in his eyes. Grumbling, he shook his head and trudged on to the trailer.

Chica made a snort of laughter.

At the shipping trailer, Hal reached up and lifted off an open lock hooked on one side of the rear doors. Keeping an eye on Scarlett, he used his free hand to shove each side open.

She gave him a docile expression, at least her best impression of one.

Light from a bright full moon spilled through the canopy of tree limbs above, offering enough light for Scarlett's sensitive eyes to quickly assess the contents.

That first glance sent her stomach to her feet.

Not because she saw six women when she'd expected three.

She'd always take on more rescues than less. The scraggly group of females smelled mostly of wolf, but she sniffed something unusual, too. The captives sat with their backs against the trailer sides, hands shackled above their heads. Clothes ranged from dirty T-shirts and jeans to a torn dress and one topless female in panties only.

Their titanium neck collars were chained to the floor.

Searching out a specific wolf scent, her gaze locked with a pair of eyes that flashed bright amber for only a second before returning to brown. Golden blond hair, filthy now and scrambled into a rat's nest, bushed out around her head. She tossed her hair to one side, exposing a badly beaten face, but Scarlett could make out the scar running from her forehead down the right side of her face to her chin.

The wolf shifter never blinked while sharing her identity then quickly hid it again by dropping her chin to let the blond mass fall forward.

These fools had no idea they possessed Jazlyn, the Golden Kodiak wolf? If they did, they'd bypass bounties offered by humans and shifter law enforcement at underground auctions, and put out a silent bid to high rollers.

They would never risk carrying that wolf shifter uncaged.

Upon second glance, Jaz looked sick or badly wounded, which might explain why they still held her captive. Those amber-brown eyes cut her way again, staring holes through Scarlett as if Jaz was trying to tell her something.

Scarlett hadn't forgotten what Jaz had done for her.

Shit. This complicated everything.

There was no way she could let these bastards take Jaz, not with the debt she owed that woman.

Hal took one look at Scarlett. "Little kitty scared? Good. You finally understand who's in charge, bitch." He grinned with predatory thrill then broke out a throaty cackling laugh.

For a crazy moment, Scarlett calculated how fast she could take this guy down before he shifted, then unlock her cuffs and free the women.

Cigarette smoke, one smell Hal hadn't emitted, drifted from the front of the truck with a rough voice. "We need to get going or we won't make Longtown by six," some guy in the cab yelled.

Scarlett knew of only one place in this part of the country called Longtown, but there could be more. She had to consult a map.

Hal called back, "Not my fault we have to go back to Atlanta and pick up one more before we come back. I didn't screw things up."

"I don't care who's fault it is. I want my money for this haul. If I have to come back there to move this along, I'm takin' a cut from your share. I caught the last two on my own."

Hal ripped off a loud hyena cackle in the direction of the cab, eyes dark with fury.

There were at least three captors, six captives. The driver had just given her the location of where they were headed, plus a window of time to intercept this truckload on her terms.

Scarlett considered the obstacles of attempting a rescue now or later.

Longtown would offer her the best chance for freeing these women, and maybe more. A far better opportunity than attempting it alone now.

Of course, all that wonderful planning depended on escaping Hal, who had more shifter buddies on hand than she'd anticipated.

"Hey! Move it," cab guy yelled.

Hal snapped out a high-pitched snarl again, teeth extending into fangs. He stepped up on the bumper to climb into the bed where he would drag her into that box to join the other women.

Chica banged to get out. *Four men. Too many.*

Four? Scarlett shouted in her mind. Her cougar had her own gift of reading scents for information.

Scarlett sent what she hoped was a reassuring look to the captured women.

The wolf with the scar on her face sent back a cold look. Jazlyn said more with a look than a judge passing a death sentence. She also knew Scarlett's secrets, one of which had to remain hidden to protect her little sister.

SCENT OF A MATE

With no time left, Scarlett leaned in as the chain pulled taut and arched hard in reverse. Her dead weight yanked Hal sideways and down, dropping them both to the ground.

Hal's head slammed into the door. He caromed off and smacked the ground hard, dazed.

She reached for the keys on a ring attached to his belt loop, breaking the small chain.

The smoker grumbled, "Hey, dickhead. Leave the fucking hoes alone and get up here."

Scarlett's heart double-timed with every second it took to find the right key.

Rumbling of hope-filled voices built in the trailer.

That sound would haunt her when she left if she failed to rescue them later.

It might also alert their captors right now and get her attacked while cuffed.

The passenger side door on the cab opened and someone cursed as he headed toward where she sat on her knees trying to uncuff her wrists.

One side of the lock unclicked.

Hal rolled over, moaning. He grabbed his head and lifted crazed eyes at her. He shot a hand out to grab her.

She fell back, booted him in the head, and threw an apologetic look at the scared faces.

Footsteps closed in from the side of the trailer.

Jumping up, she streaked out of there as fast as she could run.

Shouting erupted. The females screamed and cursed.

Heavy steps slammed the ground fast, running close behind her. A hyena couldn't stay with her. She heard no eerie laughing or the howl of a wolf.

That guy chasing her didn't sound like a bear shifter would when running.

Glancing over her shoulder, her heart sank as the guy shifted into a cheetah. He rolled forward as he finished his change and picked up speed.

Shit. She approached a twenty-foot drop she'd seen on her way in to find these kidnappers, leaped across the creek, and shifted on the fly, too.

Chica burst into life, landing surefooted on the other bank

without missing a step.

Scarlett's cat cornered hard around a stand of trees. That gave her a chance to estimate her pursuer. The monstrous cheetah on her ass chewed up ground at an insane pace, faster than seemed possible.

Unless he had juiced on Jugo Loco, an illegal shifter drug.

Didn't matter. He could eventually catch her.

Turn cheetah into rock, Chica yelled at Scarlett.

Scarlett wanted her cat watching where she went. *There are worse things than being hunted by another shifter, Chica. Just pay attention.*

If she failed to kill them all, she'd be outed.

If she failed to die, she'd bring a higher price on an auction block than Jazlyn.

More coming. You could help us, Chica pointed out.

Scarlett shot back, *Why don't you focus on saving our asses? Doing more than you!*

Sarcastic bitch.

Her cougar made a sharp right and barreled through thick woods then leaped on a half-fallen tree. The tall oak tree had probably lost its footing in the recent heavy weather and leaned over trees growing down a hill.

Was that a hill?

The sound of water trickled beneath the foliage.

Chica immediately slowed as if tired.

What the hell? Her cat was not out of gas. Scarlett told her animal, *Get going.*

No.

Growling followed them, growing louder as the cheetah climbed, panting with excitement.

The tree bounced with every heavy step forward, but Chica had a firm grip and curved her thick neck to peer behind them.

As if smelling a quick kill, the cheetah smiled, showing off his fangs. Saliva dripped from his jaws.

He slowed, crouched, and leaped.

At the same moment, Chica twisted to the side, shoving off the narrow trunk. She went airborne, legs sprawled like a feline daredevil and smashed into a pile of limbs, scrambling for purchase.

Limbs snapped and cracked like gunfire.

The cheetah, more accustomed to running in an open range, failed to land with a grip on the trunk and fell more than sixty feet. The cat howled in pain throughout the crash, then a sudden thud.

Silence.

Had he hit head down and snapped his neck?

All that barely registered with Scarlett as Chica continued sliding down, claws scarring the wood, unable to make a solid grasp to save them from the same fate.

Scarlett held her breath and silently said, *I trust you.*

Chica growled, muscles bunched. Claws extended all the way out and curled, her cat fought through the limbs cracking under her weight.

Chica slipped, then her chest slammed against a wide branch, knocking the breath from her cat, but stopping them.

As her limp cougar body started to slide off, Scarlett yelled, *Wake up!*

Chica's head came up. She shook her head hard.

Too late. Her feline body slid off the branch.

Chica!

One massive paw slapped a desperate grab at the branch. Sharp claws dug in. That ended her slide. She swung another paw up and pushed the razor sharp claws deep into the wood.

But Scarlett could feel her animal's claws tearing from the paw. *Come on, baby, you're the baddest cougar alive*, she whispered to her feline half.

Chica whined once as a claw ripped free. The coppery smell of blood filled her senses.

Making a painful growl, Chica freed a paw and reached for a better hold. She swung up her hind legs next, hanging upside down while she caught her breath. While still suspended, she freed her damaged paw and licked it.

Giving in to a moment of relief, Scarlett told her animal, *That was pretty amazing.*

Chica made a happy purring sound, delighted with herself. *Good cat. Fresh fish.*

There was her easily distracted cougar. As if Scarlett didn't indulge her as it was. She laughed and said, *Yes, you get your second favorite dinner, but we have to get out of here first.*

Oh, Chica said and stretched her head, looking everywhere then down. Her cougar gave a loud yeow, a sound she made when she liked what she saw.

Scarlett heard it as *wow.*

The sprawled body of the cheetah lay upside down across the jagged rocks. All four legs flopped to the sides. His chest made tiny movements. He'd live, but he'd have to heal a broken back. That was no fun.

Scarlett grinned. Chica had earned her meal.

A hyena's loud laughter blended with a wolf howl.

Rallying her short-attention-span animal, Scarlett told her, *Get us to the ground. I'll kill the scent trail when we cross the creek.*

She'd use that gift when she believed it would only confuse someone and not finger her as *different.*

Let this bunch of traffickers wonder how a cougar shifter had escaped.

Chica lowered her legs to a limb and twisted until she could climb down the tree. In the next minute, they left the wolf and hyena in their dust.

While her cougar ran at a comfortable pace toward the exit point, Scarlett started planning. The truck would arrive by six. Because the shifter had said "come back" to Longtown, she took that to mean the town in South Carolina, east of Ridgeway. With current time close to three in the morning on Tuesday, she calculated them driving to Atlanta then back and deduced the time period to be evening.

Tonight, to be precise.

This sounded like a larger operation than she'd originally planned to do alone, especially if these guys were dropping more captives.

She couldn't free that many on her own and wouldn't risk their lives trying. To save a group that size, she needed serious muscle.

With her paw healing, Chica's stride smoothed out. She asked, *What about women?*

Scarlett admitted, *We can't do this one alone. I'll call in a marker from that Gallize Guardian.*

Tiger owes us.

What? No. Scarlett didn't need a freakin' messed-up tiger to get in her way. She'd gone with a Gallize teammate to save Gan's sister and witnessed the Gallize Guardian call a monster Siberian tiger out of Gan. Those men met their animals as adults, often with no idea they were not born entirely human. Gan had been a captive his entire life and hated shifters. He had not been happy.

Had he figured out how to manage that tiger by now?

Or had he been put down, the only option if he couldn't gain control. Her heart squeezed at that possibility. With one penetrating look, he'd dragged up a reaction she hadn't felt in a long time.

Her cougar purred, *Want tiger.*

Scarlett snapped out of her momentary insanity. *No. Don't be a hussy. Gan was a jerk. I would only call him if I had a dire emergency!*

Make emergency. Tiger will like me.

You hated the last tiger.

Bad choice. Your fault. Not mine.

Scarlett didn't need this crap right now. She ignored Chica and returned to thinking through her next move.

The Gallize Guardian had negotiated ally status for her with his bunch of apex predators.

But which shifter would be the best to take with her?

They were all as powerful alone as any alpha backed by a pack or pride. She didn't fear them, but their Guardian gave her pause. Those shifters were loyal to their boss and would not follow her orders if he overruled her.

The Guardian lived in a black and white world.

Scarlett couldn't afford that luxury.

Jaz had saved Scarlett's ass one time and performed a huge favor a second time.

Scarlett had to take someone with her. Which Gallize shifter could she work around to free Jaz?

Gan, Chica reminded Scarlett.

I am not asking for Ganbaatar, Scarlett replied silently. *Besides, he's supposed to be out west at some compound learning how to manage his tiger. He's probably killed everything in sight by now.*

Chica sighed. *He will help. He smelled nice.*

For all her cougar's faults, her animal had occasional clairvoyance and shared random information she gleaned. She possessed a stronger ability in clairolfactance where she perceived knowledge via smell.

She'd been purring over his scent from their first meeting.

Scarlett had no place to say much. She hadn't forgotten the smell of fur and wildness that shot straight south to her core.

Between plotting this intel trip on the female shifter trafficking ring and battling to stay alive, Scarlett had enjoyed a short reprieve from thinking about him.

That damn arrogant tiger.

Even in human form, he had a feral look with dark hair sticking out in all directions, gold speckles in his brown beard, and a thundering voice. The look in his crisp blue eyes when he'd blatantly ogled her had been stuck in her head for weeks.

Bad enough to deal with him haunting her when awake, but the jerk showed up in her dreams at night.

Dream tiger, Chica cooed.

More like nightmare cat, Scarlett corrected.

Liar.

Scarlett dismissed the hussy and returned to the question of which Gallize shifter.

Gan did owe Scarlett for playing a major role in rescuing him and his sister. But why call in that debt when she had an open IOU from the Guardian?

The Gallize had other shifters just as powerful as that tiger.

Gan had only been a shifter for a few weeks. He would be a bad choice.

Chica purred, *Sexy tiger.*

Right. Scarlett didn't need two cats who wouldn't listen.

Time to test her alliance with the Gallize.

But she would not allow anyone to take Jaz.

CHAPTER 2

———

Bighorn National Forest, Wyoming

GAN LAY FLAT ON HIS stomach against the smooth boulder he'd picked for a lookout point. He held still as death, barely breathing in and out. Crisp air ahead of snow season brought him a mix of scents from evergreens to rich soil to small animals playing farther away.

He rarely thought of his new life as a shifter with any pleasure, but he did enjoy his heightened sense of smell.

It had been August when he arrived just over two weeks ago. In that short time, the temperature had become more tolerable.

A bison calf romped and played thirty feet below.

Gan's tiger banged his insides. He dug his fingers hard into crevices in the rock, shaking with strain to hold his human form.

Change now! his tiger shouted in his head. The animal shoved so much energy through his body to force a change that muscles bulged in his arms until veins stood out.

Nooo! Gan ground out silently. Every time he freed that maniac, he fought the beast nonstop. The tiger would inevitably win the battle for control, but only until he tired. Once the beast rested, Gan would force the change.

But that only lasted until Gan reached exhaustion.

He hated shifters and hated having a tiger inside him.

As if life hadn't been bad enough, his tiger had started talking to Gan in his head.

Like now. The beast shouted his favorite word. *Kill.*

Talking to the other part of him amused Gan when he wasn't struggling to keep his human body intact. Just to distract the crazy tiger, he silently asked, *Kill what?*

Calf.

Gan asked, *You hungry?*

Always.

He didn't believe the animal. That beast had blood lust. It would kill for entertainment.

Gan said, *You lie, tiger.*

Weak man. Tiger strong!

Shut up, bastard, Gan snapped at the crazy animal.

His tiger snarled and roared, still slapping at his insides with Gan grunting in pain.

If that bison and its mama could hear the uproar going on in his head, they would be long gone.

Maybe he should yell and send them away.

Not yet.

He only had one day until the Guardian returned. He had to convince that eagle shifter he could be trusted around humans. Only then would the Guardian free him.

If he failed to prove he had control, he'd either be put down as a rabid animal or left here longer … *then* put down.

Bad possibilities all around.

He never asked to be a Gallize shifter, but he was stuck with this four-legged Siberian misery inside him.

His insides quieted except for a low rumbling growl that never went away.

Sweat streamed down his face and soaked his beard. The cool breeze did little to help in spite of being naked.

He hadn't cut his scraggly hair or shaved since being locked in this compound. Why should he? The Guardian told him to relax and enjoy the great outdoors of Wyoming.

"More like great prison," Gan muttered under his breath.

His muscles slowly eased, but he kept them ready in case the tiger forced a fast change.

Had he not allowed that beast to run free for hours last night and yesterday? Had he not encouraged him to feed well, to take down a big elk?

Any food, as long as it was not mama or baby.

Tiger must understand rules.

All he'd asked of the beast was to stay under control until Gan got out of here and escaped the Gallize. If the tiger worked with him, Gan would find a place where the animal could run free and not harm humans.

Or baby bison.

Gan sighed. The foolish little animal wandered near the perfect ambush spot.

His tiger came alert immediately, banging and roaring until Gan waited for his head to explode.

For the fourth time in fifteen minutes, he locked every muscle he could to keep from changing. His tense body trembled hard against the rock.

If he could keep his animal from breaking free to kill the little bison, Gan could claim he had control of the tiger and it would be true.

If not, the Guardian and his shifters would smell a lie.

Hate you, his tiger sent back and railed against being locked up.

Gan breathed through his nostrils to keep from making any sound. His heart thumped wildly with the effort to remain in human form.

He told his beast, *Did not ask for you to be inside me. You unhappy? Your fault. I did nothing wrong. I spend whole life as prisoner, then escape only to end up shifter. Now I am stuck with you and prisoner again.*

More snarling and ripping up Gan where no mark would show.

On his next deep inhale, he sniffed the air.

All safe for now.

He might be a monster, but he did not harm babies. No one had protected his brother, killed along with their mother.

Gan had never known, until recently, that he'd had any family or that his mother had been a tiger shifter. It should not hurt to lose someone you never knew, but he'd wondered his entire life why someone had not saved him.

He'd survived a village slaughter in another country. The Gallize Guardian told him the place was called Ukraine. His family had moved there from Russia to hide, but crazy people with powers, known as the Cadells, found them and attacked the village, killing all but him as an infant. He went from baby to adult being sent from camp to camp where jackal shifters kept him a prisoner.

This Wyoming land was no different.

Still a prison.

No place would ever be home until he was free to live as he chose.

The mama bison strayed twenty yards away to a trickling creek where soft green leaves lured her to nibble. Her two-month-old calf noticed and headed her way. It ran under a low-hanging branch and jumped away, startled, then eyed the gently swaying branch as if it had been a threat.

He could teach that little one about true danger.

But the baby bison had more freedom than he had. Any natural animal could trot out of this area, right through the magic wall that stopped him.

While that bothered the hell out of him, he wished the mama and baby would move along and get out of here before his tiger pushed too hard and broke free.

A low snarl reached his supernatural hearing.

Oh, no.

He cut his eyes to the right, in the downwind direction from the calf that had no idea what evil headed his way.

Lifting inches off the rock where he'd been lying since his last shift, Gan eased up on his knees. His tiger surged. Gan almost lost his balance while trying to hold the beast in.

He leaned forward. Dug his fingers in, desperate to hold his position.

Energy buzzed along his skin and through his chest.

Sharp claws extended. *Ah, hell.*

Stop! Gan ordered.

The furious energy inside him wound tighter.

Everything overhead quieted. No birds chirped. No squirrels scrambled through the trees.

Even the wind paused as if sensing that death approached.

The bison calf weighed maybe a hundred pounds now. It pranced around clueless and might as well have an arrow pointed at it that said *Come and Eat Me.*

Gan's chest ached from his internal battle.

Sweat ran down into his eyes.

A tiny sound of movement from the right rode along the light breeze.

No natural animal or human would have heard it, but he had. His tiger hissed and clawed harder. Gan tightened his muscles, struggling to hold the beast at bay.

He tossed a fast glance at the little bison, then to the mama busily chomping the leaves across the creek.

In the next second, a blur of brown slashed into view from Gan's right.

He reacted without thinking.

Diving head first into the setting, a fourteen-hundred pound Siberian tiger exploded out of him before reaching the ground. Too fast. His insides felt ripped in four directions.

The bison calf lifted its head and froze.

Its mama bellowed and pounded across the creek.

Gan slammed into the massive preternatural wolf just before it reached the calf. The collision sent his tiger and the wolf rolling in a mangled ball of gnashing teeth and claws tearing skin.

They crashed through the woods.

Small trees broke like twigs.

His animal outweighed the wolf, but he had not been a shifter as long as that red monster. Gan expected his tiger to know what to do when it fought, but the beast had no real skill.

Just claws, fangs, and a desire to bleed anything alive.

The wolf's jaws locked onto his tiger's throat and yanked.

His animal slashed over and over at the wolf's shoulders and sides, leaving a bloody path down the red-brown coat.

Gan warned his tiger, *Bleed too much.*

Those words made no impression.

His animal fought on for another minute, slashing the wolf until the two broke apart. His tiger stumbled away, heaving every breath and bleeding from multiple places.

When the wolf didn't jump up, Gan's beast roared in triumph, but the sound had little power. Allowing one last look at the motionless wolf, his animal limped over to the creek where no bison remained in sight.

Dropping down into the cold water gurgling around a rock outcropping, his tiger washed blood off until the water ran pink. Throat muscles began healing and skin mended ahead of new fur that would grow back.

His tiger was lucky the wolf had not bitten deeper and ripped his throat out.

Gan had yet to get used to healing so quickly, but it was a good thing since his beast fought like a crazy fool. He told his tiger, *You are lucky. Wolf will win one day because you fight stupid.*

Kill wolf, his tiger said with too much confidence.

Gan spewed a curse at the hardheaded animal and argued, *Wolf watches. Studies for weakness. Fights smart. One day he wins.*

His tiger ignored him.

Foolish animal.

Once his tiger had inspected the major gashes and decided they would heal soon, he stepped from the creek.

Gan wanted to shift back to his human form. His last shift from tiger to human had been just before daylight. To do this again so soon would flatten him for a while and allow the tiger to grab control, but he couldn't fight the tiger all day without resting in his human form.

Turning toward the bank, they came face-to-face with the wolf.

Fangs bared, the wolf breathed out a demonic snarl. He'd healed completely, because that one had been a shifter much longer than the mere two weeks Gan had, even if it did feel like an eternity.

Gan's tiger snarled, *Kill wolf.*

Madness rolled through the wolf's light gray eyes.

Tiger was stupid.

Living here was stupid.

Being a shifter was stupid.

Gan and this wolf shifter, Adrian, couldn't stay out of each other's way. He'd stopped the wolf from killing a juvenile animal twice. Three times, counting today.

His tiger hunted the wolf every chance he got in this form.

The wolf prowled, searching for his tiger as well, which meant no sound sleep even when Gan found a branch high enough that would hold his weight.

He tired of this constant battling. Someone had to end the fight for superiority. Might as well do it today. He yelled in his mind, *You want die today, tiger? Fine. Go ahead. Attack crazy wolf.*

Adrian's gravelly voice punched into Gan's mind. *Bring it, you overgrown house cat.*

Gan added stupid wolf to his list.

His tiger started forward slowly, leaving the water behind. He didn't slow when he dipped down on his front paws, bunched his shoulders, and leaped at the wolf.

The wolf held back a half second then launched underneath to reach the tiger's throat again.

His tiger slapped a huge paw across the wolf's head, knocking it aside before landing and flipping around.

Huh. Gan admitted that move surprised him.

Hackles stood along the wolf's shoulders. He shook his head and took a stumbling step.

But Gan watched the wolf's eyes and warned his tiger, *Do not jump!*

The tiger had gone airborne before Gan got the words out.

They paid for that mistake when the wolf quickly sidestepped just before the tiger landed on him. Then the wolf leaped on the wide back of Gan's tiger, slashing claws deep and ripping his back open.

His tiger screamed and jumped around, trying to shake off the demonic wolf.

Gan ordered, *Roll over on him.*

Lurching sideways, his tiger rolled hard, throwing the wolf beneath his crushing weight.

Bones snapped under the pressure.

But when his tiger finished the roll, Gan's animal was no better off. His beast lay on its side panting. Warm blood flowed from the wounds on his back.

The wolf struggled to get up on three legs. The fourth flopped with broken bones.

Making mixed sounds of groans and guttural snarls, Adrian's wolf limped forward growling a hideous noise.

Gan could feel every bit of his tiger's pain. Maybe dying now would be better. He could not live as a man or as a shifter.

Not with this beast.

He'd regret never seeing his sister again … or Scarlett, that sassy cougar shifter who helped rescue both of them from being auctioned off. When he closed his eyes at night, he could still recall one scent above all others that first day as a shifter.

Hers.

His heart thumped hard.

Screw it. He would not die today.

Not in this place as a prisoner. He would fight and leave to find a better life. When he died, it would be on his terms.

As a free man.

Painful-sounding gurgles came from the wolf. He limped, favoring his broken leg. Blood dried on his rust-colored coat and fresh blood leaked from his mouth. His growls had a death rattle.

That was only right.

Maybe the stupid eagle shifter would not put two monsters in the same place again.

As the wolf neared, Gan's tiger lay still except for labored breaths.

Two steps away, the wolf's muscles bulged and rippled. He whined, but still gathered power for a last attack.

Gan's tiger tried to move. Not possible.

They were doomed.

Maybe he and the tiger would both die today after all.

Through the tiger's sharp hearing, Gan picked up the sound of something moving above them.

Adrian's wolf dropped down on its hind legs then lunged up and froze mid-leap.

A giant eagle, too large to be natural with a ten-foot wingspan, swooped down, landing perfectly, and barely rustling the foot-tall grass. Before its talons touched down, the eagle shifted into a man dressed in a suit. He appeared in his forties, which was a lie.

That eagle man, known as the Guardian, had seen many centuries. Gan's sister had told him this. She'd mated with a Gallize shifter, even though he told her she could do better.

The Guardian held all power over Gan and the wolf right now.

Eagle eyes in the man's human face sent cold chills up Gan's spine, especially when the man's head moved and angled as a giant bird would. He zeroed in on Gan's tiger bleeding on the forest carpet then glanced at the wolf's damaged body dripping just as much blood.

This was the Guardian's fault for showing up a day early.

Closing his eyes, the Guardian muttered something to himself, then opened them. "I put you here to regain your humanity and take control of your bodies, but you are determined to fight like insane animals."

Gan would have shrugged and pointed out that they *were* insane animals, but he wanted to die with all his body parts intact.

Also, his tiger couldn't move a muscle.

The wolf moaned, but the sound got trapped in his throat.

The Guardian continued lecturing them. "This was your chance to prove you were capable of living in the human world. I came expecting to see progress, to maybe take you out of here."

Gan got excited at the idea of not staying here longer until he noticed the grim look of an executioner when those eagle eyes turned to him.

CHAPTER 3

———

GAN'S TIGER STRUGGLED AGAINST BEING held in place and tried to snarl. His throat muscles would not work.

The Guardian had some kind of magic to hold his tiger and the wolf like two stuffed creatures.

Hate spiraled down at Gan's tiger from the wolf still suspended above him.

How long would they have to stay this way?

The Guardian's voice came into Gan's head as if he'd heard that question. *I could leave you stationary for a week. Or a year.*

What the fuck? Gan would have shouted the words if he could have spoken. He didn't like people in his head.

Those inhuman predator eyes pinned Gan's tiger with a glare of warning.

No more thinking around eagle shifter, Gan silently told himself *and* his animal.

Adrian's voice jumped in Gan's head next. *If you'll shut up, we might get out of this.*

You shut up, wolf.

You're as crazy as your tiger.

Unable to move, Gan shouted back mind-to-mind, *Your animal not right in head either.*

The Guardian shouted out loud, "*Silence! Both of you!* You are giving me a headache. Say one more word telepathically and you will not enjoy what happens next."

Gan's tiger growled, but the sound never left his chest. Then the beast telepathically said, *Kill eagle.*

The Guardian's sharp gaze slashed at Gan's tiger.

Gan quickly told the Guardian mind-to-mind, *Not my words.*

Tiger say bad things all the time.

Cranking up his glare, the Guardian spoke through clenched teeth. "It is the job of every Gallize to manage his animal. I explained that when I delivered you to this reserve. You have allowed yours to run free. You have clearly not attempted to bond and work with your animal."

This man thought Gan should become friends with crazy tiger?

Continuing, the Guardian said, "Your tiger's words are *your* responsibility, Gan. I suggest you keep him quiet while I think."

Gan felt his tiger's fury rising. This would not end well. Drawing all his energy to his muscles, Gan clamped down to hold control over the tiger.

If his animal was still locked in Gan's body, the tiger would be clawing his insides right now. He managed to keep the beast's crazy talk and aggressive sounds muffled.

The Guardian paced back and forth, occasionally tossing a disgusted look at both animals. He finally paused and lifted a finger to his chin, supporting his elbow with the other arm.

Still he said nothing.

From down here, Gan could see the wolf's face with intelligence staring out. Those stormy gray eyes threatened to rip him apart as soon as their bodies were freed.

Speaking now as if he'd been waiting on his chance instead of riding the silence, the Guardian said, "I don't believe anything will change if you spend another sixteen days together. You leave me only one choice, which I am not happy about. I would rather not put you both down."

Gan's tiger started growling viciously.

Be quiet, tiger, Gan warned. *Do you not understand that this man just said if we do not fix problem he will kill us?*

Finally, the tiger quieted, but it would be foolish to think the beast had the sense to recognize a true threat.

Gan could see his chance to escape this place, alive, slipping away. Adrian knew so much more about being a shifter. He would convince the Guardian Gan was the problem, not him.

Hoping he didn't make this worse, Gan spoke to the Guardian telepathically again. *We are better. We will show you.*

Adrian said nothing.

Eagle man turned a frown on Gan's tiger. "Actions speak louder than words."

Sometimes words explain actions, Gan argued.

After a moment, the Guardian dropped his hands to his sides and stared up at a smooth blue sky above the tall trees as he spoke. "I am tasked with trying to keep Gallize shifters alive as long as possible. I can only do that if you show a willingness to do your part."

After a quiet moment, the Guardian lowered his chin and spoke directly to them. "For that reason, I will allow you an opportunity to convince me of this improvement when I see no evidence of such. I will release you both to shift, give you ten minutes to gather yourselves and heal, then come talk to me. Adrian, you have been here as long as I can allow. Gan, I do not believe you will improve if left alone. Choose your words wisely."

The wolf's gaze lost the murderous edge and flared with surprise.

This Adrian thought he would be saved? What would make him more valuable?

Gan had no time to contemplate the wolf's reaction as his tiger was immediately free to move.

What did the beast do first? It snarled at the Guardian and tried to push up to bite Adrian's wolf that had yet to be released.

The Guardian grumbled to himself and snapped his fingers in the direction of Gan's tiger. In the next instant, Gan shifted back to human form involuntarily, hitting the ground hard when he fell back.

Changing too fast hurt bad, really bad, but Gan would not make a sound and appear weak.

Also released, the wolf fell, landing to the side of Gan as if pushed aside while in midair. Adrian also shifted to his human form. His wounds were once again healing quickly.

Not Gan's. Everything ached.

Why did someone not tell him how to heal fast?

As Adrian rose to his feet, jeans and a black T-shirt appeared on his body. His black hair bushed out and he wore a thick beard, looking just as wild as his animal.

Gan got the same clothing treatment, but with a gray shirt that blood seeped through. The air reeked with the fresh metallic odor.

Sometimes he liked his new extra senses and other times, like now, they annoyed him. He couldn't see the damage to one leg, but with every move he could feel torn muscles in his limb.

"Let's go, Psycho Cat." Adrian's voice sounded as if he'd eaten rust for breakfast, but Gan had not heard his human voice until now.

"Where?" Gan crossed his arms and grunted in pain at the ache in his chest.

Jabbing his hands on his hips, Adrian said, "I'll make this simple. Our clock is ticking. The Guardian does not toss out false threats. Don't ever underestimate him. We now have nine minutes. You can walk away with me to discuss this or stay here and wait out your last minutes. Make a decision."

The Guardian said nothing, just stood motionless like a fancy statue.

Heaving a deep sigh, Gan nodded toward the woods. "Go."

Adrian growled at being given an order, but took off.

Gan limped behind him. When they reached a copse of trees, he asked, "Why not talk where we were?"

Adrian yanked his shirt off then used it to wipe his face. "The Guardian thinks we're going to join forces to stay alive. He's been more than fair with me, so I didn't want to insult him by admitting there's no way I'll work with you, asshole."

"You wish to die?" Gan asked.

Adrian shrugged. "Not answering that, just stating the obvious."

All the time the Cadells held Gan captive, he'd studied the guards and those in charge. He'd learned one thing. Everyone wanted something, even Adrian.

Gan wanted out of here.

What did Adrian want?

Gan pointed a finger. "You said be quiet and we get out of this. Why say that unless you care?"

"Some days I want to live. Some days I don't care."

"What is today?" Gan asked. "Care or not care?"

Adrian slashed a suspicious look at Gan. "What if I care? Why would you give two fucks?"

"Me? I give no fucks about you, but I want to leave this place."

Snorting a dark chuckle, Adrian pointed out, "The Guardian isn't going to let two screwed-up shifters out of here."

But Gan had heard a crack in Adrian's hard shell, something

that told him the wolf did care. "Where would you go, wolf, if your Guardian would release us?"

"He's *your* Guardian, too," Adrian grumbled.

Gan ignored that, allowing the wolf to think he agreed. He repeated, "Question is where would you go?"

Adrian blinked at the question, probably because they had just said more words in the last two minutes than the entire time since Gan had been dropped here.

When the wolf took too long to reply, Gan said, "I have plan. I know where I will go. Help me get out and I will help you go where you want."

Adrian studied him with the dark gaze of someone who had seen bad things then shook his head. "We can talk all you want about going places. You don't understand that the Guardian won't trust either of us to keep our animals under control."

"My tiger is controlled," Gan boasted.

Adrian's jaw dropped. "You're joking, right? You just attacked my wolf, again, for no reason."

Gan raked a handful of sweaty hair off his face. "I had reason. Your wolf hunt baby bison."

"What my wolf does when it's hungry is no business of yours," Adrian snapped back. "I should have finished you off and let you bleed out after attacking me for the third time."

"You could try, wolf." Gan followed that taunt with a smug look. Wind brushed the early morning chill across his skin. So much nicer than hot weather.

Adrian eyed him with disbelief and grumbled, "You have no idea what you're fucking with."

"Tell me? Why should I fear you?"

Adrian studied him a moment, then spoke softly. "I didn't turn into a shifter yesterday. I'm trained for combat. If I want to kill your tiger, I can do it."

"I have been shifter two weeks, not yesterday," Gan pointed out calmly. "Your wolf bad, but you are shifter longer. Your wolf should not hunt tiny food. You should have more control and pick bigger prey."

"Fuck you, tiger. I've given you plenty of space since you showed up. Sucks enough just having to be stuck here then I get your crazy ass dumped on me. All you had to do was stay out of my way. In fact, get the fuck out of my way." Adrian stomped past him.

"Wait, wolf! I need more about this eagle man and Gallize."

Adrian stopped short, swung around and stared at him. "What have I said to give you the impression I want to be friends?"

Gan pointed at a squirrel scampering along a branch. "That animal born free. It owes no one. I was captured at birth and free only two days before your Guardian called tiger out of me, making me prisoner again."

Adrian's gaze shifted for just a moment.

Gan thought he'd seen understanding. The moment passed in a blink.

Shoving dark hair off his face, Adrian snapped, "It's not like that. The Guardian is fair. He could have put you in a titanium cage, but he didn't. He put you here so you could gain control of your animal. An assignment you failed, by the way. Every Gallize is dangerous if he can't control his animal. Even more so with someone like you, because your tiger should have been called up sooner."

Gan straightened. "How do you know about me?"

Adrian opened his arms wide. "He told me. The boss wouldn't drop a freakin' Siberian tiger on my ass without some background."

Distrust crawled along Gan's neck.

What else had those two talked about? Should he trust this wolf or that eagle man at all?

Forcing himself to stay with his goal, Gan said, "I think Guardian believes you have control. He knows you longer. He will save you and kill me."

The wolf shifter dropped his hands and stared away. "Told you, the Guardian is fair."

"Maybe for you."

The Guardian's voice came into Gan's head. *It is time for both of you to return to speak with me.*

Adrian snapped his head around, all serious again. "You get that message, Psycho Cat?"

"Yes." Gan started out of the woods, still limping. His tiger growled and pushed to break out.

That would be the fastest way to die right now.

How would he convince this Guardian, the one person standing between him and freedom, to not kill him?

"I have a letter for you, Adrian," the Guardian announced as they reached him.

"What?" Adrian acted as if eagle man had said he expected the wolf to sprout wings and fly. He took the wrinkled white envelope offered and stared at it.

The Guardian suggested, "Why don't you step aside to read that while I talk with Gan?"

"Yes, sir." Adrian sauntered off holding the envelope as if unsure about opening it.

The crackle of paper tearing followed.

True worry hit Gan's stomach like a boulder shoved down his throat. He jumped in first. "This is wrong."

Cocking his head in that strange birdlike way, eagle man said, "Explain."

"I did not ask for tiger. I do not want to live as prisoner forever. Why am I punished when I did nothing wrong?"

Adrian came jogging up. "You just don't get how much trouble you're in, do you, Psycho Cat?"

But the wolf shifter's words were not angry this time. His upbeat tone encouraged Gan.

What caused this change in Adrian?

Gan could hear the wolf shifter's heart beat fast. Why did Adrian seem excited now when he had shown no concern about dying just minutes before?

Adrian clutched the letter tightly, bending the paper.

The Guardian must have noticed something, too. His sharp gaze shifted from Gan to Adrian. "Gan deserves to say his piece."

"True, boss, but he doesn't always understand the language or that he's digging a hole." Looking over at Gan, Adrian frowned. "Put the shovel down."

Gan held his arms out with his hands open rather than explain to the wolf that he made no sense.

"Give me a break," Adrian muttered. "It's a saying. It means once you're in trouble, stop making it worse."

"Stupid saying. I cause no trouble."

"Never mind. You could have been explaining what we discussed instead of criticizing the Guardian."

For a moment, Gan thought he heard something entirely

unexpected in Adrian's voice. Hope. But he hadn't spent enough time around other people, especially shifters, with these new senses to understand what he picked up.

His tiger said, *Kill wolf. Kill eagle. Eat now.*

Gan sent back a silent, *Shut up or we die.*

Not afraid of eagle or wolf.

Gan replied, *Tiger not smart enough to be afraid.*

"Psycho Cat?" Adrian said, but not as a taunt. The wolf sounded concerned, as if he actually wanted Gan to go along with him.

Looking confused seemed to be Gan's best option, which ended up being easy to do since he didn't understand what was happening. "I have problem with words. You explain."

Addressing the Guardian, Adrian said, "To be honest, I'm sick of eating fish and elk."

"And bison. You should not eat bison," Gan added. His tiger banged his insides and growled, but he ignored the irritating monster as he would a child acting up.

Adrian turned on him. "What is it with you and the bison?"

The Guardian cut that short by saying, "I'm waiting to hear what you two came up with."

Gan wished he had more words in this language, but he gave it a try. "To stay here make our animals crazy."

Turned slightly away from the Guardian, Adrian rolled his eyes, but allowed Gan to finish.

"This place has much land, but it is still cage. We have not killed each other when we could. We should be free."

Adrian muttered something that sounded like, "Way to go, shit for brains."

"You're saying you can control your tiger?" the Guardian asked.

"Yes."

Sounding disgusted, Adrian said, "This was a waste of time. I am not helping you when you can't help yourself. I'll speak for myself with the Guardian when you're done. Leave me out of anything you have to say."

"What is wrong now?" Gan demanded.

"You said you could control your tiger. I told you we can tell when you lie."

"Do I lie?" He looked at both of them. When no one accused him of lying, he explained, "I fight with tiger every day, but I have control."

"Prove it," Adrian shot back.

The Guardian watched them with curiosity.

Gan drew in a deep breath, accepting that this would be his one and only chance of surviving. "Did my tiger attack wolf when you sleep? No. He could. We pass your den every time your wolf sleep."

Adrian whispered, "You don't know where my den is. I would have scented you."

Enjoying a moment of confidence, Gan pointed to the west. "Your den is there, across creek, and past where big tree fall. Two tall rocks on one side of mouth to cave. You did not smell tiger, because he come by trees when we got close. Every. Night."

Adrian started to speak then stopped and shook his head.

"Adrian? Is this true?" the Guardian asked.

"I, uh, do have a den for my wolf in the spot he described. My wolf never liked the cabin."

"I got that impression when you burned it to the ground," the Guardian said in a dry tone.

"You burn cabin?" Gan had wondered why this eagle man had left them with a damaged building. "I do not think you are crazy."

Adrian's eyebrows climbed his forehead. "Is that supposed to be a compliment?"

"Maybe. Not crazy. Only idiot burns own house."

Adrian cursed at him.

The eagle shifter ordered, "Language, Adrian."

He got a "yes, sir" in return.

Rubbing his forehead, the Guardian said, "I must admit that I originally came here hoping you two had managed a truce while sharing the same space, which would allow me to reintegrate you into the human world."

Gan's pulse jacked up. "Yes. We can do this."

"However," the Guardian said, leaning hard on the word, "I arrive to find you battling each other. Had I not stopped you, one may have died."

Adrian looked around and back to the Guardian. "We have our moments, but like he said, we haven't killed each other when we could have." The wolf sent Gan a warning look. "Either of us could have done that. Our animals have no outlet for releasing energy except to fight another male in their territory." He swallowed hard. "We can manage our animals, sir."

Was that truth? How was Gan supposed to smell a truth from a lie? No one told him these things.

Maybe that had been the truth, because Gan had just proved he possessed some control. He failed to mention he gave his animal plenty to chase all day and into the night before his tiger found a perch to sleep where he could watch Adrian's den.

Then Gan would shift back during the night and allow Adrian's wolf to slip out unbothered.

He did not understand Adrian. That man seemed unsure from minute to minute if he wanted to live or die.

Through the silence that stretched, Adrian slowly crushed the letter in his fist.

What words had been in that letter to sway the wolf when all Gan's arguments had fallen on deaf ears?

Eagle man locked his hands behind his back and paced a few steps, turned, and paced back.

Adrian asked, "Will you consider allowing us to leave, sir? I honestly feel ready."

Pausing, the Guardian turned to face both of them. "I'm considering it. I believe you've been ready for a while, Adrian, but you never showed any interest in leaving. Am I correct in thinking something in that letter has spurred this change of mind?"

"Yes, sir, but I'd rather not discuss it."

Nodding, the Guardian took a long moment before continuing. "If you tell me you are ready to be around humans, I'm willing to take that risk."

A big sigh of relief wheezed out of Adrian. "Thank you, sir. I won't let you down."

Gan's mouth dropped open. Just as he'd thought, this Guardian would help Adrian and not him.

Fury boiled in his gut at years of being a prisoner and never getting a chance at life. Why couldn't he have one day of freedom? Pain ripped across his chest at all the unfairness.

Gan crossed his arms. He would not continue this way. He demanded, "Kill me now or free me, but give me fair death."

CHAPTER 4

———

Downtown Spartanburg, South Carolina

SCARLETT TAPPED HER FINGERS ON the scarred surface of the table in Twilight John's, a shifter bar. Humans would happen by occasionally, but even with their less developed senses, they quickly realized they'd stumbled into a room filled with predators.

Some stayed.

Mainly the human adrenaline junkies, who thrived by living on the edge. It was a game for them to see how long they could sit in the bar until the excitement rushing through their veins turned to fear. Their breathing would pick up until they were panting, hands would tremble, and they'd start looking around with paranoia pooled in their eyes.

Big John would escort them out, explaining how predators hear the heartbeat in frightened prey.

Many would admit they'd been waiting for a shifter to break out claws and fangs for a show.

Too many humans saw shifters as strange entertainment.

Fools. Laws prevented shifting around humans. Being in the right did little for a dead person, because not all shifters obeyed those laws.

Only the ones who preferred life above ground.

Being stuck in a titanium-reinforced cage underground drove a shifter's animal mad until they died.

No one dared break out their animal form in here with a grizzly shifter for a bartender.

She swept a glance around the dark interior of the bar with

more mirrors than pictures on the rough-cut wood walls. Heavy oak barstools and chairs constructed with an eye toward strength over design wore the scars of past battles. Dim lighting cost little and kept the intended clientele happy.

Three male wolf shifters huddled in the far corner discussing the upcoming hockey season. It was only early September. Didn't hockey start in October? Probably debating fantasy team picks.

A female fox and a male mountain lion shifter sat two chairs apart at the bar, definitely not together. She drank a lemon drop martini.

Scarlett scrunched her nose. Too sweet for her taste.

Big John, the bartender who owned the bar, kept an eye on everyone while he washed wine glasses, even though he never lifted his gaze while doing it.

She checked her watch. Her window of time continued to shrink. Her resource in Longtown had come through, barely. The guy had sounded nervous, which she understood. Her contacts never wanted to let her down and face the consequences. She'd hit him with little time to ferret out details she needed for tonight, but assured him she would not hold it against him if something unforeseen popped up. She had a reputation for her intelligence network and liked to keep her contacts on their toes.

But in thirteen minutes she'd have to come up with a plan B, which would have no odds of succeeding.

That eagle shifter would get an earful if he failed to deliver after confirming he'd send backup.

The door opened, allowing a streak of late afternoon sunshine to shoot inside.

Big John stopped drying the glass he held and raised his head.

Everyone sent a pointed look toward the intruders.

Scarlett recognized Vic from the Gallize shifters. She waved him over, signaling to the room she expected him. Everyone went back to what they'd been doing.

Before the door closed, two more men walked in.

One she'd never met, but the same Gallize power rolled off him.

That arrogant Siberian tiger shifter brought up the rear. Damn his soul, he snarled softly under his breath.

Shit.

Then his gaze landed on her at the same second she inhaled his scent. That sexy look hit her in the gut … and lower.

Chica came alert and purred. *Yum, tiger smells good.*

Double shit.

Chairs scraped the floor as the three wolf shifters stood and turned as one. The couple at the bar slid off their stools and swung their backs to the bar, clearly united against a potential foe.

Big John put his hands on the bar and stood still, but he had a double-barrel shotgun full of titanium loads within reach.

He made sure that was common knowledge.

Scarlett drew in a slow breath. Aggression flooded the air.

What was the one thing she hated?

Drawing unnecessary attention to herself.

Standing away from the bar, she announced, "They work for me." Technically, that was true. "Can I use your back room, Big John?"

The fact that he didn't respond immediately meant the bartender hadn't made up his mind about allowing those three to stay.

Or her, for that matter.

She had serious doubts about this working, but rule one in any con was to own it. "Well?"

Big John eyed the three strange shifters for a long moment. "Sure. Long as there's no trouble."

"There will be no trouble, unless someone crosses me, and that only happens once," she said for everyone's benefit. She took her time eyeing every shifter in the room, daring them to cross her. "We have business to discuss."

The aggression backed down a notch.

Probably because all the shifters not standing behind the bar had sized up the three Gallize shifters. With the exception of Scarlett, no one else in this bar would know what the secret group of shifters were, but instinct told them taking on just one of the strangers alone would be a tough battle.

They had no idea.

Those three shifters were apex predators.

Big John nodded toward a door on the opposite side of the room from the entrance. "Let me know if you need drinks," he said, just his way of letting everyone know no one scared him.

She turned to meet Big John's gaze and gave him a nod. "Thanks."

Dominance game over, she swung her attention to the three Gallize and ordered, "Let's go."

That annoying tiger had better not argue. The Guardian kept all of his people in line, but she had serious doubts anyone had turned Ganbaatar into a "yes, sir" man by now.

She stepped ahead of her group and opened the door to a hallway, standing to the side.

Vic went first. Then the unknown shifter looking freshly shaved and smelling like a wolf passed by, then Gan, whose scent gave off mixed messages. Was he angry, confused, or both?

She didn't care as long as he didn't start trouble.

He paused beside her with a smoldering look and murmured, "Scarlett."

Of all the things she expected to come out of that mouth, hearing her name in a deep bedroom voice hadn't been on the list. She tamped down on the wild desire to rip his clothes off.

Damn the Guardian for sending Gan.

"Keep moving," she ordered, while holding his blue-eyed gaze.

He didn't blink, that sharp stare reminding her of his hardheaded, demanding, and aggravating side.

All true, but damn him, Gan exuded sex with everything from a simple hooded look to the pheromones sneaking past her defenses, teasing her hormones to come out and play. His beard had been trimmed in a more civilized style. The shock of dark hair falling past his ears she'd seen on him the first time had been cut. Now he had jagged black locks longer on top than the sides. Whoever did that for him probably thought he would style it.

No chance. Not unless washing his hair and shaking his head like a wet dog could be considered styling. Why did that uncombed look boost his appeal?

Chica hadn't stopped purring. She said, *Happy for tiger.*

That was because Chica did not have to deal with him. Scarlett had no idea why Gan was here, but he had no place on her mission.

She'd made mistakes in her life and would make more.

Ganbaatar would not be one of them.

She jerked her head to the side, trying to get him moving into the hallway.

He took his time. His eyes twinkled. Damn tiger enjoyed being a pain in her backside.

Did the Guardian really think she would take *him* on this mission?

Chuckling, he headed down the hall to the only open door. Those broad shoulders did wonders for a T-shirt.

His words whispered back to her. "Is nice see you, too."

Egotistical hardhead.

Had she missed the sound of his broken English? What was that accent? Slavic?

More important. What was she doing thinking about it?

Slapping her business face on again, she followed the men into a twenty-by-forty room filled with kitchen and bar supplies stacked on shelves lined up across most of the room. That left them a twelve-foot-square area with four metal chairs.

This had to be quick or she'd choke on the testosterone flooding the air.

Her window of time continued to shrink.

Shutting the door, she stood in front of it while two of them sat. Gan leaned against a metal shelving and crossed his arms.

"This is not what I asked for," Scarlett said in Vic's direction. "I got a message Tess couldn't make it for this meeting. Why?" She'd been friends with Tess longer than the Gallize. Her friend had recently mated with a Gallize wolf, which was how Tess became Scarlett's liaison to this group.

Vic's reddish-brown hair had grown out since she last saw him. He now wore it pulled back in a ponytail. He filled out his six-foot-plus size with a lanky build, but never underestimate a shifter based on his human body, especially a Gallize. He had the kind of clean-cut, nondescript face that would put others at ease if they missed the apex predator staring out through his gaze.

He explained, "Tess is hugging a toilet."

"She's got morning sickness?" Scarlett knew about Tess being pregnant but hadn't expected someone as strong as her to get morning sickness. Guess having a baby was having a baby, regardless of being nonhuman. Tess was not a shifter, but a Gallize female who carried a crap load of power.

"Cole says it's been going on nonstop the last two days and she's wiped out. You get me instead."

With a look in Vic's direction, she allowed, "You can stay, but I only asked for one of your team to take with me."

"You're getting all three of us actually. You know Gan and this one is Adrian." Vic pointed at the brooding wolf shifter sitting on his left.

What the hell? She'd actually asked for Tess to choose a Gallize for her, because Scarlett hoped to get Tess to agree with her terms that she called the shots, no exceptions. Tess would help Scarlett work things out with the Guardian if Scarlett had to push his man to stand down so that she could sneak Jaz out without anyone knowing.

Shaking her head, she had to straighten this out now. "Call the Guardian and tell him this isn't what we agreed to. I don't need a group." They were insane to think she'd take three apex predators with her. "I'll take two at the most."

Taking Vic would be a problem, though, because he wouldn't risk pissing off the Guardian if she needed him to bend a few rules. She'd bet Adrian would be the same as Vic.

Tiger will help, Chica said, popping into Scarlett's head right when she did not need a distraction. *I want tiger.*

She had to get her cat out of her head. *I will consider the tiger, but only if you leave me alone to think.*

Chica rumbled a laugh, but went quiet.

Scarlett eyed the tiger shifter with the smoldering gaze. Could he not look at her without sending out silent let's-get-naked messages?

Of course, those messages might be originating with her. She could close her eyes and the room would still feel too small with him here.

She scolded herself. *Stop thinking about Gan naked and get back on track.*

Maybe she should consider taking him. He hadn't been a Gallize shifter long. Had he been turned into a true Gallize or was he still angry at them for making him a shifter?

Vic crossed his arms and leaned back. "I get what you're saying, Scarlett, but this would be doing the Guardian a favor while affording you plenty of backup."

Adrian had been sitting calmly, but he'd started growling softly like an animal ready to strike. "She doesn't want us, Vic. Let's head back to headquarters and let the boss send someone else."

"She doesn't want *you*, wolf," Gan clarified, clearly happy with his jab. He looked over at Scarlett and winked.

What the hell did he think was going on here?

She hadn't given him any encouragement.

Standing, Adrian's arms fell loose at his sides, the way a fighter would to prepare for an attack. "I don't recall *anyone* saying they wanted you, Psycho Cat."

If these two shifted and wrecked Big John's back room, they'd have to explain to the Guardian why she canceled the alliance with the Gallize. She didn't need this crap and definitely not two idiots who would draw the attention of every shifter out front.

The minute Big John showed up with his shotgun, she'd clear a path for his aim.

Vic growled. "Cut it out you two. You agreed to do this. The Guardian told me to remind you that your options are limited."

After a tense moment of staring, Adrian sat hard.

Hold it. She took in every face at that comment. What had he meant about limited options?

Vic told Scarlett, "The Guardian asked that you take all three of us."

Gan smiled at Scarlett. "You did not know Vic or the wolf would be here. That means I am right. You did ask for me."

How did that overgrown arrogant ass come up with that logic? His ego could not be allowed to run free unchecked. She gave him a pleasant smile. "How clever of you to figure that out."

That boosted Gan's grin.

She settled her gaze on Gan. "Don't you want to know *why* I asked for you?"

He nodded, eyes full of gloating. "Yes. Explain for wolf and Vic. They are confused."

Vic slapped a hand over his eyes and shook his head.

"It's simple, Gan," she continued. "You owe me a favor and I figured the Guardian would prefer I chose the one he could best afford to lose."

Vic dropped his hand to cover his mouth where a grin peeked out past his fingers.

Adrian snorted. "Oh, man. I like her."

Gan's blue eyes turned dark as a stormy winter sky.

She leaned back against the door with her arms crossed. "Now that your ego has deflated enough for us to breathe and have a conversation, back to the discussion at hand. I still don't understand why there are three of you."

Vic explained, "Gan hasn't been a shifter long enough to be in public without backup. Adrian has been out of circulation for a while healing, but he has extensive prior training and needs the field work. I'm here mostly to observe these two and report to the Guardian on if they're ready to work on their own, plus help with anything you ask of me."

That wasn't entirely the truth, but she wouldn't pin Vic down on which details were colored outside the lines until she had a chance to speak with him alone.

Gan clenched his jaw then flinched as if he had a sharp pain.

What the hell?

Had she made a mistake in bringing the Gallize in on this?

Having Adrian and Vic would offer a better chance of the women surviving the rescue with minimal harm, but Scarlett had her doubts about sneaking Jaz away before one of them recognized her.

Gan, on the other hand, hadn't been around shifter law enforcement before now. She doubted he would have any idea of Jazlyn's identity.

Getting the infamous Golden Kodiak wolf past him would be easy.

Chica purred. *Yes, bring tiger.* She made a slurping sound. *Smells delicious.*

Scarlett sent back, *Floozy.*

Chica chortled. *Hermit.*

If Scarlett turned down this much muscle, the Guardian might get suspicious. She liked the idea of someone with that eagle shifters resources owing her. He must have flown Gan here by private plane to arrive so quickly.

She opened her arms wide in capitulation. "Fine. We all go, but while you may be overseeing them, Vic, I want all three of you to understand that this is *my* operation. I've seen the women they captured. I know where they're going now and we don't have much time. Once they reach their destination, I have no idea where they'll head to next if we miss this opportunity to save those female shifters."

Vic stood. "We're ready to roll. You want to ride in our SUV?"

"No, thank you." She needed space from all of them, especially Gan. He eyed her as if she'd slapped him with her paw. He needed to be taken down a few notches, but she hadn't meant to cause that hurt look in his eyes.

She didn't date and her lack of social skills showed at times. Still, she wouldn't have fed an ego that large. She did him a favor if he ever expected to have a relationship with a female shifter.

Her gut lurched at that thought.

Whoa. Where had that reaction come from?

Pulling out her keys with a brisk move, she dictated, "I'll drive my truck. Meet you outside after I settle my tab."

They filed out of the room, down the hall, and entered the bar again. As the three Gallize crossed the room headed for the door, Scarlett walked over to the bar.

She slapped down a fifty, more than covering one drink. "Thanks, Big John."

He gave her a nod. That was as much as anyone got from him.

Outside, Vic stood next to his Ford Expedition with Adrian and Gan milling around. Vic called over, "Where are we going?"

Stepping close to keep it as confidential as possible near a shifter bar, she said, "Longtown, North Carolina."

She gave him the major roads to reach the interstate exit. "At that point, you'll have to follow me. We'll go deep into the woods, park and hike in. I've got a place to hide our vehicles. Let's get moving."

Scarlett headed to her truck.

When she opened the driver's door, the passenger door flew open, too. Gan jumped in.

She leaned in. "What are you doing?"

He tried for an innocent look, but she doubted he even knew what the word meant. "I am ready to go. What is hold up?"

"Go ride with Vic."

"Why?"

Because this tiger shifter had her cougar clawing to get out and do more than play nice. Telling Gan that would be a mistake since he already thought everything circled around him. His ego would expand and break her truck in half if he got any indication about her attraction.

An affliction she intended to cure.

She clenched the doorframe. "Get. Out."

"No. I am tired with Adrian. Too angry."

She let her fangs drop down. "Then you aren't going to enjoy riding with me at all."

CHAPTER 5

———◆———

GAN HOPED SCARLETT WOULD NOT make him leave. He had to start working on a way to escape the Gallize. That wouldn't happen riding with Vic and Adrian.

He needed a friend.

When he looked at Scarlett, he wanted more than a friend, but she'd probably claw him up one side and down the other if she could see into his head. He hadn't been with many women, and only camp whores at that. They saw him as a toy, a prisoner who would do anything they asked for food.

He'd been ashamed to be used that way, but he'd also been hungry.

Never again.

But Scarlett … she was different. Special in a way no other woman could be. He had no idea why, only that she made him feel things that made him happy and confused at the same time.

Gan spoke in the nicest voice he had, which was not difficult when talking to this woman. "Much nicer to ride with you than those Gallize."

Vic and Adrian waited in their SUV without looking his way. They were just as happy to be free of Gan as he was to dump them.

He held his breath, hoping Scarlett would give in.

He'd missed her silky hair the color of caramel woven in braids. Today she had them pulled straight back and tied with a band to fall as a ponytail. Soft cheeks and full pink lips had been made for an angel, but one look at those deep green eyes and no one missed the warrior inside.

Looking down, she muttered, "What am I doing?"

She raised her voice when she faced him. "Let's be clear, Gan. I'm not nicer than those two or happy to have you riding in my truck."

He had suffered worse comments and simply asked, "Why do you not like me?"

Blush rose in her cheeks. "I didn't say that."

She did like him? He kept himself still, not smiling. Sometimes smiles got him in trouble.

"It's just that I didn't want a large group for this operation."

She was not saying everything she thought.

He decided to help her make up her mind and clicked his seatbelt in place. "Are we in hurry or not?"

Sounding resigned, she said, "Dammit. We have to get moving." She jumped in behind the wheel and slammed her door.

His tiger snarled at the loud sound, but the animal had quieted the minute Gan sat in her truck.

Even Scarlett winced at the noise, but cranked the engine and got her truck moving.

With her busy driving, Gan wanted an answer. "Explain."

She glared at him. "Explain what?"

"Why cougar does not like me. Has never met me."

Scarlett checked her watch, taking her time to answer. "She doesn't like tigers."

"Why?"

"We had one try to kill us."

Gan crushed the seat with his fist.

She glanced at his hand. "Hey, stop that. I remodeled this truck myself. It's a classic."

"Sorry." He dropped his arm to the seat. He'd protected women in the camps, like the one he called sister, but he'd never had a rush of anger hit him so hard as hearing some shifter had hurt Scarlett.

"Who is tiger?" he demanded, determined to hunt down this predator.

She gave him a wary look. "Why?"

"I will make him never touch you again."

They drove along in silence until she said, "I don't need a white knight. I can take care of myself."

"I am not white knight. I am tiger and I do not want you hurt.

Ever."

Scarlett's scent changed after his words, but he didn't know how to read what it meant. She still had the wonderful smell that belonged only to her, but he sensed less anger than before and more … curiosity.

That was good. Cats were naturally curious.

Should he take that to mean she wanted to know more about him?

"What's wrong?" She sent him a couple pointed glances. "Is it your tiger?"

"No, tiger is not problem."

"He was bothering you in the meeting."

"How do you know?"

She laughed. "I could feel the energy building around you, but then you moved around like you had something inside trying to break free."

"Yes, tiger does not care what I need."

Her gaze stayed on the road while she spoke. "But most of all, I smelled your … worry."

Why did other shifters know these things, but not him?

"There it is again," Scarlett noted.

"There is what?"

"You're aggravated about something."

Shaking his head, he looked at her. "You smell that?"

"Sure. Our senses are heightened so we pick up more than just a smell. Don't you?"

He propped his head on his fist and looked at the trees passing by. "I don't know."

His tiger rattled his insides and growled softly. *Feels good.*

Gan wanted to ignore the animal, but they had never spoken calmly to each other. He silently asked, *You like truck?*

Like her.

Before he could ask his animal more, Scarlett grumbled, "What have they been teaching you the last few weeks, Gan?"

"Nothing."

Her voice went up a notch with an edge. "You can't be out in our world without understanding how to use your senses."

He blinked, surprised she had started talking to him. Like a friend. He sat up and paid attention. This might not happen again.

"How do you smell lie?"

She shut down.

What had he asked that was wrong?

Grumbling under her breath, she offered, "Let's try something easy to begin with, okay?"

"Yes." He would welcome any information.

"When you met me the first time and again now in the bar, you didn't sense any aggression from me, right?"

He shook his head, his eyes studying everything about her. When she lowered her guard and talked to him in this relaxed way, his chest warmed at a new sensation of feeling normal.

She continued as she drove, working her way around slower traffic. "If I allowed my cougar to rage, even inside me, that would agitate your tiger. Your tiger picks up things from you, me, and other shifter animals. It may take a while, but your tiger can help you with what is going on around you."

Not his tiger.

That animal only cared about being a tiger. He didn't care if Gan suffered or needed help. But Gan didn't want her to stop talking so he said, "I understand."

Her eyes narrowed. "That smelled very close to a lie."

He covered his face with his hand. "Hate this. I feel everyone see me, but I see no one."

"I can understand," she admitted softly. "But you have to learn to be able to tell if another shifter is acting hostile, friendly, or trying to trick you. Your tiger acted hostile in the meeting. Fortunately, the other two Gallize held their animals under control. So did I. If not, we'd have been at each other's throats."

"You feel my tiger now?" he asked, curious.

"Yes."

"Not angry now."

Shaking her head, she admitted. "No, he's very quiet. That's what you want when you don't have a threat to face."

He wanted to tell her that she had made his tiger calm, but she might stop talking again. Instead, he said, "Tiger does not want to kill you."

"I hope not or you'll need a driver," she joked.

But he was not joking.

When he said nothing new, she turned to him. "You're …

unhappy with me."

She sounded surprised that he could be unhappy. She had no idea how much of his life he'd spent unhappy.

Running a hand over her hair, she said, "Okay, I missed something. What did I say wrong?"

Because she did not dismiss him, he gave her the truth. "You are first person, or animal, tiger does not want to kill. Is nice to sit here and be quiet inside."

He waited to see if that was all the talking. He knew so little about this world and how to deal with people. To simply talk with her was a gift.

She changed the subject. "Remember the Black River pack wolves who were hunting you after you escaped the Cadells?" At his nod, she continued. "Please work with the Guardian and his shifters to learn all you can. You'll eventually meet that wolf pack again. If they capture you, they'll use you in their lab experiments."

She worried about him being safe?

The warm place in his chest returned. He liked that, but brushed off her worry. "Will not capture me."

She smiled at him. "If your ego expands in here, you'll destroy my truck."

"I do not hurt truck."

"Never mind." She sighed and added, "You better hope you never get captured. The Black River pack breeds shifters with premium genetics to create their soldiers and slaves. They know what a Gallize is and that makes you a prime candidate."

He muttered, "Am not Gallize."

"That's going to be hard to prove to the Guardian and those guys following us." She stared straight ahead, driving in silence for a bit until she spoke so softly he wouldn't have heard without his new hearing. "Do you have to fight everyone?"

Yes, but not her.

He had to fight to gain freedom, but he would not ever harm her. It hurt to think about how he was going to leave as soon as the women were saved. Scarlett would not be happy, especially when the Guardian and his shifters came hunting him.

He would have to be sure no one could fault Scarlett when he escaped, but that meant he would not get to say goodbye.

There would be no one like Scarlett when he disappeared.

CHAPTER 6

———

MANEUVERING THROUGH TRAFFIC BECAME EASIER the farther north from Spartanburg Scarlett drove.

Evidently Gan was no happier with the Gallize than he had been that first day he met his tiger. After helping hundreds of female shifters in trouble, she knew that look of despair. She just never expected to see it in the face of a male shifter, much less one as powerful as a Gallize.

Seeing him unhappy struck a painful chord inside her.

She should stop worrying about him, get the females to safety, and then put distance between her and Gan.

Lots and lots of distance.

No matter how much she wanted to dismiss him as a jerk, he had a way of being sweet when she talked to him one on one. He made her want things she had set aside long ago to keep everyone in her world safe. She couldn't risk getting involved with anyone, especially a tiger shifter.

She snuck a look at him leaning against the door in nothing more than a T-shirt and jeans.

Women looked at Gan and probably thought about sex.

Definitely thought about sex.

But she kept seeing something new as she peeled back layers on him. The man hidden away for all these years slowly appeared. She wished they were sitting on a cliff looking out over miles of canyons and talking about … everything.

Watching him open up and hearing the sincerity in his voice as well as despair, made her want to help him any way she could.

A purr rumbled. Her cougar weighed in. *Yes, help tiger. Tiger help us.*

No, no, no, Scarlett argued silently, clamping down on her wayward thoughts.

You need man, Chica answered her.

Scarlett replied, *I wasn't asking you.*

Who do you ask then?

Never mind. Please be quiet, Chica.

Her cat grumbled, but settled down.

She kept trying to ignore what Chica said, because Scarlett had gone a long time without a man. She'd been around plenty of attractive and sexy men during that time and had never dreamed of sex with any of them.

Why Gan?

While he stared out the passenger window, Scarlett took the opportunity to sneak a better look. No one could blame her for wanting to enjoy eye candy. He wore a snug camo T-shirt, meant to blend into the terrain. That was the only thing the shirt hid. Thin material stretched over a carved-up chest, thick arms, and shoulders a mile wide.

Being a shifter, she liked a solid man.

She missed the long feral hair, but the short black locks didn't look any more domesticated. That and his beard warned a heathen had resided in that body since long before he gained his tiger and he had no intentions of changing.

He had the kind of body that made a woman want to live dangerously.

Nope. She'd stayed alive and kept her little sister safe a long time by sticking to her plan. She couldn't screw up now, but she could teach Gan shifter survival tips on this mission.

The Guardian should have taught him how to use his senses by now.

What did they expect? That he could just go out in public without any idea when he encountered a threat?

Could he keep his tiger from breaking out and engaging?

"Gan?"

He turned to her. "Yes."

"This is important. It has to do with the mission. These women have been through a difficult time. I can't guarantee one or more won't change the minute they're free. They could turn aggressive, especially around male shifters if they feel threatened, even unintentionally. If I didn't have control of my cougar, I would be at the mercy of predators. You can tell me if you have trouble managing your animal."

"Tiger is fine." Now he sounded grumpy.

No help there.

Female shifters were so much easier than boneheaded men. Scarlett hit the palm of her hand on the steering wheel.

He flinched. "What is wrong?"

"You."

"I did nothing."

"You claim you have control of your tiger." She hadn't meant to sound frustrated, but he shouldn't be at anyone's mercy. Who would keep Gan safe if he met a shifter that keyed in on his control issues and used that against him?

"I have control." But this time he sounded less confident, wary even, as if he realized she'd figured out something.

"Really, Gan? Remember when you flinched during our meeting? All of us picked up on the effort you were putting out to keep your animal locked down. That is *not* control. That's flying by the seat of your pants. Around shifters, that will get you killed and maybe even others depending on you."

Gan turned away, ignoring her, but she caught anger pouring off him.

She hadn't said that to make him angry, but to wake him up to the fact that he now lived in a more dangerous world than ever. The predators he would encounter had spent years sharpening their senses. Those shifters would catch the scent of vulnerable prey.

He might shift into a monstrous Siberian tiger, but Black River wolves fighting as a pack would take him down.

His life could end in a matter of seconds, no matter how much power he possessed.

The idea of Gan dying under the claws of vicious shifters infuriated her. She clenched the steering wheel until pressure forced the sound of a crack.

Dammit. Crushing the steering wheel that took her six months of digging through junkyards to find would cap this freaking day.

"I smell anger," he announced, sounding pleased with himself.

She took a deep breath to calm her racing heart. She never

allowed her emotions to run free, not around any male shifter.

Wait. He'd admitted smelling her anger. To cover having exposed her emotions, she claimed, "Good. I would have been disappointed if you hadn't."

"You do that on purpose?" This time he laughed, taking any accusation out of his words.

"Yes, I did." She'd own her claim and dare him to prove otherwise.

"Okay. I pass test. That is good."

She burst out laughing. "You think that qualifies you to understand scents?"

"You have nice laugh."

Four words shouldn't throw her off track.

Simple words anyone could have said, but when he spoke, her body listened. No one had complimented her in so long she forgot what it sounded like. Men in bars would talk trash, telling her how hot she was, but they wanted in her pants.

They didn't mean a word they said.

She had sharp senses when it came to sniffing out a lie or hearing the truth.

Gan's words had been genuine.

She tried to brush it off, pretend she hadn't been touched, but he'd made her feel good with the simplest of words.

He dragged in a deep breath.

She couldn't ignore it from the sound he made to the way his chest expanded.

"I like your smell, too." His voice had a rough quality that made her think of cool sheets on a dark night, tangled up skin to skin.

Shit. She clamped down on that thought before he …

"Uhm. I know *that* scent." He sounded *very* proud of himself this time. "Smells good like soft woman."

Where was a tart comeback? She waited. Got nothing, maybe because deep down she liked what he'd said.

What kind of mess had she gotten herself into? She could not carry out this mission with him thinking he turned her on.

Even if he had.

In a moment of panic, she bluffed, "That makes no sense."

That cocky bastard grinned.

Failed bluff, especially with her rubbing her legs together like a cricket.

Still two miles out from the turnoff, she had nowhere to hide her purely feminine reaction to him. It wouldn't dissipate as quickly as it had steamed to the surface.

That meant she had to kill this here and now.

She gave him a quick double take, then chuckled as if she had a private joke. "Oh, wait. I know what you're thinking. Sorry, Gan. Nice try, but you're wrong. Don't make that mistake around another female or you'll embarrass yourself."

Anger filled the cab. "I *hate* being shifter. Make *no* sense."

She did a mental fist pump at solving her problem until the silence built enough she forced herself to glance at him.

The self-loathing in his face punched her in the solar plexus. He'd been listening to her.

What happened to helping him?

Fuck. Guilt slapped her for lying to him.

How was he ever supposed to understand his senses if he got bad feedback?

He would never trust his nose if she didn't come clean with him. How did she get herself into this situation?

Growling, she said, "Okay, dammit. You did have that scent correct, but don't make more of it than a physical reaction. I'm only telling you to help you figure out your nose. Also, you should have realized I just lied to you a minute ago."

Could she be any more irritated?

Her cougar slapped her insides and snarled, *You lie. You bad.*

Now she was thoroughly pissed.

Where was a rewind button for today?

She put on her blinker and pulled off the interstate, then took a right turn on a country road surrounded by woods on both sides.

Keeping her eyes on the road where they should have been this whole time, she muttered to herself, "Where's that red ribbon tied on a branch?"

"There."

Gan spoke that word at the same moment she saw the marker for the turn, but she felt compelled to say, "Thanks."

She drove pass the small scrap of material waving gently in the wind to where she found an old pine tree with the top half burned. Probably a lightning strike.

She slowed as a logging truck approached, waited for it to pass, then eased her truck onto the shoulder.

Turning left, she dropped into a short ditch then back up the other side, and motored slowly into the woods, scanning constantly. Her intel indicated she'd find a path once she got out of sight of the highway.

She did.

That resource had a bonus coming from her. This source had lived in the area since childhood and was well known. She didn't tap him often because he had too many clients. She preferred contacts with smaller lists, but time hadn't allowed her a wide selection of resources.

She'd been so busy managing the truck over the terrain that she'd forgotten about Gan for a moment.

Why was he quiet?

Sliding her gaze sideways, she caught him staring her down with a curious look. "What?"

"You confuse me."

"That won't be a problem for you after today," she said with certainty.

"Why?"

"This is the only time we're working together. It clears your debt to me, even though I had not planned to call that marker in, just so you know. Everyone leaves happy."

Her cougar said, *You happy? Big lie.*

Chica's irritating comment pulled her back to the moment where she had a simple goal. One that had nothing to do with getting naked with an arrogant tiger shifter.

Easing into a lower gear, she pushed her truck to climb a rough hill that should allow both vehicles to disappear from highway view once they cleared the downhill side.

"How many women?" Gan asked, giving her a start with the change of topic.

"Six I know of, but there could be more."

"What is trafficker?"

She spared a quick glance to be sure he was not being obtuse. No. He clearly didn't know what that meant. "It's a group of people who kidnap or buy innocent shifters, or humans, to put into sex rings, slavery, and involuntary lab testing."

"These women. How old?"

"There's no limit to the age with shifters, but most are between teenagers to mid-thirties. The traffickers like to get young ones who are easier to handle." She wrenched the wheel to dodge the base of a tree that had fallen. The movement dropped her side down sharply and sent Gan sliding over into her.

She bunched her muscles, expecting to be slammed by all that body, but Gan shoved a hand behind her that stopped his forward motion.

As if that fixed anything?

She felt him right next to her. Smelled his warm skin. Her heart thudded at the closeness. Too close. Heat rushed through parts she'd kept locked down from any man for a long time. Every inhale acted like a lock pick, opening her up.

What was that crazy man doing to her?

He inhaled deeply then exhaled slowly.

Her cougar vibrated with a low rumbling.

Scarlett couldn't tell what that meant, which was odd. She always knew what her cat had in mind.

When the road leveled out, she turned her face to find Gan's crystal blue eyes inches away. She'd expected him to be smiling, ready to make a verbal jab.

But his eyes were wide as if she'd surprised him somehow. Irritated to be knocked off balance, she said, "Get on your side."

"Comfortable here."

"I'm not. You're cramping my space." This man had no sense of personal space. Ever.

"What is cramping space?"

Wrangling the wheel to stay on what little path they had, she shot back, "I'm not your urban dictionary. I'll use simple words. *Move!*"

Chuckling, he slid back to his side.

He thought that was funny?

No more helping the clueless tiger. He could suck wind.

Finally, she found enough open space for parking both vehicles. With the engine off, she jumped out and reached behind the seat for a tactical vest loaded with ammo. Titanium loads might not kill a shifter, but it would stop one long enough for her to contain him.

She popped in her earplugs.

Even with earplugs, she could hear conversation among the team, or Gan getting out of the truck on the other side and closing the passenger door.

She'd need her head enclosed with concrete to block him out.

Without earplugs and the suppressor on her custom 9mm CZ-75 B, the sound of this weapon going off would rupture a shifter's eardrums if they stood too close.

She loaded the magazine, chambered a round, and shoved the weapon into the holster on her vest. The vest seams closed with Velcro, allowing her to rip it off in seconds to shift if need be.

The only way releasing her cougar would happen was if this operation hit full FUBAR level.

Vic walked up to her wearing a similar tactical vest, carrying another one and with two comm sets in his hands. "With four of us, we should be able to capture some, if not all, of the kidnappers. We could definitely use the intel, especially if this is connected to the Black River pack."

"The kidnappers I ran into early this morning were Pagan Nomads. They sell to the Black River pack, but I don't know if this is a meet point for the two groups or someone else."

"Pagan Nomads?" Vic nodded. "They're hard to find."

Scarlett informed him, "I bump into them more often than I like. I've taken their bounties six times this year."

Sure, that sounded like she bragged, but it helped to remind these Gallize that she had street cred.

"No shit?" Vic asked.

She nodded. "I was surprised to see them in the Great Smoky Mountains, which concerns me that they're expanding their attack zones." Scarlett took the comm set Vic offered. She clipped the control box on her vest and put her headset in place. She added, "I'm packing titanium loads."

"I am, too. Adrian is carrying tranq loads." Gan had made it around the truck and stood with his arms crossed, looking as if he hadn't a care in the world.

Vic handed him a vest and a comm set. "Put the earplugs in first, then the headset. These are tuned to shifter hearing so they won't blow out our eardrums. All you have to do once we activate the sets is speak softly." He finished explaining how to set up the gear.

Gan gave a long look at the vest and other apparatus, then shrugged. He put on the vest, stuck the control box for the headset in a pocket, which was wrong, but Scarlett just let it go.

Once he had his headset in place, she expected him to pipe up with an opinion.

When he didn't, she returned to discussing the operation with Vic. "I'm all for taking kidnappers alive as long as the captives are kept safe first and foremost. If any of these shifters are on Jugo Loco or the equivalent of that nasty substance, I won't allow them to kill captives to prevent the women from running their mouths once they're free."

"That works for me. Gan's not carrying a weapon."

"Why not?" Gan asked.

Vic gave him a hard look. "Have you trained with guns?"

"I never shot weapon," Gan said, now leaning against the truck bed.

"That makes you a liability. We won't have time to cover you and the captives."

"I do not need gun or cover. I will be fine." His eyes never moved from her as he made that casual statement.

Vic said, "We have plenty of muscle, Gan. You're here to observe only. Don't take any risk. Scarlett is capable of handling herself. The Guardian wants you to get some training in the field." Pausing to give Gan a long assessment, Vic clarified, "Don't engage unless you're attacked. Whatever you do, don't allow your tiger out. Are we clear?"

Gan swept a look over all of them. "Yes. Not wise, but you are boss today."

Scarlett heard truth in Gan's yes, but she also sensed he had something on his mind he was not sharing.

He shouldn't be going with them unless he was prepared to engage with the enemy. In spite of Gan being a headache, she didn't want the mouthy tiger shifter to get hurt.

Shit. Why couldn't life ever be simple?

When Vic walked back to his SUV where he spoke to Adrian, Scarlett's conscience had her circling the bed of her truck to talk to Gan.

He leaned an elbow on the truck and propped his head on his

hand, completely unconcerned about what they were about to do. She didn't understand everything about the Gallize, having just recently been brought inside their confidence, but she'd met enough of them to know something was off about Gan.

Non-Gallize shifters were normally born with their animal and they changed as a child, as she had. She'd seen that eagle shifter Guardian call the tiger out of Gan as a grown man only weeks ago.

That might have fried Gan's mind.

She couldn't live with herself if he died because of her own agenda. "Gan, I've changed my mind. Let's call your debt paid. I'd like you to stay here with my truck."

"No."

She tried again. "A bust like this could go very wrong. You have to carry a weapon if you're not going to shift. If you shift, I can only imagine how bad the consequences would be with your boss. I can't ensure your safety if you go with us."

Vic called out, "Ready?"

Gan stood away from the truck. "Time to lead us to innocent ones."

"Why are you going when I'm telling you that this is a death trap? You could get killed, dammit."

He moved to step past her, but leaned down and spoke softly at her ear. "Your cougar has not met me, but I do not think she hates me. I am learning to understand smell. For now, I will do as told and observe. You will keep me safe."

His grin gave him away. He had zero fear about what they were about to face.

CHAPTER 7

———

Near Erie, Pennsylvania

"WE MAY HAVE FOUND HER, sir."

At the sound of Tantor's shaky voice, Robert paused from hammering a thick rod of steel he'd heated repeatedly in the forge where coals glowed to white hot in the center.

Tantor stood erect, filling the doorway to the forge Robert built on his property south of Erie, Pennsylvania. Beautiful blacksmith country, even if it didn't look much like his native Scotland where he had superior guards.

He would not rip those men from their homes so he created a new regiment here.

Tantor made him long for his men in Scotland.

That guard continued to be a disappointment. Tantor tackled any task he gave the man, but even if Robert were not a Power Baron, he would still require someone with more ability.

Someone capable of surprising him with creative thinking.

This one could be described as sturdy as a rock, dependable as hell, and as loyal as a Border Collie.

But the guard feared taking a step outside a safe boundary.

Robert functioned outside all boundaries, certainly the mark of a powerful man. Having a strong second was, too. He placed the steel back into the searing heat.

"That's no what I want to be hearin', Tantor," he said, proud his thick brogue had not diminished one bit in the past thirty years he'd spent in the United States. He missed Scotland, a land worthy of his undying loyalty, and the castle he claimed a century ago. When shifters came out to the public eight years ago, he patted himself on the back for having established a residence. He would never have left his beloved home for such long periods, but he made the strategic decision to become a member of the newly formed Power Council.

Tantor's voice cracked when he said, "You said … you wanted to locate her." He paused then cautiously added, "You've had us hunting her for years."

"Aye, but I'm no interested in maybes. I want only absolutes. Do ya know where she is or no?"

Sweat beaded immediately on Tantor's head even though Robert kept this room at a pleasant temperature in the sixties in spite of the heat generated by using the forge with few breaks.

A true second-in-command would have never shown up with anything less than specifics. Vague details were sloppy.

He had no room for sloppy in his world.

Sweat drizzled down the side of the guard's face.

When Robert spoke this time, his voice came from deep inside where his power lay coiled, waiting for his command. "Ya seem a bit warm, Tantor. Must be too hot for ya. I'll cool ya off."

Lifting a hand, he waved it from right to left and uttered words he learned as a child.

A rush of icy air blasted Tantor. He shivered. His teeth chattered. He clutched his sword, one Robert had crafted, but didn't move to wrap his arms around himself.

Of all the Power Barons dealing with the US government, Robert had carved out his niche as a mage of the first level. Anyone that low on the magic wielding scale could not call up a tenth of Robert's power. The human officials liked him. They thought he was the least intimidating of the council.

Robert smiled at such naivety.

His fault, of course. He allowed that blowhard Seamus to rule the council unchallenged. Seamus had plenty of power, a trait expected of someone who had wielded magic for 230 years.

But that old sorcerer only formed the council to make life easy as a Power Baron, to avoid conflict with the humans, and wallow in their adulation.

Robert joined the council so he would be in position to take over at the right time and rule humans as well as preternaturals. Underestimating him would be their greatest mistake.

"S-s-sir? You want m-my report?"

Robert snapped his fingers. The icy coating on Tantor's body shattered and tinkled as it piled around his feet.

"Aye, but be brief about it."

Tantor licked his blue lips and drew in a shaky breath. Drawing himself up, he said, "We've followed intel for months that speculated at her true identity. I've received recent intel that the Pagan Nomads might also be hunting her. They could have her even as we speak."

"Ya mean that rogue pack of mixed shifters has found her first?"

Relief smacked Tantor's face. "Yes, sir. I can confirm they are a mixed group of shifters."

Robert envisioned Tantor's big head sitting in a jar.

Completely missing the sarcastic expression Robert gave him, Tantor nodded like a bobblehead doll slapped from behind.

Some days Robert hated being yes-sirred to death almost as much as he disliked the name Robert, but maintaining that identity in the human world was key to moving around undetected.

The council knew him as Teàrlach, the Scottish Terror. Seamus made a point of sharing that the council knew of Teàrlach and his history.

He smiled over that foolish notion.

They knew what he'd spent considerable time planting for their underlings to find and report.

The council had sworn a blood oath to shield their power identities from all others outside the council. Each took a simple name for dealing with human governments.

The reputation of every Power Council member permeated the supernatural underworld, making them more formidable as one unit.

Even so, he'd waited a long time to get his hands on the one female capable of being his true second-in-command, an executioner who would do his bidding.

When he got his hands on her, he would make her a legend to be feared by all.

Once that happened, she'd fulfill a destiny only he could orchestrate.

Tantor cleared his throat. "I will have more for you by tomorrow."

"Why would ya be thinkin' that is possible?" Robert asked.

SCENT OF A MATE   71

"Because I'm not sleeping until I hand her to you. I'm running the men day and night." Tantor stood straighter after that boast.

Robert folded his arms then lifted a finger to his chin. "So yar men know what must be done? They are no confused?"

"Oh, no sir. I've kept them informed every step so they won't miss anything important."

"Weel, then, that gives me great confidence in yar operation," Robert said with pleasure.

A wide grin of relief split Tantor's face. "Thank you, sir."

Robert pointed at the fool and murmured a simple chant.

Tantor's sword flew from his hand and clanged on the stone floor. His face blanched.

Pointing at the sword he'd left heating in the coals, Robert called it by name. "Rise, Bhfeice." As the sword withdrew from the coals, the metal glowing red, Robert gave it instructions in Gaelic.

Bhfeice flew slowly to Tantor, whose eyes doubled in size and crossed as the blade paused at his neck.

He shook hard as a leaf in a summer storm. "Sir?"

Robert calmly whispered a command.

Tantor's hands came up to shoulder height. He stared at them as if they were foreign to his body.

Robert snapped his fingers.

Tantor reached for the scalding hot blade and screamed as smoke boiled and flesh burned from his hands. Stench filling the air took Robert back many decades to happy times of destroying his enemies.

Tears poured from Tantor's eyes. He babbled and screamed, *"Please don't, sirrrr!"*

"I hate that word, Tantor. It grates on me nerves for ya to address me as if I am a lowly English lord who would be willin' to accept such poor performance."

Shouting his final words, Robert ended the constant wailing when Tantor shoved the sword through his own throat. His eyes stared at nothing, blood ran from his quivering lips that finally stopped moving.

"Good edge," Robert mused.

As he watched the last trembling breath wheeze out of Tantor, Robert told the mindless idiot, "Ya shouldna ever train an underlin' to do yar job, Tantor. That only makes it simple to replace ya."

However, now Robert had to choose someone in his force who would locate his female protégé and bring Isleen to him.

CHAPTER 8

———

GAN HAD A NICE VIEW of Scarlett's backside that swayed side to side when she picked up the pace to a fast jog.

"Keep up or find your own way," Scarlett snapped at him without even a look over her shoulder.

She thought he lagged behind because he could not stay with her?

His grin widened.

With her prickly nature, she should have a porcupine inside of her instead of a cougar.

She could pretend it never happened all she wanted, but she'd been aroused in the truck. He hadn't been sure until she wrenched the wheel left and he'd almost slammed into her body. He could credit his shifter reflexes for how quickly he blocked himself from hitting her, but he'd always been careful not to harm a woman.

He'd never forgive himself if he'd caused Scarlett to wreck. Sure she could heal herself, but having bones broken hurt.

In that tense moment when she'd realized how close he was, she could not stop her natural reaction any more than a waterfall could change directions and run uphill.

When her arousal hit his senses, he forgot about shifting, hunting kidnappers, and even escaping to find a place to live free.

His primal response to her scent wrecked the war that had raged between his mind and body for weeks, forcing a truce. All he could think about in that moment was her.

Being close to her affected his animal just as much.

The same tiger that had been slamming Gan's insides and roaring to get out during the meeting at the bar quieted the minute Gan jumped into her truck.

With one deep inhale, his crazy beast had surprised him by receding for the first time since Gan had become a shifter. If he had to guess, he'd say the beast had suffered confusion.

His tiger had met someone he didn't want to kill.

A light wind snuck through the pine trees, dragging a fresh citrusy smell from the forest. His animal rumbled with a peace Gan was glad to have, but didn't trust.

He had to stay on guard that his animal didn't catch him relaxing and force a change.

Gan kept pace with Scarlett, determined to protect her from whatever they faced.

Vic and Adrian better be as capable at fighting unknown shifters as they acted. If either one caused Scarlett to be injured, they'd face worse than Gan's tiger.

The team ran silently through the forest until an eight-foot-tall chain-link fence came into view beyond the woods. Grass grew to knee-length inside the enclosure. It appeared to be a large empty pasture separating them from more woods.

Adrian eased up to the fence first and hovered his hand above the wire. "No electrical tingle."

"No livestock. What is fence for?" Gan said more to himself than anyone else. "Why not jump fence? Keep moving."

Scarlett studied the area. "Looks to be ten acres. Could just be a pasture someone is allowing to grow in before they move livestock or horses to graze here. But this could be camouflaging a security system to catch someone like us sneaking across it." She shrugged. "My resource didn't mention the fence. Since we can't be sure it's just a harmless enclosure, I say we go around."

Adrian gave Gan a smug look. "She's right. You'd know to consider these things if you had any experience in the field."

Gan's fingers fisted. Claws pushed out, stabbing his palms. He didn't need experience to wipe that smile from Adrian's face.

Scarlett wasted no time taking off and circling the fence. When they reached the other side, she turned onto a path worn down by animals. Most prints appeared to be made by hooves. She slowed her speed, sweeping a look from side to side as she continued toward light sliding between trees to indicate open ground soon.

Gan kept watch, too, as he had every day around jackal shifters in the camps where he'd been held prisoner.

Jackals couldn't be trusted.

Not even to follow camp rules.

His nose picked up so many smells out here. Too many to separate, except Scarlett's. He could pinpoint hers in a cluster of scents.

He'd only focused so closely on one other female before now. When he met Siofra, a young woman in his last prison camp, he kept an eye on her as he would a little sister around predators. In return for his friendship, she helped him improve his English and watched his back when he'd have seizures.

He had no idea at the time that a tiger was trying to break out of him. It would never have happened had he not met the Gallize Guardian who called up his beast.

No one had been more shocked than Gan when his body started changing.

He had yet to decide if he should be thankful or not. Before his first shift, he'd suffered constant head and body pain that had begun to worsen until he'd black out.

After his shift, he felt better physically, but returned to life as a captive for someone else.

There had to be a way to live as a free person.

He could not get rid of this tiger, but he would not be ruled by the animal either. If he could just get to Maine, then maybe Canada, he would live out what days he had left in the wilderness, a better place for dealing with his animal.

Scarlett stopped.

Gan sidestepped to keep from running her over.

Vic whispered, "Pay attention, Gan."

He sent Vic a glare of warning. His tiger snarled, *Too close.*

Gan ignored Vic to converse telepathically with his tiger. He asked, *Too close to what?*

Woman.

That's when Gan noticed Vic slowly closing the distance between him and Scarlett.

His tiger erupted with anger, lashing Gan's insides.

Gan hissed and grabbed his side with one hand. He held up the other one palm out to Vic and Adrian. "Stop."

Adrian's eyebrows lifted in a look that dared him to give that order again.

Vic shook his head. He reminded Gan, "Observe. That means no talking."

He'd spoken softly, but Scarlett turned to Vic then to Gan. She noticed his hand on his side and lifted *her* eyebrows in question.

Gan quickly told her, "All good. No worry."

"Then be quiet, dammit," she said in a terse whisper.

Why was everyone yelling at him? Gan told his tiger, *You heard. Be quiet or you get Scarlett hurt.*

His tiger kept up low rumbling snarls, but at least he stopped using Gan's insides like a punching bag.

She waved them to follow her then moved forward.

Gan stayed closer to her, keeping the other two Gallize behind him. When the trees thinned, he saw horses huddled at one end of a fenced area, a large barn, and a farmhouse with white siding and red shutters.

Was Scarlett sure about this place?

It didn't look like a trafficking business, based on what she'd described. He inhaled to see if he could smell anything that would hint at what to expect. He almost choked on filling his lungs with the stench of fresh horse manure.

She squatted down behind a pile of brush that had been cleared from the trail and turned to them.

Gan dropped to one knee next to her.

Vic and Adrian did the same, but faced her.

She checked her watch. "It's almost six. The truck should be here by now. What I heard them talking about sounded like they were making a specific stop here, but maybe this was just a pickup point. I hope the truck didn't arrive early, pick up more women, then leave."

Vic suggested, "Or they could have dropped women here to leave for someone else."

"Or the truck could just be late. Only one way to know," Adrian murmured. "I'll go look."

"No." Scarlett surprised everyone with that, even Gan.

"Why not?" Adrian demanded. "I'm normally the first to insert."

Gan didn't understand her refusal either, but he didn't like Adrian questioning her. "She is in charge. You agreed."

Adrian growled at him.

Scarlett's look of thanks to Gan lifted his spirits. He'd gotten something right.

She explained, "I'll go."

"No." The word jumped out of Gan's mouth before he could think, but she was not going down there without someone watching her back. Namely, him.

Her moment of appreciation dissolved under an acidic scowl. "You don't get a vote. As you just pointed out, *I'm* in charge."

"Is bad idea to go alone."

"The idea of some time alone sounds good right now," she shot back at him.

Vic's too-sharp gaze flicked from Gan to Scarlett then back to Gan.

Adrian huffed out a deep breath and sat on the ground. "What exactly *is* the mission at this point?"

Vic opened his mouth, but Scarlett jumped in first. "I'm going down there to do recon. If no one is in that house or barn, then this is a bust." She had a sick look on her face at that possibility.

Vic looked past her at the too-quiet property. "What if you find captives down there? Are we extracting them now?"

"Yes, but I'll free them first so they'll be calm before any males walk in."

Gan didn't know why, but he sensed she had not shared all her thoughts. Did she hide something?

Did he really know?

He hadn't been trained as a shifter or for any of this. His suspicious reaction could be nothing more than wanting to argue against her going alone.

"The truck could be late and show up in the middle of the extraction," Adrian pointed out. "If the captives have titanium neck cuffs, they won't be able to shift and protect themselves."

Gan could see the wolf's point, and hated to admit that, but he agreed with Scarlett about rescuing those women as soon as possible.

"I realize that, Adrian." Scarlett spoke with a calm voice. "That's why I need you and Vic to scout the entrance road back to the highway and give me a heads-up if a truck shows. If so, I'll figure out how to secure the captives while we deal with the kidnappers."

Scarlett's plan sounded fine, except for not acknowledging that Gan would be her backup.

That was his plan.

His tiger bumped him, but not hard. In fact, it felt like a nudge of approval. Gan shook it off as another misread on his senses. His tiger never agreed with any decision Gan made.

Adrian shifted a look in Vic's direction. "Does that work for you?"

Scarlett's calm gaze sharpened. "Careful, wolf. This is not a Gallize operation and Vic is not in charge."

"Understood, Scarlett, but we answer to the Guardian. I'm not disrespecting your position, just making sure that my CO has nothing to add."

Gan's tiger said, *Kill wolf! Protect her.*

Clenching and unclenching his hands, Gan forced his irritated tiger to stay put. His chest muscles were tight, holding his form against the battering he suffered. He didn't like the way Adrian had challenged Scarlett, but he couldn't deal with a screwed-up wolf and a crazy tiger at the same time.

Vic's gaze shot to Gan's fists. "We're following your lead, Scarlett. Adrian and I can cover the road, but you should have backup."

"She has this. I will go," Gan said, shutting down any argument, at least in his mind.

All three said, "No."

Scarlett rubbed her forehead. "First of all, I'm not some vulnerable female. Nor am I stupid. I'm not going to walk alone into a building filled with shifter guards. You haven't been in a situation like this, Gan. That's why the Guardian wants you to *observe*. Besides getting yourself killed, you put the rest of us in danger by not knowing how these operations work. Just listen in on your headset and pay attention. Other than that, you don't have a role today."

Anger churned in his gut.

His tiger scratched and growled.

So much for Scarlett's presence calming the beast.

But she had just humiliated him when he offered to protect her back and help rescue the women.

He didn't understand being a shifter. If not for the tiger stuck inside, he would not be here. This was not the time to get sidetracked by a woman who did not want him around.

The three of them wanted to go down there without him?

He would let them.

He had offered to make good on his debt to Scarlett and been refused. That cleared his mind of any guilt. He offered to help save women, but all three treated him as an idiot or child.

Scarlett's lack of respect pained him the most.

He had been a fool to think she cared for him. She might like him sexually, but he really thought she saw him differently than camp women. Maybe not.

Lesson learned. Trusting shifters was never smart.

Time for him to stick to the only plan that mattered.

Seeing that logging truck on the way in reminded him of when he'd cut trees one summer with other prisoners. Everyone in the camps worked at whatever they were told to do. He might not know much about modern life, but he understood living off the land.

While these three were busy sneaking down the road and around that farm, he would remain to observe ... for a few minutes. Then, he would backtrack to the highway where logging trucks were running. With his shifter speed, he could catch one as it passed him and leap onto the load.

That should get him out of the area quickly without leaving an easy trail to track.

CHAPTER 9

———

SCARLETT WEAVED HER WAY THROUGH the trees bordering the land cleared for an attractive country home with a tall
barn a hundred feet deep. When she'd reached a spot in the trees
at the closest point to the house, she dashed for the back porch,
heart racing. She forced her body to relax and not televise her
presence to a shifter.

Tiptoeing across the worn wooden planks to the screen door
shielding a closed wood door, she paused to glance behind her
and listen.

Chica grumbled, *Mean to tiger.*

Stuff it, cat, Scarlett sent back silently. *He would be in danger
down here.*

Stupid. You lose him. Chica loved to get the last word.

Damn cougar picked the worst time to start some crap. What
had she meant by lose him? She didn't have him to begin with,
but she'd fix this when she got back to Gan.

She could do without an additional helping of guilt. Yes, she'd
seen hurt flash through Gan's eyes before he wiped away any
emotion, leaving cold anger in its place.

She hadn't meant to insult him.

She'd only wanted to keep him safe.

If not for stress over the status of the female shifters, Scarlett
would have done a better job explaining to Gan, which she'd do
when she saw him again. At least he'd still be alive for her to
make amends. He had no idea how crazy some shifters could be,
especially if they were jacked up on Black River Pack drugs.

Two steps from the screen door, she picked up a nasty stench.

What the hell?

Listening first for voices or footsteps, and hearing none, she eased the unlocked back door open and slipped inside what appeared to be a mudroom. Still smelled bad, worse actually. Two steps forward, she reached the door to the kitchen and opened it slowly.

Disgusting odor clouded her face.

Bile raced up her throat.

She slapped her hand over her mouth and ran out to the porch, gasping for air.

She knew that stench.

Death.

Probably the humans who had lived here until predators showed up and killed them. Could have been a day ago, based on what she smelled.

This definitely fit the MO of the Pagan Nomads. They rarely used a location more than once. That chaotic movement of never staying in one place too long had kept them out of her reach.

The Pagan Nomads had finally made a mistake and she intended to capitalize on it.

She would bonus the contact who had gotten her this location so quickly.

Forget the house.

Not that these shifters wouldn't stash their prisoners in a place where the women would suffer that disgusting odor. Those bastards would do it if the jackal shifters didn't have to also suffer breathing that tainted air.

Drawing in a couple quick breaths through her mouth only, she made her way off the porch and around the house where the shade darkened each minute. On the other side of the house, she faced having to cross a long open space to the gigantic barn.

Chica piped up. *Not good. Leave.*

Scarlett shook her head and sent back to Chica, *We have never saved women from a good place.*

Feels wrong.

What had set off Chica more than normal?

She sniffed the air, focusing on identifying everything from the new growth on trees and fresh cut straw to the natural smell of horses. She liked horses, but they normally backed away from her the minute they realized she only looked human.

Animals sensed a predator.

The horses she'd seen when she first arrived were still huddled together. From this point, it was clear they stood in the back corner of the paddock.

The farthest point from the barn.

Could that be a sign the animals smelled shifters in the barn?

The equine fear might be what Chica had picked up on from the mixed scents Scarlett inhaled.

With daylight tossing in the towel, the twilight would help shield her movements. Taking quick steps across the opening, she reached the barn and stopped, watching in every direction. Vic and Adrian would have the road covered.

Just as Adrian suggested, the truck could be late.

A tingle ran along her spine.

That could be nothing more than excitement at possibly catching members of the Pagan Nomads tonight.

Two large doors on the green metal barn were closed with no lock in place, but that seemed natural for a farm. She'd have been more concerned if the building had been secured.

A walk-in door had been installed on the left side where she went next.

Placing one hand against the door to keep it from opening too quickly, she turned the knob and pulled. A tiny creak sounded. Her pulse jumped.

Any sound traveled farther for shifters.

She listened.

Nothing. She'd expect to hear murmurs, chain clinking, something to indicate life if the female prisoners were being held here.

Were they already gone?

Her stomach dropped. She'd never find Jaz now.

Regardless, she had to clear this building for sure. Pulling the door wide enough for her to enter, she opened all her senses. Scents of saddle soap, horse, hay, and dust hung in the dormant air.

And a weak scent of human sweat. Not that old, which supported her thought that the humans were killed during the last twenty-four hours.

Could captives still be here? She remained very still, focusing only on her sense of smell. There … she caught a lingering scent of shifters. Not strong enough for her to identify anyone, but shifters had been here.

Stay out, Chica warned.

Damn cat. But her cougar knew things at times. Without moving a muscle or making a sound, Scarlett replied, *Why, dammit? We have to find Jaz. There could be some clue for finding her and the others.*

Not safe. Get tiger.

Scarlett wanted to scream when her cat got stuck on one track. *Really? You want to bring up Gan now? What about saving the women?*

Stop! Get tiger now!

No. Looks like the captives are gone. Be quiet so I can focus on searching this place for any intel, Chica. Why would I bring Gan here when he can't even use his nose?

You stupid. Tiger will leave.

That's what had her cat worked up? Gan wouldn't just walk off without a word, would he? Maybe. He complained about being a prisoner again.

Scarlett's heart jumped.

Nothing, not one thing, was ever simple.

She couldn't get distracted. She didn't think Gan could drive after spending his life in camps, so even if he went back he wouldn't go far.

Screw it. She'd let her cougar have the last word, again, just to shut the cat up if she wasn't going to help.

As her sensitive shifter eyes adjusted to the semi-darkness with so little light filtering through skylights, she took a quick assessment. The barn definitely had held shifters at some point.

Dammit.

Alert and on her toes, she looked from side to side as she headed down the center walkway separating stalls that lined both sides. Dust and loose hay covered the wood planks here and there. The deeper she went into the building, the more she sensed the smell might be fairly fresh, as if they'd been here recently, but not strong enough to indicate they were here now.

Saddles were stacked on the right wall with other riding gear. An indoor shower stall large enough for a horse stood clean and dry on her left. These horses had it better than a lot of people.

Scarlett moved through the walkway, inspecting each empty stall as she made her way toward the rear. A finger of warning tapped down her spine. What had happened here? At the far end of the barn, a second set of barn doors and single walk-in access mirrored the end she'd entered through.

She paused at a muffled sound. Could be the building, but she didn't think so. She glanced all the way around, waited for the sound to repeat.

When it didn't, she eased forward on soft boot taps.

At a third of the way into the structure, a second twitch of noise sent her heart rate spiking. That had not been the building.

She drew her weapon along with a couple deep breaths to steady her. Never good to allow her heart rate to race when hunting predators.

Chica slapped at her insides. *Call tiger!*

Shit. Had her cat been picking up on a threat and not just nattering about Gan?

Now would be the worst time to even whisper into her comm gear.

Scarlett started to pin her cat down for specifics, but her gaze reached inside the next stall, freezing her.

Seconds slowed as she realized the captives were here.

There were ten women piled across the stall, blindfolded, and with horse blankets wrapped around each one. That had camouflaged their shifter smell. All of them wore titanium collars. Rope had been wrapped tightly around the blankets to mute any noise. Their mouths had been sealed with duct tape.

Chica banged her insides. *Run! Run! Run!*

Boots slapped the boards at both ends of the building.

One glance confirmed her worst fear. Four jackal shifters in human form blocked the exits.

She'd been lured into a trap.

CHAPTER 10

—◆—

SCARLETT KEPT PERFECTLY STILL WITH her gun still raised. She could take out both jackals facing her but not before the two behind her took her down.

One of the jackals, evidently their leader, walked toward her, leaving his partner thirty feet away. The two on the opposite end were farther back than that.

She hoped his boot steps pounding through the building would cover her whispered words as she kept her lips still. "I'm trapped in barn."

Just short of six feet tall, the ruddy-skinned jackal shifter with a dusting of beard and a man bun of wiry red hair paused his forward motion. He touched his ear and chuckled before closing the distance.

Showing off a grand smile, he asked, "Think your two buddies are going to come save you, Rambo Bitch?"

Damn.

He knocked her gun aside and snatched off her headset. Claws jutting out from his fingers sliced across her ear.

That had been intentional.

She gritted her teeth, but sucked down any reaction.

Chica had stilled. For an easily distracted cougar, she knew when they were in deep trouble.

Grinning, he spoke as if they met to talk over drinks. "You can call me Carver. We've been trying to catch you for a *whiii-ul.*" He dragged out the word with a Southern twang, but his accent had a fake ring. Evidently he didn't think so, because he stuck with it. "Took some time to set this up. Did you really think that squirrelly informant would find out about this location and our operation unless we wanted him to?"

She cursed.

He said, "Hey, it's not nice to speak badly of the dead. He had no idea he was a cog in a well-designed operation."

When she put all of this together, the realization hit her with the power of a fastball to the head. The Pagan Nomads must have been planning this for months, taking time to test one of her resources to determine they could get the results they wanted.

The amount of effort and preparation to catch her should be flattering. Nope. Not feeling proud to be a prize.

Had those men with the over-the-road trailer known who they'd almost captured and had that triggered this setup? Or had the Pagan Nomads been sending teams out with trailers, just waiting for her to stumble in?

The poor guy who had fed her intel for years from this area was dead.

These female shifters were sacrificial.

As for her? She could not be taken alive.

Scarlett glanced to her right.

When she found Jazlyn, the wolf shifter had worked her blindfold down on one side probably by rubbing it on the hard wood.

She peered back through a swollen and bloody eye. She shook her head at Scarlett, sending a message to save herself. There was no hope for them.

"See what happens when you interfere with our business, bitch?" Carver's bushy red eyebrows climbed high with the taunt.

Chica waited at the edge for Scarlett to release her. *Kill jackal. Rip head off.*

Scarlett would like nothing better, but Carver and his men hadn't killed her for a reason. That meant she had a window of time to figure her way out of this if she had any idea how.

Power tingled at the tips of her fingers, ready to do her bidding. She could disable this shifter, but the others were too far away for a blast of power to work on them. All she'd succeed in doing would be to expose that she was far more valuable than just an irritation to punish.

Working to buy time, she said, "You caught me. What do you want?"

"I have what I want." He laughed, opening his arms wide. "I get to hand you over to the boss for one hell of a bonus. Your little reign of terror has come to an end."

Someone banged on the doors at the end of the barn facing the house.

Carver yelled, "That our guys?"

"Yep."

"Let 'em in."

One door swung wide, backdropped by the dusty light of encroaching darkness. Clouds had rolled in today, which would stifle the moonlight.

Two jackal shifters dragged in Adrian, who looked like hell. Blood dripped from his stomach where he had his hands clasped over a hole. If that wasn't healing, he must have been shot with titanium.

Another shifter guided Vic forward with the handle of a sword shoved into Vic's back. Eighteen inches of the wide blade tip protruded from his stomach.

Did the Pagan Nomads know they'd captured Gallize shifters? Probably not. That meant they would torture them for information before killing the men.

Both were pale from blood loss and titanium poisoning. Every minute that metal stayed inside their bodies slowly killed them. The sour smell of tainted blood reached her.

Scarlett couldn't believe this mess. They were screwed.

Chica demanded, *Change now!*

Did her cougar really believe they could defeat these odds?

A deafening roar exploded into the barn as Gan burst through the opening in his Siberian tiger form. He came in as a striped tornado, claws and fangs lashing at everything in his way.

She'd never been so happy to see that monster tiger.

He slapped the shifter Carver had left by the door. That guy hit so hard his head cracked open.

High-pitched howling erupted as the three jackals left shifted.

Scarlett ripped her vest free and unleashed Chica, who could be far deadlier faster rather than wasting time trying to reach the gun.

Titanium might not kill.

Chica would.

Carver had whipped back around, his animal's mad eyes glowing yellow. He'd changed to a light brown jackal, but she had a step on him.

Chica screamed with fury and tore into Carver's jackal.

Gan's tiger slashed bodies and hammered anything in his path. Jackal howling and cries shook the air.

Scarlett's cougar fought with relentless determination to finish off this jackal, but Carver's animal had training. He attacked, spun to the side, and attacked again. Scarlett felt the bite of sharp claws across Chica's shoulder.

But Chica could be wily. She dodged one attack, rolling, then coming to her feet to leap on the jackal's back.

She spun her paws like a shredding machine as the jackal jumped around, trying to dump her.

Two more jackals dove into the fray. That had to be the pair from the other end of the building.

One clawed her back and the other locked her hind leg in his jaws. Chica's legs were getting mangled, but they were still trying not to kill her.

Scarlett wouldn't return the favor.

Her magic thrashed inside her, urging her to tap it, just once. Stop suffering and help her cat.

Chica shouted, *Need magic.*

Scarlett's resolve faltered then she stopped. No.

If the Pagan Nomads could capture her, so could a greater danger who wanted her magic.

But her cat was getting bludgeoned. She reached for her magic, sick at the risk she had to take, then …

A giant shadow crossed overhead then a huge body crashed down behind her.

Fangs released her cougar's legs.

Jackals slung around howled in pain.

Chica doubled down on tearing through the neck of Carver's jackal. He shoved up hard, trying to dislodge the cougar killing him, but Chica opened and closed her jaws again in a split second.

With a firmer grip and fury driving her strength, she yanked her head back and forth. She might not have the jaws of a tiger, but she had the heart of a lion. Chica tore through muscle and crushed bone. When the jackal's head fell loose and hit the floor, the headless body collapsed.

Chica heaved one breath after another. She pushed up.

Her back legs functioned, but her body trembled from the damage until she turned to search behind her.

Scarlett watched through Chica's eyes as the last jackal died.

Gan's tiger held down the body of a still-fighting jackal with one huge paw, opened his wide jaws, and bit the head off. He flung it aside like a child's ball.

Tiger eyes glazed with murderous intent swung toward them.

Oh, shit. No humanity in those crazed eyes.

Chica purred in happiness. *Tiger come back.*

Her cougar took a step toward him. *No, Chica. He's dangerous.*

Tiger good, her cat argued.

Blood dripped from his jaws. Hair tufted across his massive back. He had to be twice the size of her cougar.

His jaws opened and he roared, an awful sound, warning of impending deaths.

Dammit. Scarlett said, *Chica, drop down and show him your throat.*

No. Never. Chica hissed at his actions.

Scarlett had always been proud of her cougar's refusal to bow to any other animal, but showing submission right now might be their only hope of survival.

Gan had no control over that tiger.

Chica took another step, which put them within the tiger's reach. *Stop*, Scarlett pleaded.

Too late. The tiger snarled and swiped a paw at her cougar.

Chica jerked back, but not before a sharp claw sliced her face.

Scarlett screamed curses Gan's tiger couldn't hear. She had to stop him somehow.

Chica wasted no time in retaliating.

Her cat snarled, arched her back, and dove at the tiger.

CHAPTER 11

————

STUCK INSIDE THE BEAST, GAN kept yelling at his tiger telepathically, but the monster ignored him. *That is Scarlett, fucking moron. Stop hurting her!*

Kill cougar.

Do it and I swear I will cut my head off when I shift back to human just to kill you.

The tiger stopped short as if unsure if Gan could do what he claimed.

That hesitation allowed Scarlett's provoked cougar to dive at him and slam a paw with all claws out across his nose.

Ouch. Her claws had cut open his tiger's face.

Gan had no way to stop this craziness.

The cougar hissed and spun, bowing up to really attack this time. The swipe at his nose must have been a warning only.

Scarlett's cougar had no fear of his tiger that towered over her. He begged his tiger, *Do not kill Scarlett. She is cougar.*

All of a sudden, her cougar dropped to the ground and started changing into Scarlett.

Confused, Gan's tiger backed up.

Good thing because Gan didn't believe he could stop his tiger from attacking Scarlett while she shifted.

The animal had fought Gan over leaving the farm.

To be honest, Gan fought himself over leaving. It felt wrong no matter how insulted he'd been.

When he saw jackal shifters taking Vic and Adrian into the barn, he knew Scarlett had to be in trouble.

Shifting could get him shipped to Wyoming immediately, but he didn't care. He would not let jackals harm Scarlett. Vic and

Adrian wouldn't have survived waiting on Gan to figure out how to contact the Guardian.

Now that Scarlett had startled his tiger into stopping, Gan dragged up all the energy he could find and forced the change. His tiger fought him, making the change miserably slow, but finally gave in when the struggle clearly hurt the animal just as much.

Scarlett lay panting on the floor.

Falling to his knees next to her, he lifted her up, sick over the wound on her cheek. Crazy tiger. "I am sorry."

She grabbed his arm and pushed him away. "What the fuck?"

He must be just as insane as his tiger, because hearing her yell at him calmed his worries. She would be okay. "Tiger is stupid. Does not understand who is friend and who is enemy."

"Are you kidding me?"

He gave her a frown. "Why would I make joke?"

She stopped seething and looked hard at him. "You're serious."

"Yes." Much like the tiger when the animal was in blood lust, his human body had no control this close to Scarlett without clothes. He'd envisioned her this way, but he lacked imagination because the real woman was so much hotter.

She asked, "Are you hurt anywhere?"

"I am good." Yes, he hurt everywhere, but with his animal calming down he could feel the wounds healing.

"That was a lie." She started searching his body, which had plenty of blood on it, but mostly from jackals. Her gaze drifted down his chest … and farther.

Her mouth opened in an O.

Having her stare down there at him made his dick even harder. He couldn't stand, much less walk around this way, but he didn't know how to fix this.

Then he had the best idea. "I knew you like me."

That snatched her gaze back to his face. Embarrassment brightened her cheeks. She scowled. "Don't kid yourself."

But her face argued with her words.

Seeing blood drizzle down her cheek disgusted him at his inability to control his beast. He touched the soft skin around the wound, glad to see it healing. "Stupid tiger. Want to kill him."

"That's not a winning proposition for a shifter," she quipped in a dry tone. Releasing a hard sigh, she wiped the blood from her cheek. The cut had almost closed. "Don't worry, Gan. I'll survive. Besides, you're bleeding, too."

He reached up and wiped the blood from two deep gouges across his nose and cheek. "Cougar not nice."

"Nope," Scarlett agreed. "She will beat down any person or shifter who harms us. You should heal without scarring. How are Vic and Adrian?"

"Wait here. I check."

"Okay. I'll get with the women."

After stepping over body parts that had shifted from jackals back to humans, Gan's body thankfully lost all desire for sex. He found Vic on his knees leaning forward. Vic had an arm extended to the floor, preventing the tip of the sword from touching the ground.

That had to be painful.

Adrian lay on his back, gripping his chest and making painful sounds.

Gan knelt next to Vic. "I pull sword out?"

Nodding, Vic wheezed, "Do it."

Jumping up, Gan put a foot on Vic's back, gripped the handle. He did his best to pull the long blade straight out. He didn't want to cause Vic any more pain than necessary.

But a sound came out of Vic that turned Gan's stomach. He helped the shifter lay over on his side, then went to Adrian.

Staring down at the wolf shifter, Gan asked, "How do I help you?"

Between pants, Adrian said, "Find a knife. Scarlett's vest should have one. Dig the bullet out." He choked out another breath and blood oozed from his mouth. "Then I'll change and heal."

Gan turned to look for Scarlett's vest.

She walked up to him, wearing the vest that covered her upper body and ripped pants tied around her waist shielding her lower half. She carried a blanket draped over one arm. In her other hand, she held a knife she flicked open.

With a glance at Adrian, she told Gan, "I'll cut the fragments out unless you have experience with removing bullets."

He gave her a half smile. "Not me. I am here only to observe."

Adrian muttered a curse.

Her green eyes twinkled. "Touché, tiger."

Gan had no idea what two shays were, but liked making her smile.

Dropping down, she ripped Adrian's shirt open and used a scrap of that material to wipe blood away from the wound. While Scarlett handled that, Gan went back to Vic who had managed to sit upright. The clenched jaws said he'd paid a price for that move.

Vic had lost his vest somewhere and now shucked his shirt. He tried to push his pants off, but winced every time he leaned forward. Face drenched in sweat, eyes weary from pain, he looked up at Gan. "I need to shift and start healing. The blade left no titanium inside me the way bullet fragments have in Adrian. If I shift, I'll heal faster. Once she clears enough out of Adrian, he'll survive until one of our medics can wash out the poison." Taking a breath, Vic glanced at his pants and explained. "Need clothes after I shift."

"I understand." Gan stepped around to Vic's feet to first pull off his boots, then yank his socks and pants off. Then he stepped back.

Vic shifted slowly, bones making horrible sounds as they broke and rearranged. His boxer shorts shredded as he turned into a giant red fox.

That looked nothing like any fox Gan had seen before.

What was Vic's animal?

The entry and exit points of his wound repositioned, but also began healing over. Vic's animal moved slowly, panting hard after the effort of shifting.

A long howl echoed through the building.

Gan turned to find Adrian's crazy wolf climbing to his feet and swaying. He snarled and drool slid from his mouth when he exposed his fangs.

Moving quickly, Gan lifted Scarlett up and put her aside then stood between her and the wolf.

That only increased the wolf's guttural snarls.

"Do not touch her," Gan warned, unsure if his words would get through to Adrian now that he was not human. "If you do, I will turn my tiger loose on you."

Adrian's wolf snapped up at Gan, who didn't even flinch, then the animal turned away. He walked gingerly over to the doorway and sat down to lick his wound.

Scarlett stepped up beside Gan, sounding amused. "Did you really think he would attack me?"

"No, but I did not want to take risk. His wolf is sick in head. Not good."

Humor vanished. "You mean the Guardian sent me out here with an out-of-control wolf?"

"Yes. And tiger. Both crazy, but wolf can behave if reminded not to be stupid," Gan said, then turned to find her staring at him and not happy.

He felt the need to remind her, "Tiger save everyone."

She blinked, catching herself. "Yes, you did. Thank you for showing up and keeping us alive …" Her voice trailed off and her gaze drifted away.

Why had she stopped talking when she had more to say?

Gan leaned in to ask her to finish, but she changed the topic. "Vic is a maned wolf?"

Following her line of sight to the tall animal with a deep red coat and black legs, he asked, "Does mane mean fox *and* wolf?"

"Maned," she corrected, emphasizing the d on the end. "It's not a wolf, or a fox, actually. A maned wolf is a specific species all its own," she explained. "They're native to South America. Pretty rare."

So many shifters. Gan shook his head. "What now?"

Adrian said, "We need to call headquarters."

The wolf had shifted back to human form. Adrian pushed to his feet, his skin pale and hair slick with sweat. He walked over and dragged his jeans on, zipping them. "The jackals tore up our comm gear and crushed our phones."

"Not mine," Scarlett said with a hint of smugness. She peeled off a layer of her vest that exposed a mobile phone, another knife, and some odd things Gan couldn't identify hidden inside.

Adrian asked, "Where'd you get *that* vest?"

"I had it made." She lifted the phone to eye level, punched numbers.

Gan could hear both sides of the conversation, another benefit of being a shifter. She gave someone at Gallize headquarters a quick explanation of what happened, plus a description of Vic and Adrian's wounds. Before ending the call, she gave directions on how to locate all of them.

Shoving the phone back into her vest, she announced, "Since you two are no longer critical, your people are coming by land instead of air so they can transport the captives, too. Should be here in less than thirty minutes."

"I heard that. The captives are *here*?" Vic asked from the side. He'd shifted back to human form and managed to wrangle his pants on as well.

"Yes. Their mouths are taped shut and they're wrapped in blankets to prevent noise. I started unwrapping them. That's where I got Adrian's blanket."

"Thanks for that and getting the pieces of titanium out," Adrian called out.

She nodded to him. "You're welcome. I need to check on the women. Why don't you both just sit tight and allow your bodies to heal as much as you can while I get the captives calm enough to be freed."

When she walked away, Gan followed.

She waved a hand at him. "Thanks, Gan, but I don't need *any* help."

"I will observe."

He smiled at hearing her muttered, "Dammit."

When he reached the stall filled with the female shifters piled on the ground, they all eyed him like a son of the devil.

Gan backed up a step.

Scarlett stood there a moment as if contemplating something then turned to him and whispered, "I need a favor."

"What favor?" He kept his voice soft, curious to find out what was going on.

"I need to free one of these women and let her go without anyone seeing her escape." She studied him hard, clearly waiting to see how he would react.

Gan cast a look at the women again, wondering which one Scarlett wanted to keep secret. He asked, "Why is one special?"

"I can't explain right now, but I owe her."

He studied Scarlett's face for a clue to the importance of this woman, but she revealed nothing. He pointed out, "Guardian will take care of all women we rescue."

Rubbing her forehead, she said, "Not this one."

"Why?"

Shaking her head and grumbling to herself, Scarlett stopped pecking at the problem and told him, "She's a wanted criminal." After making that statement, she crossed her arms and waited.

Now he understood, but had another question. "Is she dangerous?"

"Law enforcement thinks so," she hissed low. She leaned past Gan, her eyes searching as if watching Vic and Adrian, but those two were in no hurry to move around.

Gan said, "I did not ask what others think. What do *you* think? Is she bad person?"

Scarlett stopped scanning and brought her full attention to Gan. After a second, she said, "No. I think she's been wrongly accused of a crime."

He knew what it was to be hunted like a criminal when he had done nothing wrong.

"I will help you," he whispered. Her eyes lit up and he wished he could do this for her without asking anything in return. "I may need favor one day."

She cocked an eyebrow loaded with suspicion. "What do you want for helping me?"

If he told her what he had in mind, she would refuse him. If he tried to pretend he didn't have a plan, she'd call him out for lying.

He said nothing.

Growling, she reached down and grabbed a blanket as if to shove it aside. "Let's do this."

Smiling, he stepped closer.

She took one look at him, then at the women in the stall who ogled him, and stood up, blocking his view. Then she stepped toward him.

His nose might not be smart yet, but his eyes worked just fine. He saw something in hers that sent his heart racing. A possessive look that slipped off his face and drifted down before she lifted her head again.

One heated look had him hard again.

He could only do so much.

This was not his fault.

She stepped close and he started leaning toward her, not caring if anyone saw them kiss.

She shoved a blanket at his chest. "Cover up."

CHAPTER 12

—

SCARLETT USED CLAWS SHE ALLOWED to break through her fingers to cut the rope wrapped around the blankets, which had been used to create female shifter burritos.

Titanium collars were often locked, but these only snapped closed, which allowed for a quick release. The kidnappers had been an overly-confident bunch.

Gan stood outside the stall with a blanket wrapped around his waist. He kept his head turned toward the barn entrance and spoke quietly. "Vic and Adrian still near door."

"Thanks." She continued releasing the women, who turned to free each other. She'd expected him to start asking why she had not kissed him when he'd lowered his head a moment ago.

If not for being irritated over the women visually sizing him up like a slab of beef, that moment wouldn't have happened.

Her brain clicked into gear in time for her to give him the blanket.

She noted a total of ten women, glad the additional ones were clothed as well as the ones she'd seen in the trailer earlier this morning. The naked female now wore a blanket toga.

Jazlyn sat up and groaned, pushing a wad of hair off her damaged face. She normally had sun-kissed skin, but not now. Dried blood covered most of the pale skin bruises hadn't formed on yet. She whispered in Scarlett's direction, "What's the plan?"

"Getting ready to explain it."

As the last women were tossing off their ropes, Scarlett addressed the group. "Listen up." She angled her head at Jaz. "This one is being hunted by everyone. She's the reason I found you and why you're going to be safe." She let that sink in before continuing.

"I need to get her out of here. I have transportation coming that will take you to the Spartanburg Friends of Shifters shelter. You'll be safe there. Right now, I need you to file out of the stall and stand in a group in the middle of the walkway. Stay close together to form a visual barrier."

After a couple questions Scarlett took the time to answer and calm nerves, each woman got up and followed the first one out, who stood just past Gan. When nine women had gathered in a thick wall of bodies, Scarlett started to stand up, too.

Jaz grabbed her wrist and pulled her down to where she knelt on the floor out of view. Licking her cracked lips, Jazlyn said, "I got caught trying to find you."

"What? Why were you looking for me instead of getting out of this country?"

"Fayth is in trouble."

Four words iced Scarlett's skin. "What happened? *Where is she?*"

"I've got her hidden, but she's injured and has been without me for three days while I was captured."

"Who hurt her?" Claws pushed all the way out of Scarlett's fingers. Red fury clouded her mind. She struggled to hold her cat inside. Someone would bleed for touching Fayth or that baby.

Jaz hurried to tell her, "Lincoln, King of the Cat Clowder."

Scarlett ground her back teeth. That miserable tiger would not stay out of her world. Cat Clowder. Only he would choose a term from the 1700s for his little kingdom.

Speaking in a fast chop, Jaz said, "He's been hunting rogue groups, killing the males and capturing the women."

"Wait. What about Fayth's mate?"

"Dead."

Poor Fayth. Scarlett's heart shriveled at that news. After their screwed-up childhood, all Fayth had wanted was a mate and family.

Panic blasted through Scarlett. She grabbed Jazlyn's arm. *"What about the baby?"*

"Safe. For now. I'll tell you everything when we get out of here."

Scarlett grabbed her head, wanted to scream and rip something apart. "I will kill that fucker and he'll beg for mercy."

Gan whispered, "Scarlett. Are you okay?"

She nodded, unable to get words out until she forced her heart to slow down. Alerting the Gallize up front would get Jaz caught. When she could breathe normally, she sniffed at Jaz. "Are you wounded?"

Grimacing, Jaz said, "No. Maybe. They did something to all of us. I don't know what, but my body is slow to heal and I hurt in places that aren't wounded."

Questions raced through her mind, but Scarlett shut down the emotional ones and fixated on what mattered right now. She had to stop that tiger from getting to Fayth and the baby. That wouldn't happen unless she got Jaz out of here, which would not be easy with a wounded wolf shifter.

Her mind would not let go of how all this happened. There was only one way Jaz would have been captured, which started a domino effect ending at Scarlett. "Who gave you up, Jaz?"

"I paid Kentucky Kirk a lot of money to find you fast, because word was that he associated with you. He must have sold me out to a higher bidder."

"He did and I'll deal with him." Scarlett's hit list kept growing. She wouldn't kill him, but he'd pay for years to come. She spit out, "The damned Pagan Nomads. They burned one of my resources here and killed him."

"Sounds about right."

"Did the traffickers not recognize you?"

Jazlyn's lip lifted on one side and winced. "Not once I fought them. Every time my face started healing, I'd do something to start a new fight, like kick them in the nuts. Blood covers a lot. The last shifter did a number on me a couple hours ago."

"Dammit, Jaz. Why didn't you or Fayth call me?"

"Fayth's phone was forfeit. She barely got out with the baby and the clothes on her back. I had even less on me. I can't spend money on phones and don't need them to live off the land. Besides, I told you I would not leave a message on your voice mail service and risk someone recognizing my voice. Not with today's technology."

Scarlett rubbed her neck. "I hear you."

"Sorry to walk you into a trap."

Scarlett pushed up to her feet. "You couldn't have known.

Sounds like they've been working hard to catch me for a while. Let's get you out of here so you can shift and heal."

"Can't shift. None of us can."

Scarlett did a double take. "Why not?"

"Whatever these men shot us with is preventing us from shifting."

Scarlett had heard enough. "Give me a second." She stepped out of the stall, noted the women standing calmly and talking softly to each other.

Gan turned to her after having waited patiently.

She explained, "My plan just changed from sneaking her out of here to taking her somewhere safe."

"Where?"

"Where am I taking her?" she asked.

"Yes."

"Why do you want to know? The fewer people who know my plans the better."

He scratched his chin. "Gallize know of this safe place?"

"No. Why?" This was not the time to give her grief.

"Is only a question," he said, sounding as if he was the sole reasonable one talking. That could be accurate. "How do I help?"

"Before you do, I need you to understand that I don't want to get you in trouble."

"Is fine."

Nothing about this was fine. But she couldn't refuse Gan's help now, not with Fayth needing her.

Scarlett would face the music if she got nailed for aiding and abetting a criminal both shifter and human law enforcement were hunting. The Guardian over these Gallize shifters worried her more than law enforcement.

But if he found out Gan had helped Jazlyn escape capture, she had to make sure he wouldn't blame Gan. Once she dropped off Gan or set up transportation to get him back to his people, she'd call the Guardian and inform him this had all been her doing. That she'd convinced Gan he was doing the right thing.

No way would she let that eagle shifter hold Gan responsible.

The Guardian would come after her and she had no idea if she'd survive. She'd sensed a level of power the first time she'd met him that felt old and dangerous.

Minutes ticked off in her head as loud as a gong banging.

Putting her hand on the roped muscle of Gan's arm, she noticed a buzz of energy and his small flinch, more a look of surprise than pain. He'd felt it, too?

She asked, "Can you get her outside while I cover for you?"

Putting his hand over hers, which caused a stronger buzz and a strange feeling in her chest, he said, "Yes. Tell Vic and Adrian I go to piss outside." Gan waved a hand at Jaz, who still hid in the stall. When she inched over to where they stood, he whispered, "You walk in front of me to back door."

She sent a look at Scarlett who nodded. "It's a good plan. Don't slow down until you get to the tree line. I'll be out soon and find you."

Once Jaz stood in front of him, Gan said, "I will put finger on shoulder so you know how close I am." She nodded her agreement then Gan must have nudged her. She walked forward, with Gan on her heels. The blanket tied around his waist should have looked absurd.

Maybe on another man, but Gan carried off the image of a warlord.

He strode casually with confidence, as if this was all his show. Not a nervous twitch or glance back once he had Jaz moving in front of him.

He trusted Scarlett to do her part.

His trust meant something.

Hers did, too.

She hadn't given another man trust since hers had been betrayed by a tiger, but there went a Siberian tiger shifter alone with a woman Scarlett would protect with her life. The same tiger that had dismembered an entire team of Pagan Nomads.

Scarlett should be second guessing that decision, but she wasn't. She knew without a doubt that Gan would not harm Jaz. He struggled with the right words sometimes, but when he made a statement, he meant it.

She stared at the muscles playing across his wide shoulders and back as he got closer to the back door, wishing she had met him at another time. He didn't hide his interest in her. No games, no question that he wanted her.

She shouldn't find that hot, but she did.

Men, shifter males in particular, got on her nerves when they came on to her, trying to intimidate her with their alpha attitude or schmooze her with their charm.

Gan didn't have those skills, thankfully, which left him with bold honesty.

He had no trouble stepping in to help free Jazlyn, a female shifter he didn't know, even after he heard Jaz was a wanted person. Gan would be a great backup if she had to face off with Lincoln's tiger while getting Fayth to safety.

But she couldn't take him.

She would not pull Gan deeper into her mess. He'd helped and that was enough. He struggled to find his way as a Gallize shifter as it was.

When he reached the back door and stepped outside, Scarlett turned to the women huddled together. She squeezed around the end. The gap she created filled immediately. Good shifters.

She'd made it halfway to Vic and Adrian when vehicles drove up fast outside, braking in a cloud of dust that caught bits of light from the overhead security lamps now in full bloom.

Doors slammed and five men, make that five Gallize shifters, in tactical gear poured in.

Gan and Jazlyn wouldn't have had time to reach the woods.

CHAPTER 13

SCARLETT PAUSED IN STRIDE, HER gaze locked on the five Gallize shifters inside the barn with weapons drawn. She held her breath, expecting to hear noise outside if an unaccounted for Gallize had jumped out to intercept Gan herding Jaz toward the woods.

No radio transmissions buzzed.

No yelling outside.

Were Gan and Jaz pinned close to the building waiting for a chance to make it across eighty yards of cleared land to reach the closest trees?

Maybe these five male shifters were the entire unit.

How could she let Gan know it was safe to send Jazlyn off on her own so he could get back inside? He had no comm unit even if she put hers on again.

The minute the five-man team entered, they split up with predetermined tasks. Two shifters immediately went to check on Vic and Adrian. A third one stood by the entrance with a high-powered rifle ready while he watched everything in the building.

She didn't kid herself.

They were protecting teammates first.

Vic spoke to the last two shifters. "The women probably need medical treatment, food, blankets. Give them whatever they need."

"Where's Gan?" Adrian asked, straining to look past Scarlett.

As the pair Vic sent to the captives passed Scarlett, she replied, "He said he had to take a piss." Good thing Gan had actually said that so these two shifters wouldn't sniff a lie.

One of the female shifters in the group yelled, "No!"

Scarlett swung around and rushed over to where the two men looked bewildered.

A stocky guy with blond hair, cut short on the sides and an inch thick on top, smelling of bear and a well-used vest, said, "I was asking to see their wounds to determine if we should treat them here or if they'd be more comfortable in the bus we brought."

Scarlett huffed out a breath. "Be patient. They've had a rough time and they don't feel good. The traffickers might have injected them with a drug, because they can't shift. You can appreciate how that makes them feel vulnerable."

"Yes, ma'am."

Ma'am? She started to tell him he had her age wrong, but he was being polite and after meeting his boss she knew where the manners came from.

She turned to the nine women. "I give you my word you can trust these men. Their boss is the deadliest shifter you ever want to meet and he expects them to treat you well. He sent his people with me so we could rescue you. Those two on the floor almost died helping. One of them got shot with a titanium load and the other had a titanium sword shoved through him from back to front."

That brought out a few cringes.

The women leaned in different directions, trying to see past Scarlett to where Vic and Adrian sat. When they returned their attention to Scarlet, she said, "I would not rescue you to hand you over to anyone who would harm you. These are all honorable men. I want you to let them help you. Okay?"

Heads bobbed with a few mumbled complaints, but they knew they were lucky to get away from the Pagan Nomads.

"Good. Please go with them out to the bus. If you feel like you can't shift, it might be something the traffickers shot inside you, and we'll figure that out. We have great shifter medical aid. If, however, you get the urge to shift and think you can, please don't. Just wait until you arrive at the Friends of Shifters shelter. We provide a safe area for our female shifters to change where you'll be protected the whole time." She seriously doubted any of these women wanted to shift around men whose alpha-level power rolled off these guys in waves.

"Are you going with us?" one thin and trembling women asked.

"Not this minute, but I'll be by soon." She hoped. That must not have rung with truth. She got a few frowns, so she explained for everyone's benefit. "I have someone else who is in danger and needs me, but I'll call to make sure the staff at the shelter is expecting you so that you have what you need when you arrive. You won't go anywhere else until you're ready and choose to make that move. Understood?"

She got a chorus of okays. "Thank you. When I come by, I'll work with each of you on what the future holds and how to keep you safe."

"Thank you," murmured again through the group.

"You're welcome. This is …" She turned to the blond guy.

"I'm Landon and my partner is Shawn. We have supplies and a comfortable bus to transport you to the Friends of Shifters shelter together. I second everything she said. We are here to care for your injuries, protect you, and deliver you safely to the shelter."

Scarlett's nose told her Shawn had a wolf inside him.

Her announcement and his confirmation cheered up the women, who had probably expected to be separated. As the group broke up their wall of bodies and began following Landon, Adrian strode up to her with a hitch in his gait and skin still gray. "Where's Gan?"

She rounded on him, forcing him to turn so that his back was to a stall. She feared the back door would open and Gan might still have Jaz with him. Using her exasperated voice, she said, "I told you he went out to take a piss."

"Shouldn't take this long," Adrian argued.

Shit. This guy didn't believe her.

"Who are you to say how long for piss?" Gan asked as he walked up from the back of the building. She hadn't heard him open the door. He kept coming until he stood beside Scarlett in a clear show of support.

Then he pointed to his jeans. "I had to get clothes. Not good to walk around naked when women already afraid of us."

Everything he said rang with truth.

She hadn't minded seeing him naked one bit, not until he'd caught her ogling him then she'd caught the captives taking in every inch of him. Had she been jealous?

Regardless of what Gan told Adrian to cover how long he was

gone, she did appreciate him coming back in dressed for the women.

She hoped his return meant Jaz had made it to safety.

Adrian cut a questioning look at Gan. "Just making sure you didn't get any ideas about straying, Psycho Cat."

Had Adrian thought Gan would run?

So had Chica. Why?

Scarlett could answer that. She and those two Gallize had treated Gan poorly even if they all had the right reasons for keeping him out of harm's way.

Gan was like any other proud man. His gaze stayed firmly on Adrian when he spoke. "Lucky for you I did not stray, or only observe."

That shut up the wolf.

Vic walked up, hissing with each move. "What's going on?"

Gan shrugged. "Nothing. You should tell Guardian how I have control."

Adrian made a sound of disbelief.

"No?" Gan challenged. "My tiger kill bad shifters and I am now human. You live because of tiger. How do you argue my words?"

Scarlett could argue that his tiger had started to attack her cougar. If she hadn't shifted to human, he might have, but the tiger had not fought back when Chica hit him hard on the nose.

Gan *had* managed to gain control after all that and return to his human form.

It didn't matter now.

She wasn't about to throw him under the bus when he needed support.

Vic ran his hand over his bark-brown hair now loose from the ponytail. "One time isn't going to convince the Guardian you're ready to be on your own."

"I know." Gan scratched the side of his neck. "But Scarlett need backup on something important. I owe her debt and want to pay back. Guardian said I would have chance to do that. Call Guardian. He will approve."

Scarlett did an outstanding job of not losing her shit at that announcement. He should talk to her before putting her on the spot. First of all, she could not take him with her. The Guardian *might* overlook Gan's help freeing Jaz, if that got out, but he would not be so understanding if Gan voluntarily went with Scarlett now to clearly aid and abet a wanted criminal.

What was he thinking?

Why would he want to do go with her anyhow?

She suffered a weak moment of wanting to accept his offer and take him with her, but guilt stomped all over that bad idea. Gan needed someone to protect him because he didn't realize what he was offering to do.

Wait a minute? She wanted to slap herself. What was she worried about?

The Guardian would not allow Gan to go with her. Gan had not spent enough time as a shifter to be allowed out on his own around humans.

Panic moment over, she sighed with relief.

"You think he's going to let you go off like that?" Vic asked Gan, sounding shocked at the tiger shifter's audacity.

"Yes. You should call him. She must go now."

Vic's jaw muscles pulsed like his head might explode. He ground out his next words. "Adrian, go with the medics on the bus with the women. You need to get back to headquarters and have that wound flushed out ASAP."

Gan said, "You can control wolf around women?"

"Yes," Adrian snapped. "I can do a lot of things you can't, tiger."

Stabbing a scathing look at Gan, Vic said, "You stay right here while I find a phone." Then he stomped off, pausing to groan and slow down.

Adrian called out, "You need help?"

Vic swung around and snarled, "No."

Shifters weren't keen on looking vulnerable, even if a teammate had good intentions.

"Fuck all of you." Adrian stormed past Vic, who followed him out at a slow gait.

Scarlett waited as the men left, glad Vic had been so riled up he hadn't asked for her phone. She needed a minute to explain to Gan that going with her would end up with him being hunted along with Scarlett and Jaz.

Additionally, she needed him to think before he opened his mouth and started making declarations and demands.

With all the shifters out of hearing range for whispers, Scarlett turned to Gan. "What the hell are you thinking? You don't owe me anything after helping my friend escape."

"This is true. You owe *me* favor."

Was he serious? She didn't have time to argue. "Okay, fine. I'm sorry, but you'll have to wait for me to pay you back."

"No. You pay now."

Everything inside her said not to ask, but she didn't have the luxury of a rational conversation right now. "How can I pay you now?"

"Take me with you."

She looked into his sharp blue eyes, wishing she could take him with her for so many reasons, but too many of those reasons were not in his best interest. "Why the hell would you ... what am I saying ... I shouldn't even ..."

How did one tiger shifter with so few words manage to fluster her?

None of those disjointed thoughts mattered. She said, "The Guardian is not going to let you go with me."

His eyes filled with pleading. "He will send me back to Wyoming land where I am locked inside invisible walls. Adrian will stay with team. No me. I will be alone again. I have been captive my whole life. Everyone control me. I am tired of no choice. Just one time, I want to feel ... free to make choice."

He said the one thing that cracked her heart wide open and made her want to grant this simple wish.

She'd lived in a different kind of captivity where she couldn't have a life. She had to hide and stay under the radar, avoid relationships. While she was free to walk around, she also suffered from lack of choice.

But if she gave in and took him with her, Gan would face punishment he didn't deserve.

Vic came hobbling up, grumbling the whole time, with a mobile phone at his ear. "Yes, sir. I'm handing it to her now."

Scarlett looked at the phone as if the plastic box had turned into a snake about to strike. If she said the wrong thing, she either crushed Gan or welcomed the wrath of his deadly Gallize Guardian.

A riled up snake would be easier to handle.

CHAPTER 14

—

"HELLO, SCARLETT." THE GUARDIAN'S RICH voice on the other end of the call sounded friendly, which he had the ability to be when not angry.

She tried to keep that in mind and not think about how a powerful being can smash everything in sight.

While she struggled to compose a sentence, because not even she knew what she was about to say, the Guardian prodded her with, "Vic tells me you want to discuss Gan."

Gan stood quietly to the side.

Two Gallize shifters from the team began picking up bloody body parts decorated with hay and tossing them into a rubber tub. A third member of the team came in with some solution he sprayed over all areas affected.

Scarlett turned away and cleared her throat. "Yes, I, uh …" She sensed Gan's eyes boring invisible holes in her back. Screw it. "I've got a lead on another person in jeopardy, someone important to me actually. I'd really like some backup. Gan offered and …" Her voice trailed off.

When a shifter lifted the giant tub and carried it deeper into the building, Gan stepped close to her.

His gaze hadn't left the phone in her hand.

He didn't have to crowd her, because he could hear both sides of this call just as any other shifter close by could.

Just having him that close pushed her.

The Guardian said, "Scarlett?"

She never got flustered. His fault it had happened twice in a short period of time.

Feeling like a kid about to get caught trying to sneak out of school aggravated the hell out of her so she rattled it out all at once. "Gan shifted into his tiger to save everyone then shifted back. I'm under the impression this was some kind of test today and I, for one, think he passed with flying colors. I'm asking for him to go with me."

Gan smiled so big she could see it in her peripheral vision.

Her heart wiggled with seeing him happy. She took a breath and added, "If you can spare him."

"What?" Vic snapped. "He's not ready."

Gan took a step toward Vic.

Scarlett moved between them and held a hand up at Gan, plus she gave him a don't-you-dare look.

The Guardian asked, "Why did Vic say he wasn't ready?"

She shrugged even though the eagle shifter couldn't see her. "You'll have to ask him, but keep in mind that while both Vic and Adrian were incapacitated and the rest of us were surrounded by the kidnappers, Gan came in and took down almost all of them or you would be short two of your men."

That knocked the gruff out of Vic. When he spoke this time, it was loud enough for everyone to hear. "She's right, sir." Then Vic glanced at Gan and said, "I should have told you thank you by now. Good job, man."

Gan said, "I am glad you live. Now I want to repay debt to Scarlett."

Scarlett almost forgot she had someone on the phone until the Guardian asked, "Are you sure you want Gan and not someone who has been in the field longer?"

"I am ready," Gan countered, voice booming.

She looked at him and slashed her hand across her throat, telling him to cut it out.

Gan's forehead crinkled. "What is wrong with neck?"

Growling at him, she told the Guardian, "I think Gan will be perfect for what I need." She wasn't lying either. Gan hadn't hesitated to help her free Jaz. He had no loyalty to the Gallize yet. That would come in time, but for now he wouldn't get mired down in details such as wanting to run anything questionable past the Guardian first.

All she had to do was return him safe and sound, and leave things with the Guardian in a way that showed Gan had helped without clearly understanding he had aided someone wanted by law enforcement. She would tell the Guardian any wrongdoing was all on her.

With Gan's lack of experience in the field, she could make a convincing argument.

"I don't need to tell you that Gan has not been a shifter long, Scarlett. You were there the day I called up his tiger."

Why was the Guardian pointing that out? He couldn't have read her thoughts, right? She said, "I do know that."

"And you're willing to take responsibility for having him around the public this soon? You'll ensure his tiger is not a liability around humans?"

Now she got it.

The Guardian wanted everything on the table. He was putting her on notice that everyone, including her, knew how inexperienced Gan was as a shifter. If she took him with her and Gan failed to control his Siberian tiger, the Guardian would not hold Gan responsible.

He'd hold her responsible.

That actually took a weight off her shoulders.

Now she wouldn't have to worry about Gan carrying any blame about helping Jaz. "I'm the one in charge," she assured the Guardian. "Any problem that arises is on me, but I think he'll be fine."

She danced close to a lit fuse with that one. But after what Gan had done today, she did believe he could do this.

He'd said the tiger had calmed around her.

Why had that animal struck Chica?

The cleanup crew had made it to the back of the building and were walking in long strides toward the front. Vic stepped out of the way, nodding at the men.

The Guardian wrapped up the conversation. "Very well. You may take him with you, but I want him back at headquarters in three days."

Gan's eyes lost their moment of thrill and his mouth flattened in a line, but he said nothing for once.

"Got it. Three days." She reached deep to sound confident.

"You have a number for me, which is answered twenty-four-seven. I have your number and expect to reach you at any time as well."

The Guardian just letting her know Gan's leash had limits.

Scarlett intended to drop Gan back the minute she had Fayth and Jaz set. "About the women I'm sending with your men tonight. I've asked your team to deliver them to the Friends of Shifters, but I know they need to clear it through you first."

"When I sent the team, I authorized them to follow your instructions. They will go to the shelter immediately and provide anything the women need in the meantime."

"Thank you. I'll alert the shelter so they're ready for the women. Oh, one more thing. Someone has to deal with the humans killed in the house." She did not want that sad job.

"I have a different Gallize team arriving to finish cleanup. I'll inform them of that task and contacting human law enforcement who will inform the families."

"That's good." Scarlett added, "Thank you also for sending three shifters with me today. As it was, we needed all of them." She glanced at Gan and added, "Gan, in particular."

His lips smiled a little at that.

Returning to his uber-polite voice, the Guardian said, "I appreciate the experience Gan is gaining, too, Scarlett. As long as he is not in danger and not a risk to others."

"Would you like to talk to him before I hang up?"

Gan started waving her off and shaking his head.

The Guardian said, "Yes, I would."

She handed Gan the phone.

He glared at her and held it near his ear. "Yes?"

"*Sir!*" Vic snarled. "Yes, sir."

Gan gave Vic a blank look and spoke into the phone again. "Are you there?"

Vic grabbed his hair and walked off making odd noises.

Scarlett could swear she heard a chuckle come from the phone.

The Guardian said, "I'm glad you were there or we would have lost many today, Gan. You were impressive. I only hesitated to send you with Scarlett for fear that you'll rush in when you shouldn't, not because I lack faith in you as a shifter."

"I am fine. I will make no mistake."

"You're allowed to make mistakes, but it's my job to manage them and keep everyone safe."

"I understand. I am good."

Scarlett noticed Gan did not agree or disagree with his boss, just acknowledged the eagle shifter's words.

What was Gan not saying?

A long sigh followed. The Guardian hadn't gotten the confirmation he'd expected either, but evidently he was willing to give Gan some room to learn and grow into being a shifter.

She'd like to think of that as a vote of confidence in her ability to keep him and anyone around him safe, but she would be foolish to think for a minute that the Guardian wouldn't keep tabs on both of them.

When the call ended, Gan handed her back the phone. "Ready?"

"I guess." That was as honest an answer as she could muster, considering what she'd just obligated to a man whose power topped anything she brought to the table. She made a quick call to the shelter to clear the way for the team to drop off her ladies. Once she found Vic and told him what to do when the bus arrived at the Friends of Shifters, Vic offered her and Gan a ride to her truck.

She politely declined, claiming the walk would be good for Gan.

"In that case, I'm going with Adrian on the bus with the medic. Three of the women said they would be fine riding in the Hummer with our men. We're ready to get your women to safety. I'll return later for my truck."

She found it interesting that Vic felt the need to keep an eye on Adrian. Could be because the wolf had been badly wounded.

She followed him out to thank the men and watched as they drove out of sight.

Now she could catch her breath and get Jaz out of here.

When she entered the building again, Gan waited halfway to the rear door.

As she reached him, she said, "They're gone. We should be all set to grab Jaz and get to my truck without anyone seeing us. Do you have any injuries you've been hiding from me?"

"No. I am good."

He seemed introspective, but not limping in spite of so much blood drying on him, so she accepted his claim and led the way to the back door.

Stepping out into the cool evening air, she said, "I need the truth, Gan. You *can* control that tiger, right?"

"Sometimes."

She groaned, but put that on the back burner to deal with if she had to later on. "Where did you leave Jazlyn?"

Gan pointed. "I took her there."

She stopped to scan the trees. "I don't see her, but she could be sitting down to rest. Let's get her and—"

"She is not there."

Her head started pounding as if tiny construction workers ran jackhammers against her skull. She rounded on Gan. "What do you mean *she's not there*? Where did she go?"

"She did not say where. She said for you to meet her. She gave me address." He repeated the address Jazlyn had given him. "She said is over line in, uh … Virginia. Yes, that place."

Scarlett could find it, but why had Jaz taken off? "What *exactly* was said before she decided to go?"

His brow creased with confusion. "You want all words?"

"Yes, I want *everything* that happened and was said once you got outside."

He looked past her as if digging into his memory to answer her. "We wait when we hear trucks. They park around building. We run to woods. When we get there, she said she must go to Fayth. I tell her you want her to wait for us. She think about it one minute, then give me address for you. Told me she would stay in trees until I walk back in building."

"*Us?*" Scarlett asked, clenching her jaw hard enough to crack teeth. She knew what happened. Jaz trusted no one, especially not some shifter she didn't know.

Giving Scarlett a nod, Gan said, "Yes. Us."

"But we had not discussed you going with me at that point." Scarlett struggled to keep from yelling at him.

He shrugged. "Was not important. I know I go with you when I talk to her."

She grabbed her head, ready to pull it off just for some relief. "Dammit, Gan. You scared her off!"

"I did nothing. I was nice. Save her from building." He crossed his arms. "How am I wrong?"

"She would have waited on me if you had not told her you were going with us, too. She left because she doesn't know you. That woman has been on the run a long time and stayed alive because she isn't an idiot."

He glowered at her. "Not my fault."

She deserved this for convincing the Guardian to allow him to go with her. "You … I … never mind. Let's go."

She set a faster pace this time. Gan had no trouble keeping up, but neither could he talk. She sped up every time he tried. She expected Jaz to track the scent back to where Scarlett and Vic had parked their vehicles.

She hadn't expected to be robbed.

"She took my damn truck!" Scarlett stomped around, cursing and ready to strangle Jaz. When she stopped, she swung her acidic temper at Gan. "If you'd kept your mouth shut none of this would be happening."

He lifted his hands. "Not my fault you have bad friend. You say so."

"*Arghhh!* You are making me nuts."

"I did nothing." He turned to the other vehicle. "You should not leave key."

She couldn't believe he was criticizing her. "I didn't leave my key out in the open. I always hide it, but that year truck is easy to hotwire."

"What is hotwire?"

She slapped a hand over her eyes. This was all her fault for wanting to spend more time with Gan and thinking he could be her backup.

She got what she'd asked for.

Gan pointed out, "She did not take both. We have ride. All good."

Most men would know when to stop talking and making things worse. Not Gan.

"No. We are *not* all good." Scarlett stepped over to him. "Starting now, no more confusion. There are rules for coming with me. You do not tell anyone anything I haven't approved. You do as I say and don't make my life any more difficult. I need to get someone important to safety. Once that happens, I am delivering you back to the Guardian. Do you understand?"

"Yes." He said a lot with one unhappy word.

But yet again, he hadn't really agreed, just acknowledged what she'd said.

Giving up, she headed for Vic's Expedition that had none of her stuff in it, plus she'd have to call and ask the Guardian to borrow the vehicle. That would mean coming up with a believable reason she couldn't use her truck.

This got deeper by the minute.

She reluctantly walked over to the black sport utility.

Gan opened the rear hatch where multiple bags had been dropped inside. He pulled out a set of stretch pants and a T-shirt he handed her.

She grudgingly took them and mumbled her thanks.

Then he opened the driver's door, which surprised her since she thought he had never driven a vehicle. He leaned down, sticking his arm under the seat and came back with the keys he placed on her open palm. "I watch Vic hide keys."

"Thanks." The word could have come out nicer, but she'd at least said it.

She asked, "Can you drive?"

"No." He went to the passenger side.

When they were both seated, she cranked the engine and backed around, working to calm herself before she tackled driving out of here.

In an innocent voice men had when they wanted to win points, Gan said, "See? I am helpful."

"Right," she snapped, unwilling to give him strokes for the keys. She wouldn't have needed them if Jaz had waited.

Jaz would have waited if he hadn't scared her off.

"Why are you angry?"

He'd finally figured that out?

Had it been that hard to figure out? "I'll tell you why I'm angry, Gan. Having you with me complicates an already difficult situation with someone close to me in danger. Then you say too much when you should have said nothing and now I have to track down Jazlyn … *with* you, which isn't going to go over well. She'll expect me to have figured out why she left and have the good sense to show up alone. When she finds out I brought you, she'll … let's just say she'll be very disappointed."

"Life not easy. Everyone has disappointment."

"You're not helping, Gan."

The seatbelt warning light flashed in the dash. He opened his door.

"Whoa. Where are you going?"

"I am too much problem. I leave."

She put her head down on the steering wheel. This was why she spent her life alone. She was no better at being with people some days than Gan.

The door closed.

Crap. She put the transmission in park and jumped out, hurrying around the truck. "Gan!"

He kept walking.

She ran after him. "Stop. Please."

He stopped. Good to know that please worked.

When he didn't turn around, she circled him until she stood in his path. Now what to say?

She should apologize, but that galled her considering he'd created this problem.

"Move, Scarlett. I want to go."

It hurt to hear those words. She'd been trying to send him back, but now he wanted to walk away. She didn't want him to do that, which made no sense, but she didn't have the time or energy to analyze her reaction.

Putting a hand on his chest, she said, "No, let's go back to the truck. Please."

He leaned his face down to hers. "No. Everyone tell me what to do, where to go, what to think. I am not animal. I was prisoner, but human for long time. I never have choice. I know what is best for me. I want no leash, not even invisible one." He swallowed hard. "I care for you. I want you safe. I try to help, but make you angry. I want to go where I can live like person. I want you happy. I will go."

Stepping around her, he kept moving.

She stood there, stunned at all he'd said. He hadn't caused this trouble intentionally, only by trying to help her.

Not just that.

He said he cared for her and wanted her happy. No man had ever cared if she was happy. In fact, a couple of them had done all they could to make her life hell.

Gan plodded along through the dense forest, but he was making headway.

She took off and caught up to him, putting her arms on his waist.

That stopped him faster than the word please.

Energy zinged under her fingers.

The skin over his taut waist was smooth and warm.

He grabbed her hands with his and pulled her closer against his back. She smiled. He might not always do as she asked, but his actions were as sincere as his words.

She moved her cheek over his back, inhaling as she did. Gan had a natural scent of a large jungle cat and something uniquely his that reminded her of early mornings when she let Chica run through the forest.

His fingers threaded through hers, pressing her hands against rock-hard abs.

She felt bad about crabbing at him.

He had a point. From the moment a Siberian tiger had been called out of him, Gan had been forced to figure his own way through all of this. Add that to the fact that he'd been captive his entire life before that and had not been born in this country so English was not even his first language.

She got the Shit Award for taking her frustration out on him.

She swallowed hard.

Maybe even a shit could change.

Her eyes and throat burned. She forced out the words. "I'm sorry, Gan."

"I forgive. I am sorry I did not understand Jaz upset. I am learning. I do better."

For someone wronged so many times in his life, Gan forgave easily. She might be undeserving, but she took his words and held them close.

He gave her fingers a squeeze then pulled her around by one arm.

She put both hands on his broad chest to catch her balance and smiled, prepared to tell him she really was happy about him going with her.

She wanted to make up for the argument.

Gan had his own makeup plan.

He cupped her under the arms and lifted her to kiss the daylights out of her. Her legs wrapped around him as if they'd only been waiting for an invitation. He might not know the language or how this world worked sometimes, but he nailed kissing.

She hadn't been kissed in a long time.

Not like this even back then.

His mouth sent shivers over her skin and heat searing between her legs.

Hell, she hadn't been with anyone who turned her on like this with just a kiss.

She grabbed his hair and clung to him, dragging him closer for more. He put a hand under her bottom, lifting her up. Perfect. She wrapped her arms around him and sent her tongue in to meet his. *Hello there, handsome.*

His other hand slipped under her T-shirt and located breasts excited to be found.

She nipped his lip.

He nipped hers back and growled at her, then smothered her laugh with his lips.

Kissing him each time just got better. She put everything into it and his lips lifted with a smile at her clearly taking control. Yes, she had a bad habit of that and it had sent other men running.

Not Gan. She doubted anything she did would intimidate him.

His big fingers played with her nipples and her body clenched. It had been too long and never anything that felt this good. His tongue slid into her mouth, tasting her, and leaving a hot path everywhere it went.

He kept playing with one breast then the other, as if undecided over which one was his favorite.

Please let him get stuck, unable to decide.

It might kill her to be teased nonstop, but she'd accept the risk.

"We need better place," Gan murmured, kissing her cheek then her neck.

"What place?" Her mind couldn't function with his hands on her.

"For take clothes off."

Clothes? She blinked when the word registered and lifted her head. "Wait, we're not doing that here."

"That is what I said. Need better place."

She dropped her head back and spoke to the sky. "I'm an idiot." Then she looked at Gan again. "I have to go save my friend. I can't be doing … *this*."

"Not now." He said that as a statement, one meant to clarify that the only thing in question was the timing.

She was not starting a new discussion. "Not now."

"Okay." He swung around, walking back to the truck.

"Put me down."

"Why?"

"So I can walk."

He didn't slow down. "No." He fought a smile then finally said, "This is what I decide. It cause no problem. You should be happy."

Well, damn, he had a point.

She held on, taking in everything about him this close up. He deserved an award for stopping if he was half as worked up as her. He deposited her on the driver's seat.

When he stepped back, she had a front row view of one major boner.

Yep. Give that man a gold star for stopping. That did not look comfortable.

She hadn't meant to leave him that way, but he'd started it after all. In fact, this made twice in one day he'd rattled her hormones, making them think getting up close and hot with Gan would be a regular occurrence, when she should know better.

With Gan back riding shotgun, she maneuvered the Expedition through the woods. Just before pulling out onto the paved highway, she stopped to plug in the address on her phone GPS. With that set, she couldn't avoid dealing with what had just happened.

They needed ground rules, which would be awkward now that she'd almost gotten naked with him. She didn't want to spend the whole time snapping at him like a shrew.

His voice held all sorts of gloating when he said, "I smell you are happy. I help again. You should keep list."

And just like that, he screwed up her good mood.

She had to pull that ego back down from outer space. "That got out of hand, Gan. We need to keep a professional relationship. We're only going to be together maybe two or three days."

When he said nothing, she looked over to find his elbow leaned against the door and his head propped on his hand, staring at her.

SCENT OF A MATE 121

She didn't trust that content look. "What?"

"We can do many times in two days."

Her jaw dropped. "Did you not hear what I said? I can't be playing around with you. It's not professional and there is no future in it. Let's just cut it out right now. I'm not blaming you. My fault for letting it get out of control. Do you get what I'm saying?"

"Yes. You want me. Place not good. Is okay. We find better place and I give you what you want."

She stared at him.

Don't kill the tiger shifter.

While it would be easy to pick a spot in the nearby woods to hide the body, she didn't have her truck with the shovel.

He spoke with authority. "You thank me in two days. Maybe in one day if you drive now."

On second thought, she had claws.

She didn't need a shovel.

CHAPTER 15

HAVING DELIVERED THE FEMALE SHIFTERS to the shelter, Adrian followed Vic and the team into the Gallize Spartanburg headquarters to debrief the Guardian.

From what he'd been told during his stay in Wyoming, the Guardian felt they needed a place of operations with so much Black River pack shifter activity going on in the southeast.

Based on what happened today, they had more than the Black River pack to take down.

Adrian had waited until the bus emptied out with Shawn escorting the women into the shelter while Landon flushed the titanium from his wound. It would have been easier on him to wait until they reached headquarters where a medic had better instruments than what they used in the field.

But he chose to suffer through it to keep Mad Red from breaking loose and destroying anything in its path.

That treatment and his wolf's reaction to the pain had been hell for almost two full minutes, but it would have been worse if Scarlett had not cleaned out most of the metal.

When Adrian's claws shot out and his head warped halfway from human to wolf, the guys understood. Excruciating pain loosened the tether on any shifter's hold.

He knew the real truth.

He'd been fighting his wolf the whole drive and allowed the pain to batter his animal into compliance. Shifting would have been easier on both of them, but he was too beat down to hope for any control.

Those women had been through hell.

They didn't need to even see Mad Red.

Walking through the two-story brick building that had stood probably as long as Spartanburg, any indiscriminate snarling and growling would get him shipped back to Wyoming.

The sign outside had identified the location with three letters. GSH, which stood for Gallize Shifter Headquarters, though no definition of those letters existed. The solid black front door remained closed, opening only when someone activated the electronic lock.

Shawn waited at the elevator for Adrian to enter. They rode down beneath the building and exited the car.

"Hey, Adrian. Good to see you." Justin stepped from an office and into his path.

Shawn walked on.

Forcing his voice to sound light, Adrian gave the bear shifter a bro hug and said, "Good to be back."

Justin cocked his head in a curious motion.

To fix the lie he'd tried to pass off, Adrian frowned. "Let's say it will be good at some point."

"Got it. No worries. You on the way to see the boss?"

Glancing at Shawn who had taken a right into a room down the hall, Adrian said, "Yes. Just got back from a field op with Scarlett and Gan."

"Where's the tiger?"

"That's a long story. Let me get through debriefing with the Guardian and I'll fill you in."

"Over beers. My treat. Cole might be back by then, too."

"Sounds good, man."

Adrian moved forward, condemning himself for being a walking lie. He shouldn't be out of Wyoming.

He shouldn't be breathing.

His Gallize brothers—Justin, Cole, and Rory—fought against the Guardian putting down Mad Red.

Adrian had asked his boss to do it, but …

The letter in his pocket wouldn't let him take the coward's way out or keep hiding. Not when he had to step up for a past brother in arms who died stepping up for Adrian. He only had to manage Mad Red long enough to make good on a promise.

For now, his wolf slept from exhaustion.

When he entered one of the meeting rooms on the floor two

levels down, he paused to grab the lay of the land. Vic sat in the cushy office chair on wheels. Landon took a spot at the table two chairs down from Vic and Shawn sat on the opposite side from Landon.

Adrian spotted another padded chair like Vic's and eased down into it. He flinched halfway there.

Vic looked over. "I don't smell titanium. Did you already flush that wound?"

"Landon did," Adrian muttered back.

The Guardian came in quickly, paused to look at Adrian, then addressed Vic. "Are you up to giving a report?"

"Yes, sir." He started to rise.

"Please sit … everyone." The Guardian stepped past Landon and took a seat at the table. "Are you doing better, Adrian?"

"Yes, sir. Wound is clean. I'm healing."

Vic recounted everything that had happened, including how the Pagan Nomads had set a trap. "They knew we were coming. They wanted to get Scarlett."

Landon asked, "Why?"

Adrian groaned when he shifted his position. "Best I could tell, she's been interfering with their operations. Sounds like their boss gave an order to grab her. This had to take a while to coordinate, which would mean burning some of her contacts."

"You don't think they've just been waiting for her to show up at one of their operations?" Shawn asked.

"No." Adrian had thought about what happened on the way back. "This was topnotch. They'd have to arrange all of that every time they were at any location. It's not logical."

The Guardian added, "Adrian is correct. One reason we work with Scarlett is because she has an extensive underground network it would take years for us to develop. For even one of her resources to destroy a relationship with her would be a costly mistake. I am going to guess that resource did not choose to betray her. For that to be the case, the Pagan Nomads probably fed their intentions of grabbing female shifters in the Great Smoky Mountains into the information network. They knew she'd go hunting those women. She told me how she'd gotten the location. She's savvy. This was not a mistake on her part or an accident, but a high-level operation."

Adrian couldn't contain his question any longer. "Knowing all that and how little time Gan has been a shifter, why would you allow him to go with Scarlett … sir. Sorry. I don't mean that to sound critical. I'm not smooth right now."

"I understand, Adrian, and it is a valid question." The Guardian steepled his fingers, appearing contemplative for a long moment. "All of you have met Scarlett. What is your impression?"

The question surprised Adrian.

Landon looked at Shawn, then said, "We only met her for a short time in that barn. She seems confident and in charge. Takes no crap off anyone. Smells like a cat."

Shawn nodded in agreement.

"She's shared that she's a cougar," their boss confirmed. "Anything else?"

Shawn said, "I think she's also an alpha. She was putting off some strong power mojo."

Grunts of agreement followed. Vic said, "Every time we meet her, I recognize her as a shifter, a cat, and strong, but it feels like she's got more under the hood that she's hiding."

Adrian had been so busy dealing with his wolf the whole time he hadn't noticed much. Just another sign that he was not valuable in the field right now, but neither was Gan.

The Guardian said, "You are all correct. I felt that she was controlling everything about herself in the first meeting."

"You mean like her heart rate, because of being around other shifters?" Vic asked.

"Yes, but more than heart rate. I don't have specifics or any evidence, but she's definitely powerful. More than she wants anyone to know, is my guess."

Coming from their boss, that was major.

Glancing at Adrian, the Guardian said, "Back to your question about allowing Gan to leave with Scarlett. Gan shifted into his tiger and attacked all the Pagan Nomads. Before handing Scarlett the phone, Vic told me Scarlett had shifted into her cougar. The cats fought together. I would have expected a tiger with so little experience in the world to have attacked her cougar. Did that happen?"

Vic frowned. "I'll be honest. I had a sword in my gut while they fought and was trying to remain conscious."

"I was in pretty much the same shape," Adrian admitted. "I couldn't help them. Hell, I couldn't move. I heard more than I saw."

The Guardian said, "Understandable. I allowed Gan to go with Scarlett because I have no doubt her cougar can hold its own with Gan and it appears Gan's tiger did not attack her cougar. If it had, I'd think she would refuse to take Gan with her and definitely not request him."

Vic rubbed his chin. "You have a point."

"I also believe Gan has a natural protective streak you all possess," their boss added. "In fact, I think females bring that to the surface for him."

Adrian sat up and regretted the too-fast change in position. He rubbed his chest. "You may be onto something, boss. The morning you came to get us, he shifted as he jumped from a boulder down to knock my wolf away from a baby bison."

"Oh, man. You were eating little bison?" Vic said in a chastising tone.

"Give me a break would you?" Adrian muttered. "My wolf was tracking the scent of the adult and saw the baby first. Anyhow ..." He shot Vic a glare to shut the fuck up if he wasn't going to help. "Gan went on and on about never harming babies or mamas."

Smiling, the Guardian said, "And that is why I decided to take a chance and leave Gan with Scarlett. She may be just the influence he needs. He'll have to control himself around her or she will insure he does."

"Damn, boss. That might work," Vic agreed.

"There is one potential problem," Adrian interjected, though he hated to bring it up. But Gan being free of Wyoming was on Adrian as much as anyone. "He may make a run for it."

"Where?" Vic asked.

"I don't know his exact destination," Adrian admitted.

The Guardian remained silent and stoic, pushing Adrian to come as clean as he could.

"I'm not saying he will take off for sure," Adrian clarified. "But he asked me about how far Canada was and made a comment about wanting to live where it was cold."

"That doesn't mean he's going to run," Shawn argued.

"No, but Gan doesn't always say exactly what he's thinking.

I'm still concerned about him being off with Scarlett even if she is a … shoot, what is she if she's not just a shifter?"

"I don't know yet," the Guardian admitted. "But I don't believe she would have chosen Gan to go with her unless she could manage him. To be honest, my concern is that might be exactly why she chose him to go with her. She may think she can control him."

Adrian shifted his shoulders and stretched his neck, not wanting to say more, but knowing he had no choice. "She may be in for a rude awakening if she pushes him too hard."

A pair of steely eagle eyes narrowed at Adrian. "What are you saying?"

A prickle of concern ran up Adrian's spine. Busted. "I don't think Gan can control his tiger as well as he claims, and I should have said so up front but …"

"You wanted to leave the compound as much as Gan did after you read the letter, correct?"

"Yes, sir." Adrian leaned over his arms on the table and lowered his head to run his hand over the scruffy hair. Stupid of him to be in this position. "I'll go bring him back if that's what you want, sir."

Silence hung over the room like heavy blanket.

The Guardian studied Adrian. "Can I trust you to not go rogue?"

Not what Adrian expected his boss to say, but he sat up and faced his boss. "Yes, sir. I'm not taking off. I would like to remain here long enough to get in touch with someone from my past. Once I get that done, I'll go wherever you wish at that point, even back to … Wyoming. No argument."

Moving on quickly as if that exchange decided something for the Guardian, he said, "Thank you for offering to go for Gan, Adrian. I'll take that into consideration. Now, do we have any intel on the Pagan Nomads?"

Vic leaned forward, tapping his fingers on the table. "Not that I know of, but we will. I'll put out word with our contacts. Scarlett may get more out of the women once she's back."

Nodding to Vic, the Guardian said, "The sooner the better. I'm concerned they may have captured more women to use as bait."

Shawn spoke up. "If you're concerned about Gan's control, how long are you going to let him be on his own?"

"I gave Scarlett three days. I want a team ready if she calls before that deadline."

Landon asked, "What if she doesn't call and he runs?"

"I would call him home, just as I would any rogue shifter."

Adrian had a chill raise goosebumps over his skin at the Guardian's tone. That eagle shifter was a man of his word and fair to a fault, but Adrian would never cross him and expect to live long.

Vic asked, "Does Gan *know* you can do that?"

Everyone looked at Adrian, who lifted his shoulders. "I don't think so."

Sounding more than a little exasperated, the Guardian asked, "You didn't tell Gan?"

"To be honest, sir, we didn't really talk until the last day when you showed up. There's a lot he doesn't know."

CHAPTER 16

———

GAN HAD KEPT TO HIMSELF during the drive, mainly because Scarlett occasionally growled softly, and not a happy sound.

Her green eyes would brighten then she'd blink, pushing her animal back down.

His beast had been restless, but not battering his insides as usual. That tiger remained settled only around Scarlett.

Gan thought hard on this and silently nudged his tiger. *Why calm now and not before?*

She is ours, his tiger sent back.

Scarlett? Ours?

Yes.

What was his tiger talking about now? Having anyone talk in Gan's head bothered him, but an animal made it even worse. Still, Gan had so few people to talk to and needed to understand this beast so he would be able to help Scarlett when the time came.

He argued, *Scarlett is not ours. She is not happy with us.*

Not happy with you, his tiger corrected.

I did not attack her cougar, Gan shot back, angry all over again about his animal hurting Scarlett. He ordered, *Do not hurt her again.*

No. Protect her now.

Scarlett sent an impatient look at Gan. "Are you having a problem with your animal?"

How could she know this? "We are fine."

"That crap is not going to fly with me, Gan. If you're struggling to hold on to control, you should let me know. I don't want to be inside this cab with a Siberian tiger looking for dinner."

"You are safe."

"Really? I should believe you after your tiger struck my cougar?"

Gan propped his elbow against the car door. He had become tired of being inside this rolling box the first hour. They were into hour number three, but getting irritated and reacting to her anger would not put her at ease.

He explained, "Yes, you should believe my words. Tiger now understand cougar and you are same. I told you, you are first person he does not want to kill."

Tension eased from her face.

She kept her gaze on the road, glancing at him once. Her thumb bumped against the steering wheel like a tiny fist pounding out her thoughts.

"Why does your animal not want to kill me?" She quickly added, "Don't get me wrong. I like not having to worry that my cougar won't have to watch for an unexpected attack. I just want to understand what is going on with you and your tiger."

So did he, but saying that would create more problems than help. "I have no answer. I only share what I know. This is first time tiger is almost quiet. Only with you."

"What is almost quiet like?" she asked with sincerity.

Gan thought on it. "At first, tiger want out every minute, mad at everyone, most of all me. I am just as unhappy with animal. I spend sixteen days in Wyoming. Tiger take control, run hard, look for wolf to fight. Red wolf hunt tiger, too. I wait one day, maybe more. When tiger eat and sleep, I change to me. Tiger wait one day, maybe more. When I sleep, he take over. Always same."

The long pause of quiet pushed his gaze to Scarlett.

She watched the road then looked over at him with disbelief. "You have to be kidding."

"Why you always accuse me of make joke?"

"Dammit." She ran a hand over her face then clutched the wheel again. "You can't live that way as a shifter, Gan."

"You think this is news to me?" he quipped, but not in humor. Everyone kept telling him how he was wrong about this and wrong about that. If they'd asked him, he'd tell them he had managed pretty good since he and the tiger had been shoved together in this body.

Scarlett's pretty face scrunched with a frown. "Hasn't anyone explained how you and your animal need to become one?"

"We have one body."

"No, that's not what I mean." Her tone turned serious. "I'm going to have a talk with that eagle shifter when I see him again."

He had no idea what she rambled about and waited for her to make sense.

"Let's start at the beginning," she said as if teaching him. "Do you call your tiger anything?"

"Prick. Idiot." He had to think what else from his limited English vocabulary. "Moron."

"No." Scarlett sounded appalled. "Do you two talk at all?"

"More like yell. He is moron many times."

"Gan, you have to find a way to become friends with your tiger."

"Why? He is not friend."

"Why?" she echoed at him. "Because failure to bond with your animal will mean being unable to live in this world. You will never have control of your animal if you allow your tiger to force the change when you're asleep. If your tiger breaks free and harms a human or shifter without acceptable cause, that's an immediate death sentence."

He knew that.

He had figured that out on his own when he fought the tiger for control of his body. But he had no idea how to be the one in charge every minute.

That was why he planned to slip away as soon as he and Scarlett took care of her friend. He would find his way to the far northeast until he reached a wilderness with plenty of snow and cold air. He was not excited to live alone, but he would take that over living under the thumb of an eagle shifter.

It was not as if he had many years.

His camp sister explained if he did not take a mate, he would die from a curse.

No woman would live in the wilderness.

His sister had given him a phone number to memorize in case he ever needed her. Once he left Scarlett, he would contact his sister and have her tell everyone he escaped, but he'd make it clear Scarlett was not at fault.

He would tell his sister to ask the Guardian to let him live in peace, promising he would not be near humans.

When he hadn't spoken for a while, Scarlett offered, "I can help you, but you have to really put your heart into it. Will you do that, Gan?"

He did not see how anything they tried would change the way he and his monster fought for control of this body, but he said, "I will try."

"Let's start out by giving your tiger a name. Don't you dare utter something mean like moron. Think of a name you'd like to have as a friend, then suggest it to your animal."

He had no friends. How was he supposed to figure that out? Instead, he asked, "What do you call cougar?"

Scarlett's lips curved. "Chica. I didn't name her at first, but my cougar and I got along fine so I hadn't thought on it much. I was working for a family of fox shifters who owned a restaurant when I was first out on my own. Any time it got busy in the restaurant, some of the workers would call me Chica, a generic name for a young girl, when they needed something. My animal rumbled happily every time they used that name so I gave it to her."

Shifting her attention back to Gan, she added, "Your tiger will let you know when a name sticks. Just start trying some out. Like I said, choose a nice name."

He wanted to keep Scarlett happy so he tried, but after a few minutes of struggling with this he ended up irritated. "Names I know not good."

"Why?"

"I did not have friends. I lived in camps with jackal shifter guards, not friends. Those names make me angry."

"Hmm. I see your point. What if I give you some suggestions?"

Shrugging, he said, "Is fine."

"What about Tigger?"

"What is that?"

"A cartoon tiger."

Gan asked his beast, who growled. *No.*

Gan shook his head.

"Are you originally from Russia?"

"No. Guardian say I am born in Ukraine. I live in different camps in other country. Cadells bring me here … I don't know how many months ago. Four maybe five. Is hard to tell time when prisoner." He only shared simple facts.

Why did he smell sadness on Scarlett?

Gan stilled at that realization. Had he just figured out an emotion with his nose?

She smiled. "Okay. Let's try regional names since your tiger was actually born there, too."

He hadn't considered that his tiger had been with him since birth, but if his mother and father were tiger shifters that made sense.

"What about Anton?" she asked with a quick look at him.

Gan put it to his tiger, *Do you want name Anton?*

No.

Again, he shook his head at her.

She kept trying. "What about Boris?"

When he tried that one, Gan's tiger said, *Stupid name.*

Gan told him*, Do not be mean to Scarlett.*

Then it dawned on him to just not repeat what his tiger said.

That went on for the next ten minutes without solving anything. His tiger did not like any suggestion. When Scarlett stopped offering them, he asked his tiger the one question that should make this easier. *Do you want name?*

No.

Gan may have failed to choose a name, but her idea had accomplished something that had not happened before now.

He and his tiger had spoken to each other in a normal way for a while.

No calling each other names or yelling threats.

He'd have to think on this some more. It would be foolish to believe he could really live near humans, but he'd like to not spend what time he had left alone.

Every day from childhood, he'd longed for a life with a family and friends. He'd had a few friends in spite of what he'd told Scarlett, but they had all died. All except the young girl he befriended in the last camp and claimed as a sister. She would have died if he had not forced her to run and escape.

The guards had beaten him for helping her escape.

He had not cared, because he wanted her safe. Besides, he also found his way out the next day.

The Guardian called his sister a Gallize female when she accepted Rory as her mate and power burst around them. She did not shift into an animal like her Gallize mate, but she had special powers, which had kept her safe when the Cadells hunted her down.

Gan would not find such a woman.

He cast a look in Scarlett's direction. She would not be a Gallize. She was already a shifter.

Why waste his time thinking on these things?

Because Scarlett wanted to make him better.

She deserved to know the truth, that he could not be saved.

He would never meet a female such as his camp sister. Not even the Guardian knew how to find these Gallize women, from what his sister had told him. She explained that becoming Rory's mate saved that jaguar from a mating curse some witch had forced on Gallize shifters a long time ago.

His sister pleaded with Gan to gain control of his tiger so he could mate. She said, based on what Rory had told her, Gan would not have much time because he became a Gallize so late in life.

Even if a woman would want a man with a crazy tiger inside him, few could accept the power he now possessed. He would not kill some woman just to save himself.

All these things had run through his head for over two weeks in Wyoming.

How could he tame a tiger that understood their life would be short? He had not told his tiger, so the animal might not know.

Or, as usual, the tiger would not accept Gan's words.

Scarlett's phone had been quiet, but it started ordering her to follow directions again.

"Where are we?" He listened to the mechanical words, but none of them made sense. He had to learn what the words meant if he hoped to find his way north soon.

"I'm getting off in Johnson City, Tennessee. Then we'll have about fifteen miles of backroads heading east. The house appears to be on the south end of Holston Lake, just below the Virginia border. The lake is located in both Virginia and Tennessee."

He listened to her phone and watched how she followed directions. If he rode with her a few times more and she played her phone, he could figure it out.

Twenty minutes later, she drove down a gravel road that ended at a house built of logs. Beyond that, moonlight danced over a lake.

Scarlett stopped short of reaching the house. Her eyes flicked back and forth quickly, taking in everything from side to side.

Gan asked, "What is wrong?"

"Nothing exactly. I'm trying to decide if I can get you inside without Jazlyn seeing you."

"Why?"

"She knows I figured out why she took off without me. If she sees you here, she's not going to be happy with me."

He scoffed. "Is only fair. You are not happy with her."

"Yes, but she's the only connection I have to Fayth right now. I don't want her delaying contact because she does not trust you."

"Should trust me. I help escape."

"I know that makes sense to you, Gan, but that woman has been through a lot just to stay alive. She's being hunted to be thrown in a titanium pit where she'll die a horrible death. On top of that, one of my contacts betrayed her and I'm betting the Pagan Nomads were behind that failure," Scarlett said in a glum note. "She doesn't know who you are aligned with and is probably worried you'll call your people in without me knowing."

He held his empty hands out. "I have no phone. You have phone. Not my fault if they come."

Scarlett waved her hand, dismissing his words. "They're not coming. I cleared taking this vehicle and your boss knows you're with me. We're good. Let's just go and hope she doesn't wait long." She got the truck moving again and parked in front of the garage.

Opening her door, she turned and asked, "You said the key would be behind door number three, right?"

"Yes. Where is this door?"

"I'll show you." When she got out, she wrangled her loose pants up and climbed three steps to the porch. Once there, she studied the outdoor furniture decorated with flowery cushions and various pots filled with different plants.

Gan followed her gaze to the flowers and leafy plants. Where was this door?

Then Scarlett stepped off the porch and strode out into the yard.

What was she looking for? He stayed with her.

She cast a long look across the land on this side of the house where large trees with big limbs must offer nice shade during the day. After standing there a moment, she moved to a garden under the tree closest to the house and seemed to find what she'd been hunting.

Stepping carefully around delicate plants, she dropped to one knee, staring at rocks.

Lifting one the size of a small melon, she turned it over and pinched a small black box free from a hole on the underside. She grinned up at him. "The key."

"That is not door."

"Saying the third door meant to look in the third place I would expect to find a key hidden by most humans." With the rock back in place, she stood up and returned to the porch. "The first spot is under the welcome mat, which is a terrible place to hide a key. The second spot is under a flower pot, another bad idea."

"Rock is third place?"

"Not for sure, but a lot of people like hiding their keys in a fake rock." Returning to the porch, she unlocked the door. "No alarm, but I would have been extremely disappointed if Jaz had set me up to open a house with security alarms."

"Still not make her good friend," Gan qualified. They had saved the wolf shifter and she ran away. How could she do that after Scarlett had risked her life for the woman?

"Actually, she is a good friend," Scarlett countered. "She did something very special for Fayth eighteen months ago as a favor to me and now Jaz was there for Fayth when her world crashed and I couldn't be. Jaz put herself and her freedom at risk just trying to get in touch with me."

"She had no phone?"

"Not normally. It's not as if she has unlimited funds even for a burner phone, for one thing."

"Burner phone?" He had so much to learn.

Scarlett explained how someone could buy a phone at a store and never connect to the phone services that would allow law enforcement to track the phone. Then she explained tracking with a GPS.

"Jaz has lived off the land for years," Scarlett continued. "I have no idea what she does for money, but I've told her time and again that I would give her cash. She refused and said not to expect to hear from her again."

"This is friend?" he asked.

"Yes. She didn't want to put me in a tight spot with the law and figured if we never spoke I'd be safe." Opening and closing closets, Scarlett kept searching the house as if memorizing everything about it as she spoke. "Jaz said Fayth didn't escape with her phone. Neither one of them would have the number for the backup phone I had hidden in my vest. My current primary phone was crushed by the shifters we fought. The first thing I normally would have done as soon as I started using a new phone would be to call Fayth's number and leave my new one, and make it sound like a spam call."

"What is spam call?" Gan followed her as she looked through the downstairs.

She circled the backside of a comfy looking sofa and stood at the large window, which looked out into a yard and dock on a lake. "Someone you don't know calls your number to sell you something. Fayth knew how to get the new number out of the message anyone else would dismiss. But now even she doesn't have this number. Jaz wouldn't let her call my voice mail service. There's being careful, then there's Jaz. I can't fault her. She's managed on her own a long time, always looking over her shoulder. She put her life on the line to help Fayth and find me."

Leaving the window, Scarlett headed for the kitchen at the other end of the huge room.

She said, "I'm thinking Jaz told Fayth to stay dark while she was gone looking for me."

"Dark?"

"Like radio silence. Don't call and risk being tracked to wherever they're hiding. Fayth is not cutout to deal with threats and will do whatever Jaz or I tell her."

Scarlett paused at a dark stone counter in the kitchen. She lifted a piece of paper from the polished surface.

He made a guess. "Is from friend?"

"Yes. She says she'll come to see me between twenty-four and thirty-six hours after I arrive."

"Why wait?" The Guardian had given him three days. Gan wanted to get whatever Scarlett needed taken care of then be gone before his time ran out.

Turning to him, Scarlett said, "Jaz will come here at some point to watch and be sure we haven't been followed or your people don't show up to grab her."

"She waste time," he groused. "We need help Fayth now."

Scarlett cocked her head at that. "I agree. I want to find Fayth like yesterday, but what is your hurry?"

He should have kept his thoughts to himself. He had to be careful not to lie. "I have three days. What if she waits too long and Guardian wants me back when you are busy helping Fayth?"

Her eyes narrowed as he spoke.

He had not lied, but it was a muddy truth.

After a moment of the staring match, she said, "We're good on time. Let's put together one bag out of what's in the back of the car and grab showers, then eat. I'm starving."

His stomach rumbled at that moment. One thing he'd learned was to not allow the tiger to get too hungry.

Resigned, he agreed. "Yes, we eat."

She handled moving clothes they needed and weapons into one bag that had to belong to Vic, based on scent, then grabbed her vest and shoved it into the same duffle. She left the other bag that smelled of that wolf called Adrian.

Back in the house, they climbed the stairs to find two bedrooms with a bathroom built between them.

Farther down the hall a doorway opened into a large bedroom with a very big bathroom.

He followed her into the large bedroom, claimed it. "I use this one."

"No. Who made you king of the hill?" She carried the bag into the bathroom, yanked out a change of clothes, and shoved them at him. "You saw that first bathroom. I'm sure it works, too."

She shut the door in his face.

His tiger made a sound Gan had not heard before. The animal snickered at him.

Gan grumbled to himself and turned back to the first bathroom he'd passed.

Maybe life without a woman would not be so bad.

CHAPTER 17

———

Near Erie, Pennsylvania

ROBERT STRODE THROUGH HIS SPRAWLING home, sharp strikes of his boot heels setting off sparks of energy. The walls rippled ahead of him as his power drove forward, sending a warning to every being it reached.

Never cross a Power Baron who considered draining the life force of a foe nothing more than sport.

Doors to his library flew open before he reached them.

Lights above flickered.

He slowed and caught his breath.

The exquisite gilt bronze-and-crystal chandelier created by the master Pierre-Philippe Thomire could not be replaced. Duplicating the original would have no value. Robert had purchased the magnificent piece for his mistress just before the artist died in 1843.

Humans had such short lives, but they could be useful.

Pulling his power back in check, Robert entered the room where heavy mahogany bookshelves lined two walls. A granite fireplace fifteen feet across and rising to the twelve-foot ceiling held a roaring fire. Comfortable leather seating nestled in the center of the room, but those would not be used this evening.

They were meant for quiet evenings with favored guests.

To the side of the seating area in the wide walkway to a wall of books he'd collected over two hundred years stood his new second-in-command.

At twenty-six, Kenneth held an erect pose, showing off his six-three height and considerable build. He made a much better first impression than Tantor.

An arm's length behind him waited a surly thirtyish looking man, who had lived almost a century in hiding until shifters came out.

Where Kenneth's lean build spoke of disciplined training with weights, the shifter's thick arms showed off muscles on top of muscles.

Two additional guards in black-and-gold uniforms matching Kenneth's, bookended each side of his guest.

Robert strode forward, observing the man with an indignant expression. He asked, "Is this the tiger shifter?"

"Yes, boss."

Expecting the usual "yes, sir," Robert gifted Kenneth with a slight smile of appreciation.

Wise young man that he was, Kenneth did not move a muscle to acknowledge receiving a prized acknowledgement. He stepped aside, allowing Robert to take his place in front of the tiger shifter known as Lincoln.

Lincoln's golden shifter eyes glowed as if on fire. "I'm here just so I can tell you I am not one of your flunkies to be called to you. You Power Barons signed agreements, blood treaties from what I heard. We don't screw with your people. You don't screw with shifters. I don't give a shit what you do to humans. They're all a nuisance as far as I'm concerned."

Robert allowed him to continue his dribble even as anger over Lincoln's disrespectful tone slid onto the faces of his guards.

With no immediate consequence, Lincoln became comfortable, shifting his weight as he crossed his arms. "You have exactly one minute to say what the hell you want then we're done."

Thank the power of the universe the man finally shut up. Few things were as welcome as silence after that earful.

Robert lifted his watch into view as if the time mattered.

It didn't.

Lincoln heaved a deep breath, letting everyone know he was being imposed upon.

After exactly fifty-eight seconds, Robert took a second read of his watch.

Lincoln's frustration hit a new level. "Enough already. What the fuck do you …"

Robert murmured softly and lifted his hand with his finger and thumb making a circle.

Lincoln paused to stare at him with confusion. Then his mouth opened wide, so wide his eyes were tearing. His hands trembled where they were still stuffed inside his folded arms. He made strangled noises.

Canting his head, Robert asked, "You prefer your mouth shut perhaps?"

The garbled noises got louder.

"I'll take that as a yes." Robert pinched his fingers together.

Lincoln's lips smacked shut and stayed that way. His eyes bulged. He continued to shake hard as a leaf in a summer storm. A wet spot formed in the front of his pants.

Shaking his head, Robert said, "That is no a pretty sight for a man, much less for an alpha tiger shifter." He made tch, tch noises. "Pay me heed, tiger," Robert started in a tone meant to broach no argument, even if the shifter could speak. "No one threatens me who does no pay a price. To end yar life would be a simple decision, but I'm no a simple man. I prefer to get more out of every action I take. Ya have one chance to spare yar life. As for reportin' me to the Power Council or any government, what happened just now is slight compared to what you would suffer for makin' a second mistake. I doona really allow anyone two."

Fury poured from Lincoln's eyes.

Shifters were not quick to comprehend. Ignoring the ridiculous threat in Lincoln's eyes, Robert continued.

"I understand ya have been raidin' rogue shifter groups. I could turn you over to SCIS for that alone. Have you ever seen the titanium hole in the ground where they put criminal shifters? 'Tis no a nice place. Some die in the first forty-eight hours once the animal goes insane. I would insure ya survived."

Threatening to contact the Shifter Criminal Investigation Service extinguished the fury in Lincoln's eyes, leaving behind what Robert had been waiting for. Fear.

He chuckled. "So much bad can happen to a shifter caught breakin' rules. And let us be clear. You are caught."

Walking over to a side table of gilded gold and marble, Robert opened his humidor. He chose a rare cigar crafted in Honduras, one of a very limited edition. Clipping the tip and lighting it, he strolled back to the mute shifter.

"I will award ya the opportunity to make up for yar bad manners while in my home."

When Robert released Lincoln's lips, the shifter coughed and gagged. Clearly not a connoisseur of thousand-dollar cigars.

Once the noise subsided, Lincoln croaked out, "What do you want?"

See? Communication was everything. When performed correctly, even a shifter understood how few words were required to have a productive conversation.

Robert released the magic holding Lincoln's body. "I understand the Pagan Nomads have captured a female shifter."

Lincoln gave him an indignant look. "Those jackals kidnap females all the time. As long as they don't touch anything that is mine, I ignore them."

"Now ya can no longer ignore them."

"Why?"

"Because they have touched somethin' of mine and ya will deliver her to me."

CHAPTER 18

A HUNGRY SHIFTER IS A BAD idea. A hungry tiger shifter with questionable control is a disaster waiting to happen.

Squatting, Scarlett dug through the freezer for something to go with the steaks she'd found. The people who owned this lake house had stocked it well. Guilt pecked at her, but she'd make good for this unavoidable intrusion.

The microwave hummed, thawing the steaks.

Corn! She snatched up the bag, stood to put the cobs on the platter, and jumped back.

"Dammit, Gan! Don't sneak up on me like that." Her heart thumped wildly, but she had to be honest. The rise in her body temperature and rapid pulse wasn't just from being surprised.

Gan wore only jeans, leaving all that carved up muscle, shock of black hair, and sexy beard on display.

She'd borrowed a pair of shorts and a T-shirt from a bag in the closet. These fit her better than the oversized clothes she'd gotten from the go bags in Vic's truck.

"I did not sneak." He folded his arms and gave her a cross look.

Bulging biceps rolled across his arms with the movement.

Her mouth dried at the sight.

What was her problem? She'd had men in the past when she'd been in the mood for a night. This blasted tiger shifter chased her through dreams, turning her body inside out with need, and … always talking to her.

Much like the real one.

She hadn't really talked to anyone, especially a man, in so long. Actually, never with a man. Not like Gan, who said he liked her and wanted her happy.

Gan was different, unique in so many ways and sincere.

He took up so much real estate in her mind it scared her a little. What would she do when all she had left were memories?

She shouldn't blame him for her erotic dreams, but they hadn't started until she'd met him.

He inhaled slowly and lost his irritation if the smile curving his mouth was any indication.

She picked up the corn and tossed it on the counter, trying to diffuse the sizzle of energy buzzing between them.

The microwave dinged.

She jumped.

"What is that?" His attention shifted past her.

"The microwave. I thawed steaks. We'll grill those and this corn. Not much for a pair of shifters, but I hate to impose on the owners of this place more than that. If we didn't need the cash I have, I'd leave them payment now. I'll send money to them with an anonymous thank-you note later."

"That is nice. You are nice."

Heat flushed her neck at the simple words that struck chords with her. She had to shut that mouth ... because she liked what came out of it too much. He said things that threw her out of step, because he meant the words.

She never thought about being happy, just being safe and keeping those she loved safe.

Right now in this tiny moment in time, she enjoyed feeling good about herself.

Simple words that tugged her heart. *You are nice.*

She couldn't let this get out of control or lead him on, so she shoved all those tangled emotions back out of the way and changed the subject. "Thank you, but I'm not as nice as the people who loaned this place to us, even if the favor was involuntary. I wouldn't like anyone using my home without permission. I'm not happy to break into this house, but I'd do much worse to protect someone I care about. I have to get to Fayth."

Scarlett didn't blame Jaz, but she needed to see Fayth and the baby. What would be the point of fighting so hard to survive if she lost the only family she'd ever had? That couldn't happen. No one was hurting them. No one.

He walked over to watch the microwave. "Who is this Fayth?"

"My younger sister."

Swinging around, his eyebrows dropped low over his eyes. "Another cougar shifter?"

"Actually, no. She's a wolf. Let's get the steaks cooking and I'll tell you about her."

She put everything on a platter then dug around for a lighter. Toting it all outside where the moon had reached its zenith, she smiled at the romantic setting painted with broad strokes of light over the black lake.

Romantic? No.

Time for a subject change in her head. "Do you know how to cook on a grill?"

He gave the cooker a once over. "Never see grill before, but I cook on fire."

What kind of life had Gan led to have not seen a grill? She had to remind herself sometimes of the gaps in his knowledge. Once she had the grill lit, she turned again to find him right behind her.

He grabbed her arms before she backed up against the grill.

She had plenty of words to say, sharp words, but not one came to mind with him so close. He smelled of the soap he'd used to wash and a natural wildness that clung to him.

His touch lightened from holding her in place to gently massaging her arms.

Why couldn't she move?

He wasn't forcing her to stand here, not unless she blamed the power of his presence. Her heart beat faster and faster. Heat began building where it shouldn't if she intended to stick to her words and not end up naked.

With him.

Slowly this time, he breathed deeply, and exhaled softly.

It would be impossible to deny her desire when he'd just scented her this close. He'd figured out that scent fast.

The hunger in his eyes stole her breath. He whispered, "I like you soft. You smell … like morning when air is fresh and full of life." He kissed her forehead then her hair.

Why was she working so hard to deny this feeling?

Or him.

Her brain had two halves that normally didn't argue, but right now the disciplined side chastised her for getting into this position while the pleasure side wanted to play this out.

Wanted to play.

She didn't think Gan had two halves, not based on what she saw churning in those eyes now a deep-sea blue.

She envied him and the way he made decisions sound so simple. His hands were slowly silencing the crabby voice in her brain and upping the volume of the part telling her to meet him halfway. Her body voted to shut the hell up and just have fun.

His lips kept up a gentle attack on her skin.

Nothing would ever come of this. Gan knew he was leaving in three days. He'd even joked about making the most of the first two days.

Her heart weighed in, drowning out her mental gymnastics and asked if two days would be enough.

Not really.

Gan kissed her cheek and chin.

She lifted her head and stifled a moan.

He didn't feel like someone she wanted to remember as a one-night stand, but neither of them had more to offer. After years of no passion, no connection, nothing that felt like this … she was alive in a way she hadn't experienced. Her body cried for so much more than mere sex.

Gan was so much more.

His fingers worked magic on her arms and shoulders. His lips caressed her cheek and teased her ear.

She swallowed. She was beginning to have a deeper understanding for Gan's frustration at not being allowed basic happiness to live as he chose.

Why couldn't she have someone who made her feel the way Gan did? Why couldn't she be a normal person? Not human, because she would not give up Chica, but normal had to be in there somewhere.

Her logical side pushed in to have a say. *You can't have anyone for the same reason you have to keep your sister far away. She would be collateral damage if you ever lose this deadly game of hide-and-seek.*

All true.

She couldn't have forever with anyone, not if she cared for that person and … she did care for Gan.

They could steal this night for both of them. She'd save it to replay during the lonely nights ahead.

Gan lifted a hand and brushed his fingers down her cheek.

She closed her eyes, committing to memory every second. She'd enjoyed sex in the past, but that had been all physical. Not like this, not intimacy where Gan touched her soul.

She could lament over what she'd never have or enjoy what she held in her hands now.

He drew her to him in a way no other man had.

No seductive games. No word play. No illusion.

Honesty.

Everything about Gan spoke to a core honor.

His lips ended the teasing and smothered hers for a mind-blowing kiss. Heat coiled and spun with the energy inside her. That strange sensation that happened when they were together sizzled across her skin everywhere his fingers caressed.

She opened up to him, kissing him with her own honesty. She'd busted on him earlier for that first kiss, but that had been her brain always on guard against any connection. She'd clung to her control, convincing herself she was happy having the upper hand, never falling victim to caring for a man.

Gan kept banging on the foundation of her emotional fortress, battling her control to keep him out.

Tonight, she would let him in.

Weary from holding a strong front for so long, she welcomed the safe harbor his arms offered, if only for this moment.

His hand cupped her cheek while he continued the sweet assault on her body.

She ran a hand up the thick muscles along his sides that flexed under her fingers, calling her closer. She went all in and slid her hand down across the front of his jeans, stroking along the thick ridge.

A heavy groan rumbled from deep inside him.

She loved that sound.

His big hand reached behind her and cupped her bottom, lifting. She bit his ear.

Gan pulled back, hesitation in his tight voice. "That is yes?"

"Oh, yes, baby. If you don't mind waiting for dinner." She

smiled at him, touched by the way he asked permission before taking the next step. For all his lack of knowledge when it came to many everyday things of the modern world, this man knew what a woman wanted.

He let out a long breath of relief. "I have one hunger. You." Backing away from the grill, he sat on a sturdy lawn chair constructed of wood.

She bent her knees as her legs dropped to each side of him. Leaning forward, she put her hands on his chest and slid them up to his neck and kissed his lips then his chin. Running her fingers along his beard, she kissed his cheeks.

His hands clutched her hips and his breathing ruffled her hair that she'd piled on her head. She threaded her fingers through his silky, untamed locks.

Wild like the man, but who wanted tame?

He allowed her a moment of doing as she pleased, then he joined the kiss, pushing his tongue gently inside her mouth to play with hers. She'd never known a man to smile so much when he kissed.

It was as if he reveled in the moment of a simple kiss, enjoying every second.

She started smiling, too, and pulled back to take in his face. In the little time she'd known him, she'd never seen this man appear so blissful.

Toying with a lock of hair that fell near his eye, she asked, "Why are you smiling so much?"

"I am happy. Have not had moment like this before."

Her brain screeched to a stop. "Have you not, uh, done *this*?"

His eyebrows drew together and he cocked his head as he studied her. Then he laughed. "I understand. Yes, I have been with women. But not like … this."

Relaxing again, she asked, "What do you mean?"

His hands massaged along her back, under her T-shirt. She needed his hands in other places, but she also wanted to hear his answer.

He shrugged. "When I look more like man than boy, women come to me. They want sex. No man says no to that, but it was only … feel good for minute. Had to be fast and secret. Sex with prisoner shame them if anyone know. When I want more back, they laugh at me. I was game for them."

Bitches! Her claws tipped out, pricking the skin of his neck where her hands had paused while he spoke.

He grunted.

"Sorry, Gan. That pisses me off for a woman to use you that way."

His eyes twinkled. "Not hurt. I like claws on sexy cat."

She shook her head chuckling. "You're certifiable, you know that?"

"What is certify …"

"Just a joke. Finish what you were telling me about why this is different."

"Because to be with you like this make small freedom for me. I have choice to want this. Want you. Did not want others. Not like this. My hand more nice to me than women."

Preferring a hand job over sex with those women was sad, but he continued talking so she kept playing with his hair, encouraging him to go on.

"That was secret sex only. No one could know. No freedom to choose woman. You are first one I am kissing and feeling skin. You are …" He looked away while he figured out the word, then his eyes returned to hers with a deep thought. "Special. You are special."

She swallowed the ball of emotion in her throat.

He pulled a hand from her back and pushed his fingers into her hair, pulling it loose to fall around her shoulders. "I am happy for normal. First time. Not prisoner. Not shifter. Just man with pretty woman who wants me." His voice dropped to a rich baritone. "Scarlett who want me first time we meet. Always Scarlett. Only Scarlett."

He wanted only her.

She had to be careful she didn't step off a cliff tonight, but tell that to her heart doing a jig at his words.

"You incredible wild man," she murmured, her stomach falling away. She held his gaze that didn't waver until she broke the connection first, leaning forward to bite his lip.

Hard.

What did he do?

Laughed and kissed her as if he intended to keep doing it for hours.

Be still, my heart, she mused.

His fingers smoothed over her back, pausing to feel her scar. "Who hurt you?"

She didn't want to talk about another shifter when he had been so relaxed.

Giving her a small pinch, he said, "Tell."

"Lincoln did that. When he demanded I be his mate, I said no. He doesn't accept no from anyone, especially a woman. He carried a titanium knife and cut my back when I ran from him."

That hadn't been the full story. She'd realized quickly he'd been a mistake to date back seven years ago when she was a mere nineteen. As she tried to break off the relationship that never quite got rolling, he'd grabbed her and demanded sex.

That's when she found out just how much he hated the word no. She struggled to get away and ran. Never a smart idea to run from a predator, unless that was your only option.

Lincoln lost his mind. He had the edge of speed and size on her. She'd felt the burn of titanium as the blade slashed the back of her shirt and her skin, then he clamped his hand on her arm, wrenching her around.

She'd panicked and hit him with her power more out of survival instinct than thought. What she discovered that day was how her power had marked his shoulder with a black claw shape. She'd heard the mark was on the back of his shoulder and looked like it had been burned into the skin.

Lincoln had been looking for her ever since.

"Lincoln must die."

Gan's softly spoken threat brought her back to the moment. She placed her palm on his face and his eyes closed, but he wasn't finished. "I keep you safe."

She heard the truth in his words.

"I don't want to talk about Lincoln." She kissed the lips she would dream about for years to come. "I want to forget he exists. I want—"

Gan yanked her T-shirt up and off so fast her hands barely left him. Was he a mind reader? No, just a man who didn't need a lot of direction.

His mouth did his best to keep her busy thinking about nothing but his lips as he worked her shorts off.

She had no underwear.

Gan figured that out quickly, running one long finger up the inside of her thigh. A zing of energy buzzed her skin. Her body tightened and ached.

He finally brushed his fingertip over her folds.

She clenched her legs and gripped his shoulders, struggling to not beg him. Her breath came out shaky. "What the hell are you waiting for?"

He whispered, "Look at me."

When she did, the heat burning up his gaze should have given her pause, but her heart thudded a crazy beat with longing for all that gaze promised.

"Do not look away," he ordered, then brought his fingers back to the center of her heat.

She gasped and trembled, but her eyes locked with his as he stroked her over and over. Clutching him, she said, "More."

He whispered, "Soon."

Did soon mean right damn now? Every second had her dancing on an edge where torment lay on one side and ecstasy on the other.

Her body couldn't make a damn decision.

She tried to reach for him to share the fun, but his fingers stopped moving.

"No, don't stop," she breathed out.

"Put hand back."

She lifted her hand immediately.

"Yes." He kissed her, a sweet brush of his lips, and resumed driving her crazy. His finger pushed her to the edge then dipped inside her.

She squeezed out a sound she'd never made.

Evidently he understood strange sounds of pleasure, because he kept pushing in and out while his thumb stroked her. The energy growing inside her twisted into a tight spring.

His other hand cupped her breast, worrying the hard tip of her nipple. He had her shaking with need.

She started riding his fingers and he changed the rhythm to a faster pace. He pushed and pulled, stroking her relentlessly.

Energy exploded through her. Sizzling frissons raced over her body and lifted the hair on her head. He kissed her as if they'd never kissed and he had to get it right.

Nailed it.

Shock waves rolled through her.

She lost touch with everything except him.

Slowly, her body realigned with the world. When she opened her eyes, he had her tucked close against his warm chest. His hand slowly moved over her bottom.

That felt insanely good.

Reaching for his pants, she found the zipper pull.

His hand stopped her.

She looked up. "Why are you stopping me? We don't have a condom or we could do more." She paused. "Do you know what a condom is?"

Snorting, he said, "Yes. Women did not want baby from me."

"Then why stop me."

"Not stop. I do this. Zipper can hurt."

Not that she wasn't glad those awful women had used condoms, but his voice had been sad as if he'd been told right up front he was worthy of nothing more than servicing them.

He unzipped his pants and pulled out a prizeworthy dick. By his gloating grin, he knew it. "Is good, yes?"

That was the sound of confidence, not arrogance. In a world where he'd been a prisoner, he'd found something to be proud of and she couldn't take that from him.

"Oh, yes, wild man. That's impressive."

She got a proud smile in reply. He wasn't gloating, just pleased that she could see something special about him.

He had no idea.

Everything about him sent her heart doing backflips.

With the first stroke of her hand, he acted as if he had reached heaven. "You are most amazing woman ever."

She had to laugh.

He hadn't come yet and she'd already gotten a gold star. She kissed him and whispered in a husky voice, "Hold on, wild man."

Her fingers glided over the smooth skin covering his thick hard-on. She took her time, returning the favor of driving him crazy and turned herself to where she could cradle his firm balls.

He played with her breasts with mindless intent, because she had a grip on his full attention. Literally.

SCENT OF A MATE153

When he lifted his hips, meeting her downward stroke, she leaned down and kissed the tip.

He sucked in air and held still.

Muscles on his neck stood out with the strain of waiting. His eyes pleaded for something he didn't put in words.

Human disease couldn't live in a shifter's body.

She covered him with her mouth and continued what she'd started. Her fingers rolled his balls at the right moment and he came hard.

Gan made a deep growl when he let go, but it was hearing her name that touched her. He knew exactly where he was and who he was sharing this moment with.

Not just some camp bitch.

When his muscles were limp and his eyes were closed, she grabbed her T-shirt and wiped her face then cleaned him as best she could. She'd deal with herself when she went back up to shower.

Her gaze roamed over Gan's sprawled body. His arms fell to the sides, legs were just as boneless-looking as the rest of him.

As she started to lift up, his hands came back to life, grasping her and pulling her to him. He hugged her and kissed her hair.

When had she cuddled with a man?

Too many years ago to count, back when she was barely out of her teens. She wrapped an arm around him, content to just be.

"Thank you," he said in a hushed voice.

"For the blow job?" she teased.

He pinched her bottom and sounded serious. "No. My words are not many, but to kiss you is gift. Yes, my dick love that. Never had before, but to hold you in my arms. That is … I have no words."

Her eyes burned with unexpected tears.

She wasn't a crier. She would kick ass and make someone pay for crossing her, but Gan's admission grabbed her heart and squeezed.

He was telling her that being with her was more than before. Different.

Just as this felt different for her.

"You're special, too." She struggled not to say more, but she acknowledged the truth to herself.

Gan mattered to her.

More than just mattered, she cared deeply for him.

It hurt to not tell him. He deserved to know, but they had no future. How much worse would it be for Gan if she opened up and then had to say goodbye?

She'd thought to share one time with him, something for both of them.

Talk about getting it wrong.

She'd just screwed up big-time.

The idea of telling him goodbye was tearing her heart apart.

CHAPTER 19

———◆———

GAN USED LONG TONGS TO flip over the steaks and turn the corn. His gaze kept drifting to the lake.

He'd had streams in Wyoming and small ponds near camps, but no large body of water. The Cadell guards feared losing a captive who swam away.

Just looking at the moon's reflection in the lake brought him a peaceful feeling.

Scarlett leaned close and inhaled. "Smells good. How long before the steaks are done?"

"Cook for you. Raw is okay for me."

"Ugh. I don't like super hot, but also not icy cold."

He grinned.

"What's so funny?"

"No."

"What?"

"My words get me in trouble." Of course, he couldn't help smiling when he said that.

Her lips tilted with a grin. "Tell me. I won't get mad at you."

"You like steak hot. You like shower hot. You like me hot." He slashed a questionable look at her. "We need condom."

Her eyes darkened.

Good woman. She had the same idea.

He shared the big shower with her this time and had sex again. He thought about it. Not just sex. Maybe this had been making love. He'd heard others talk about that when no one realized he snuck around the camps.

He'd asked one woman to explain.

She said it was having sex with someone you loved.

He had never experienced love, wouldn't know what it looked or felt like, but this ache in his chest had to be something important. He shook off the thought. He confused what people said. Scarlett had said he was special to her.

But did her words mean the same to her as his did to him?

He would not ask her about love. Not when she was happy with him. He made problems too often when he spoke.

Still, he didn't like the idea of leaving Scarlett in a few days, but he couldn't stay. Once they took care of Fayth and her baby, he had to go or he'd miss his only chance to get away from the Gallize.

Why did just thinking about leaving her hurt?

Stay with me, his tiger said in Gan's head.

He had not missed the animal, but while he continued to cook the steaks, he asked, *Stay with you? What do you mean?*

Mate go with me.

Mate? Is that what Gan hadn't been able to put into words. Was Scarlett his mate? Could she even be his mate?

Would she want to be?

She'd have to run away with him. She had a sister, Jazlyn, and women at a shelter all depending on her.

He could not take her from all of that.

Lifting the steaks and corn off the grill, he turned the knob she'd used to change temperature until the grill turned off. That would have been nice to have in a camp.

Scarlett had the wooden patio table set for the two of them with a candle glowing.

Today had been a gift, too.

He'd never enjoyed one day in the past. Even with the fight inside the barn with bad shifters, he proved he was more than someone to sit and watch. He'd saved his people, protected Scarlett and the female shifters.

His people? No, the Gallize were not his people.

Placing the platter on the table, he loaded each plate and sat, looking at the bowl of berries. "What are those?"

"Blackberries. I found a bush on the far side of the house." She spooned some on each plate.

He tasted one and was sold. "I would like these every day."

She paused in cutting her steak. "They aren't always in season, but a lot of them grow wild."

Saving the sweet treat for last, he started on his steak. "They grow in cold land?"

"I think they grow as far north as Maine," she replied, not looking up.

Maine. The land that had snow and wilderness, but blackberries? He had to go there to live.

Stay with mate, his animal growled.

That tiger could not let him be happy even for one minute. Gan silently replied, *If you want to live, we must be far from people. You want to kill all the time. You are reason we must leave.*

Gan finished his meal and the tiger still had not responded.

That was odd, but he had no complaint.

Scarlett jumped up and cleared the table. Gan picked up what she'd left and delivered the rest to the kitchen.

His tiger said, *Want water. Want swim.*

Gan did, too, but he couldn't turn his tiger loose. Maybe the animal could enjoy the water with Gan swimming.

He asked Scarlett, "Want to swim?"

She finished loading the dishwasher and turned to him, casting a long glance at the lake. "That's a great idea. My cougar needs to get out and stretch. She loves water. Let's let our animals out for a break."

She wanted him to free his tiger?

Mate good to me, his tiger crooned.

She waited for his reply.

Gan had to tell her the truth. "I never turn tiger loose."

"Maybe you should, Gan. I'd like to see how much control you have when you aren't in the middle of a battle. If you can't control your tiger to go swimming, I need to know that so I don't take you somewhere you, or anyone else around, will be at risk."

He considered everything she said. "What if your cougar does not like tiger?"

Scarlett smiled, making him think he worried for nothing. That was until she said, "Oh, my Chica does not like your tiger at all after he slapped her with a claw, but she's capable of handling your tiger if he makes another bad decision."

Gan wished he had stayed quiet. He shouldn't do this.

"Come on, let's do this. Show me what you got, wild man."

His damn tiger had boxed him in a corner. He told the beast, *You must do as I ask or this will not happen again.*

In response, the tiger hammered his insides, raring to be free.

Scarlett flipped off the overhead lights in the kitchen leaving the subtle under-counter lights on, then left the house. Gan walked outside behind her, watching as she neared the lake.

She took a moment to look everywhere. "No houses close enough to see even during the day. We should be good out here in the dark." She turned to him. "You first."

Determined to prove he could do this, Gan tossed off his pants. He drew hard on the energy he had become accustomed to feeling like a furnace thundering in his body. Even so, he'd expected this to be a slow change.

His tiger must have wanted out bad. The shift seemed to happen in half a minute and not as painful as usual.

His animal came up on all fours and stood eye level with the top of Scarlett's head. She stepped forward and raised her hand to brush her fingers over his ears, scratching the backside.

His tiger lowered his head, emitting a soft growl that rumbled peacefully.

Scarlett said, "Whatever you two are doing right now is working. That's what you need to think about Gan. How to make this work."

He told his tiger to nod.

The animal actually obeyed.

Backing up a few steps, she pulled off her T-shirt and shorts, making her shift quickly. When finished, she rose gracefully as a stunning cougar. Her long tail swept back and forth as if content, but the cat's eyes showed other thoughts.

His tiger's tail moved in the same happy sway.

Gan told his tiger, *Be careful. Cougar does not like you. You hurt her.*

Mate likes me, his tiger replied with no doubt.

Arrogant animal.

When his tiger walked forward and moved his head to sniff the cougar, Scarlett's animal sidestepped out of his path and walked away.

His tiger's jaw dropped and his tail drooped to the ground.

Gan chuckled. *I thought you want to swim.*

In a growly sound, his tiger said something Gan couldn't figure out, then headed for the water.

The cougar jumped in, splashing and paddling around, ignoring the tiger that sulked at the edge of the lake. But it took only a moment for the tiger to forget the rebuff and start splashing too.

Before now, Gan had struggled and fought every day with his tiger from the first second of realizing what he had become. He'd endured long miserable weeks in Wyoming, never rested and never happy.

But to have his animal behave so … freely had Gan sitting back to watch and think. He had not wanted the tiger, but the tiger had not wanted him either.

They had both been wronged.

Regardless, they both had to figure out how to make this work for what time they had left to live. Why spend every minute of being free in a battlefield?

What would happen if he and the tiger could find a way to survive together?

An hour later, the cougar stepped from the lake and shook the excess water from her coat.

Gan's tiger had been only a few steps behind her, pausing to shake before he reached her.

When his tiger did not move, Gan asked, *What is wrong?*

Cougar does not like me.

Gan would have laughed at the forlorn words, but after the past hour he'd gained some understanding for his animal.

If Scarlett didn't like Gan, that would hurt, too.

He told his tiger, *She is good like Scarlett. You must be nice to cougar.*

How?

His tiger had never asked his opinion on anything. Gan said, *Walk up to her and show her you are sorry.*

Taking a tentative step, his tiger padded toward the cougar then past her, turning to face Scarlett's cat. They stared at each other for several heartbeats.

Gan started to worry until his tiger dropped his head and held it there for a bit. When his animal lifted his head, he carefully moved closer.

Then his tiger licked the cougar's cheek and pulled back quickly, waiting.

Nothing happened.

Gan felt bad for his tiger, because the animal was confused and unhappy. It surprised him to realize he could feel the animal's emotions.

Her cougar started to walk past his tiger, then paused and swiped a fast lick over his cheek. She continued another step, stopping only to slap a paw at his tiger's rump.

His animal snarled, but without any heat.

When his tiger swung his big head around, Gan could swear Scarlett's cougar smiled then continued on to the patio.

His tiger said, *She likes me.*

Gan laughed. *Do not make her angry again.*

If I do, I make her happy again.

Where did his animal get so much confidence?

Watching Scarlett shift back to human form, Gan told his tiger, *I would like to be human again. That would make Scarlett happy.*

I will do for mate.

Gan asked, *Why do you think she is mate?*

His tiger countered, *Why do you not see her as mate?*

The shift back to his human form started before Gan could reply, but he had no answer to that question. He could feel Scarlett in his chest as if she were a part of him, but was that mating? Would she ever feel that way about him?

Once Scarlett had her clothes on again, she said, "I can't sleep unless I wash after that swim. Let me do that and dry my hair, then I'll be back."

"Leave wet. Please."

"Why? It's a mess to brush out."

He ran his hand over her wet hair. "Is natural. I like."

Was she blushing? The woman who battled like a hardened warrior and made love as if the world ended today? He smiled to himself at that.

Yes, she had made love to him.

Kissing her hair, he suggested, "I wash for you."

She laughed, pushing him away. "Not this time. Save that thought for when we find a condom."

"Why need condom to wash hair?" he said, teasing her.

"Yeah, right, wild man. We both know what will happen if

we're in the shower together again."

"What happens?" he pressed, trying to sound serious, but failed. He couldn't keep a straight face no matter how hard he tried to smother his smile. He had never enjoyed being with a woman so much.

Just looking at her made him happy.

She stepped over and hooked a hand on his neck, pulling him down nose-to-nose. "You know exactly what would happen. Also, you should never play cards. You have no poker face."

"What is poker face?" He didn't care. He just wanted to keep her close.

"Poker is a card game where players bluff often. Bluff means to hold losing cards, but pretending you have winning cards."

He rubbed her nose. "You are right. I would not be good bluff person. Hard to find right words to tell truth."

Her eyes twinkled. "That's okay. Your words are just fine. I like truth and honesty when I talk to someone."

"I like truth, too. I think about wash more than hair." He grinned.

Her laugh hummed through him like a deep breath of spring air. "I knew that," she admitted. "I would be game, but we need to get some sleep and be ready for the minute Jazlyn shows up tomorrow. You can use the big shower after I'm done."

He sighed. "You will miss me."

Scarlett kissed him hard and shoved off, striding to the door. "We're going to have to work on that self-esteem problem."

She'd confounded him again. "What is this? I have no problem."

Opening the door, she said, "That's called a joke, Gan. We'll work on your vocabulary so you know when someone is only teasing."

Shaking his head, he waved a hand. "I hope you wash hair better than make jokes."

The door slapped shut, but not before she yelled something that sounded like, "You. Are. Impossible."

He wanted to say, "And you make no sense." But he knew she teased him. Some people had said cruel things to him as a young boy trying to understand languages everywhere he ended up, but Scarlett had a kind heart.

She played with words, using them to know him better. She

knew exactly what he'd had in mind for washing her hair.

He should have asked her where they could find a condom.

Standing there as he thought through all that had happened, he realized he had never been at peace like this. He'd never just stood still because he wanted to or swam. He'd suffered mental and physical torment nonstop in camps before the tiger showed up. Then he fought Adrian's wolf in Wyoming or had to follow Vic's directions when they traveled with Scarlett.

No one had ever walked away from Gan, trusting him to just do what he wanted.

No one until Scarlett.

She had not told him stay here, go inside, don't shift, or many other orders he'd been given in the past.

Taking his time looking at the property that had short grass and a walkway from the house to the lake, he considered the size of the land. Fifty yards out on each side of the house, short grass spread out until it stopped at a straight line of thick woods.

Turning in a circle, he took it all in. This would be somewhere to raise a family. He would never have a family, but he could see it in a place like this.

A dark cloud passed over his soul.

No, he would not be sad on the best day of his life.

Gan had an idea for another first.

He took a walk, just because he could. He would hold fiercely to every freedom, no matter how small.

After circling the left side of the land where he followed the grass near the trees, he walked the edge of the lake then started back up the tree line on the right side.

He'd made it halfway back to the house when he felt energy brush up against his.

His tiger said, *Change now. Kill wolf.*

Gan struggled to hold the tiger in while still watching for what had set off his animal. "Who is there?"

Adrian emerged from the black shadows. "What the hell are you up to out here, Pyscho Cat?"

"How are you here?" Gan squeezed out when his tiger battered his insides. "Go away. Tiger want out."

"Shit. I knew it was a bad idea to let you go alone," Adrian grumbled. "I just saw you shift back earlier. This is important,

Gan. Hold your tiger in."

His tiger banged back and forth demanding, *Free me. Kill wolf. Threat to mate.*

Gan snarled at Adrian. "Tiger was good. You make him angry. *You* leave!"

Adrian stood with hands on his hips. "I can't do that. The Guardian knows you lied about having full control."

"You lie, too."

"True, but I admitted the truth to the Guardian and I can keep my wolf in right now. He wanted to send Vic to check on you, but I asked to come instead."

"Why? You hate me."

"I don't hate you, but I was sick of your tiger making life insane the last two weeks in Wyoming. You said you want to be free. That won't happen if your tiger takes control. I can't help you if I have to call in the Guardian."

Gan grabbed a fist full of his hair. "I will not live like this."

"Like what?"

"I was prisoner whole life. I will not live as prisoner again. You do not understand. You were trained. You live free life. Your wolf not stranger. You are free to come here alone." Gan glared at him, angry the wolf shifter didn't get it.

"It wasn't all roses," Adrian shot back. "My wolf and I *were* close at one time. I have enough control to be here now, but I'm going back to Wyoming as soon as I do one task."

"Why?"

"My wolf can't be saved. I was captured by an enemy force and locked in a titanium cage too small to move or shift in for most of a month. It drove my wolf insane. We were close once, but no more. I know I have to be put down, but I've got to take care of something first if I don't screw up and get sent back early."

The tiger raged on. Curling his hands into fists, Gan spoke through clenched teeth. His tiger was determined to kill the wolf shifter. He held his chest muscles tight to the point of trembling, squeezing out, "Do not go back. Run. Be free."

He couldn't believe he was trying to help this wolf shifter.

Adrian cursed. "That reminds me of something you need to know. Running won't work for me or you. The Guardian would just call me home."

"What?" Gan cocked his head. His teeth chattered from strain. "What is call home?"

"Our boss has the ability to call any of us to him, no matter where we are in the world, at any time."

Disappointment hit Gan so hard he struggled to stay upright. Cold clutched at his heart.

He would never be free.

Never.

His tiger must have sensed his distraction. The animal battered him a second time. *I save mate!*

Gan struggled to think past losing the one thing he'd lived for this whole time. To be free. He told his tiger, *Stop. Wolf will not harm Scarlett.*

Wolf bad. Wolf sick. I kill.

Claws shot out of Gan's fingers. He mentally yelled at the tiger. *Stop!*

His tiger roared and slammed his insides.

Muscles began twisting and bones cracked with the impending change.

Adrian pleaded in a hushed voice, "Don't do this, Gan. Stop your animal so I can tell the Guardian you're doing okay."

Gan's jaws stretched. His teeth elongated.

CHAPTER 20

———

SCARLETT FINISHED TOWELING HER HAIR.
Was she really not going to dry her hair because a man had asked her to leave it natural?

Evidently so.

Even stranger than that? She laughed at the woman in the mirror.

She was no insecure female who had to prove a point by not doing what Gan had asked.

That was the bottom line.

In his blunt way of speaking, which included an explanation that sounded like a compliment, he had *asked* her to let it dry naturally.

Chica purred happily.

Not that it was unusual for her cat to be content, but this purr sounded like she had something on her mind.

Scarlett asked, *What's going on, Chica.*

Tiger is two.

Pulling on shorts and a knit top, Scarlett headed to the bedroom to do some stretching. *What do you mean two?*

Human, tiger, human.

Scarlett had found a bottle of skin cream and paused in smoothing it over her arms. Her cat could be highly perceptive. For that reason, Scarlett listened closely when Chica wasn't distracted by a butterfly or catching a whiff of raccoon. For some reason, Chica liked those critters as much as deer.

I don't understand, Chica. Why two humans and one tiger?

Not two. One shadow human and tiger.

Scarlett put the lotion back and stretched her legs out to bend and twist at her waist. Could her cat be talking about a ghost? She asked, *Could you see through the shadow human, Chica?*

Yes. Chica purred some more.

Scarlett asked, *When did the shadow human show up?*

Always with tiger.

Scarlett stopped twisting and straightened. She struggled to make sense of that, but what if Gan's tiger wasn't just like other shifter animals?

Could that be one reason Gan and his tiger fought for control?

Chica came alert. *Tiger in trouble.*

With no hesitation, Scarlett raced downstairs and out the back door, took one whiff and turned to her right. Seeing Gan, she headed toward him.

His shoulders twisted out of shape.

No. No. *No!*

Gan howled, "*Stop!*"

She tore across the yard to help him.

He couldn't hold the tiger in.

She called up her energy, the one she kept secret. No one in the far houses could see any of this. She hit Gan with her energy ten feet before she reached him.

His back arched.

She stopped and held her breath, but his body kept moving. What? Had her power not worked on him?

He stopped shifting, but he should have frozen in place like a statue.

In the next three steps, she released her magic's hold on Gan's body. Misshapen parts shrunk back to human size.

She sucked in air from panic more than running. As a cougar shifter, she could run fast for long periods. Worry over Gan had rattled her more than she would have expected.

Gan gripped his head, holding it while he breathed deeply. "I feel not right."

Shit. Her magic had definitely hit him.

She should explain how that was a residual effect of magic forcing him to stop mid-shift. She wanted to, but telling him about her extra gift would not go over well. He hated people controlling him, which she never wanted to do.

But she would not back away from keeping him safe.

Climbing off her guilt trip for a moment, she asked, "Are you okay, Gan?"

"Yes, better. Tiger wanted out. I try to stop change."

"Looks like the change did stop," she said carefully so she could skirt the truth.

"But ..." He shook his head. "Why?"

"Do you think your control is getting better?" She hated to tangle the truth with a leading question, but she had no idea how much his ability to scent a lie had improved. What would he say if she told him she had actually prevented his shift?

Would he look at her like everyone else who had stolen his ability to choose what he wanted done or not done?

Chica said, *You change human.*

Scarlett had a moment of dread. She'd marked Lincoln with a black claw shape on his chest. The tattoo-like mark didn't appear for a day after she'd hit him with a load of her power and the mark couldn't be removed.

Rumor was he'd tried.

She searched Gan's neck and moved around to his face, trying to see what Chica saw. She finally asked her cat, *What change?*

Head glows blue. When you stop shift, his head turn blue like bright sky. Pretty.

Shit. Had she also put a claw mark on Gan that would appear later? Scarlett worried on that for a moment, then pushed it off. All she did was help him manage his shifting.

What was a little blue aura?

No harm, no foul, right?

She'd need scuba gear soon to breathe under the load of guilt she kept piling on.

Yes, she'd provided him control surreptitiously, but she'd rather he feel stronger about his ability to manage his animal than to think she could control his body.

That hadn't been her intention at all.

Deep down, she had a feeling this was going to eat at her for a while. Hadn't they just talked about being honest with each other?

This proved she couldn't have someone in her life, not if she couldn't share all her secrets without getting that person killed.

Chica said, *Wolf close by.*

That's when Scarlett turned her attention to her senses. She knew that scent.

She gave it another sniff. Not Jazlyn.

Adrian.

Her pulse jacked out of sight. She turned toward the woods. "Might as well come out, Adrian."

Gan groaned. "Hate that wolf."

"That's not nice," Adrian said as he stepped back into the moonlight. "Hi, Scarlett."

"Don't hi me, wolf. What are you doing sneaking around out here? And how did you find … ah, shit. You tracked Vic's sport utility."

Twisting his neck until it popped, Gan asked, "How did you follow truck?"

Scarlett answered that. "They used an electronic device. I'll explain it later, but first I want to know why the Guardian did this after I called to clear taking Vic's wheels."

Raking both hands over his head, Adrian explained, "This is not about you, Scarlett. I helped Gan convince our boss that we were okay to get out of Wyoming. I had to come clean with the Guardian and tell him I'm still questionable on control. I'm good for now, but if I'm out in the public for very long I'll be fighting my wolf more and more. After that conversation, he realized Gan would have less control than me."

"Maybe not," Gan argued.

"Really, tiger? Because I just watched you almost break out claws and fur a moment ago."

Scarlett held her breath.

What had Adrian seen?

Opening his arms wide, Gan said, "I am not changed. Your wolf has problem, but I am not tiger. Is good, right?"

Scarlett studied Gan. He would normally be chiding Adrian, but Gan sounded angry. Or hurt?

Adrian locked his hands behind his head, his dark gaze jumping from Gan to Scarlett. "What do you say, Scarlett?"

"I'm guessing you were probably here when our cats went swimming. That should answer your question." She gave him a look that dared him to counter her point.

"I saw." Adrian's sharp gaze slashed over at Gan. "I admit I was surprised at the control you showed changing back right after Scarlett finished her shift."

"Now you know. You are done." Gan made that statement in a flat tone, but Scarlett could hear the anger simmering beneath his words. "Go home. Remind Guardian he said three days. I have two more."

"Shit." Adrian dropped his hands and stalked one way then the other, looking like a wolf pacing in a cage. He stopped short. "I hate being in this position. He wants me to shadow you for a few days, but not in secret. He's too fair for that. He felt if you knew you were being observed you'd do your best. I'm only following orders and doing what I'm told. If you make it through this initial period, you'll understand later on when you have to do the same for another of our shifters."

Scarlett didn't miss how Adrian avoided saying the word Gallize. They had shared some details with her weeks ago when she and the Gallize had rescued Gan and his foster sister.

She expected to learn more later on as long as her friendship of the Gallize status remained intact.

Gan sent a sad glance at Scarlett. "I did not ask for this. I want to help you, but I can only make Adrian leave if I go."

He was reminding her that she couldn't allow Adrian to be nearby when Jazlyn showed up tomorrow.

Why did everything have to get so screwed up?

She'd been looking forward to spending a night with Gan beside her while they killed the last of the twenty-four hours Jazlyn had set as a minimum.

Was that too much to ask?

Now he would be on edge with Adrian so close and she needed Adrian gone way before Jazlyn's window of time to meet.

Warm fingertips brushed across the side of her face, pushing her hair out of the way. Even though they were all shifters, he whispered, "It will be okay. I will go."

His words were only for her.

Her stomach hurt at the thought of him leaving.

Once again, she had to do what was right for everyone else, though. Would the day ever come that she could do what was right for her?

No. She would always take care of those she loved.

Licking her dry lips, Scarlett said, "I want—"

Something came crashing through the woods on the far side of the property.

They all jumped around, prepared to face a threat.

Scarlett recognized the person who burst from a thick stand of trees at a full run.

Jazlyn.

The smell of fresh blood hit her.

She took off to meet her friend.

CHAPTER 21

—◆—

SCARLETT RACED ACROSS THE LAWN with Gan at her side and that blasted wolf shifter following right behind. She didn't have time to shield Adrian from seeing Jazlyn.

Her friend had to be in bad trouble to show up now and this way.

"What happened?" Scarlett called out. As she closed the distance, she realized Jazlyn carried a bundle wrapped in a brown cloth.

Jazlyn stumbled.

Scarlett reached her in time to grab her arm and pull her upright.

"Take her." Jazlyn shoved the bundle at Scarlett just as the baby whimpered. "They have Fayth."

Denial screamed through Scarlett. She had failed the one person who needed her most. "What happened? Who did this? *Where's Fayth?*"

Jazlyn swiped a wash of blood out of her eyes. Her body had been clawed and beaten. "I had her safe in a house down the lake." She swallowed between rasps. "I don't know how they found us. I covered my trail. Someone tripped a wire I'd set for security. I gave Fayth directions and sent her to you, but she wouldn't leave, fucking hardheaded woman. She hid the baby in a closet upstairs and dug out a bottle she'd had ready with a mild sedative. She'd anticipated needing to keep Lily quiet at some point. I would have grabbed them and run here, but I couldn't risk there would be more than three or four coming for us. I was right. I couldn't shift, but I had a titanium knife. She had barely shifted seconds before eight shifters ran into the front yard. She didn't want them in the house to find the baby. We took off and made a hundred yards in different directions to split them."

"You should have called me," Scarlett shouted, hands fisted and needing to hit something.

Jaz snapped right back. "I did. Got no answer."

"Dammit. Sorry. I forgot. That was the phone that got trashed." Scarlett had to stop panicking over Fayth and calm down so she could think.

"We'll find her," Jaz assured her. "We fought them, but I got separated from Fayth. I heard her scream when they dragged her away. I threw the knife and hit one shifter in the throat, then the second one came for me. When I took him down, I went after her. Another cat shifter hit me. I gutted him. By the time I broke free, Fayth was gone. That left one I drew away from the house then doubled back to catch him."

Scarlett didn't ask if she'd killed that one.

That was understood.

Jazlyn took a fast breath. "By then, everyone was gone, probably thinking the one they left behind with a vehicle would bring me in." She grabbed Scarlett. "Fayth made me promise if anything happened to her to get Lily to you. Take the baby and get out of here *now*. I'll find Fayth."

Adrian said, "Were they all cat shifters?"

Jazlyn seemed to just notice the men. "What are those two doing here?"

Scarlett dismissed that question. "It's a long story. Right now, we need information."

Gan asked, "Who did this?"

"Lincoln, dumb shit," Jazlyn shoved a furious glare at Gan. "Just like you. Another fucking tiger shifter."

Scarlett racked her brain. "How could Lincoln have found Fayth *now* when he clearly hadn't while the Pagan Nomads had you?"

"I don't know. Someone figured it out." Jazlyn coughed up blood and spit it to the side.

Adrian repeated his question. "Were all the shifters cats?"

That drew Jaz up short. She frowned with her eyes flicking back and forth as she thought. "No. I smelled a wolf and a hyena, maybe two."

Scarlett clutched the baby to her. Worry jumped a new level. "Hyenas and wolves? Lincoln hates anything that isn't cat."

Jaz cursed. She grabbed her head, staring down. She started mumbling, "I got clobbered with a limb … I killed that one."

"Back to hyenas," Gan reminded her. "How do they find you?"

Scarlett clarified, "No, they found Fayth."

Jaz froze and growled. "Shit. Who has a knife?"

Gan and Scarlett said, "Why?"

"I just realized why my shoulder is burning and I can't shift. If the odd shifters belong to the Pagan Nomads, they could have stuck a tracker in me, in all of the captives." She turned her back. "Knife now. Right shoulder. Look for a lump from—"

"—a capsule," Adrian finished as he flipped open a switchblade. "Not my first rodeo, wolf." He ran his hand over the back of her shoulder. "Found it."

The only indication that Adrian cut into Jaz came from her quick intake of air.

"Looks like a tracker." He smashed the small capsule between his palm and the butt of the knife. "They were tracking you."

Jaz added, "But the cats were looking for Fayth. I heard one say Lincoln said to be sure to find the baby." Turning to Scarlett she rushed on. "You have a head start. I'll stay and block for you. I can get away again."

Scarlett believed her, but she also believed the tinge of doubt clinging to her friend's words.

Gan shifted his gaze to Adrian then to Scarlett. "We need to go but have plan to meet again."

Adrian announced, "I'll stay with this one and help cover your ass."

Jaz leveled him with a disgusted look. "I did not ask for help."

"And I didn't ask your opinion," Adrian countered.

Scarlett felt better that Jaz wouldn't be alone. She started to work out details about meeting up when Jaz lifted her nose and turned sharply toward the woods she'd just emerged from.

Adrian stepped past Scarlett who inhaled as Gan did the same.

Chica warned her, *Danger coming fast.*

Four shifters jumped from the trees in a spread-out formation, racing at them.

Two more followed on their heels.

CHAPTER 22

———

G AN CALLED UP HIS TIGER and for once they were on the
same page. Bones snapped and rearranged. Muscles elongated and thickened. His jaws stretched and filled with fangs. His
tiger roared and stepped in front of Scarlett who couldn't shift
with a baby in her arms.

Two of the attackers changed on the fly. Crazy fast.

Both were black, like a panther female Gan had seen captured
by the Cadells, but these males were far larger.

He smelled hyena on the air, hardly pausing to note that he'd
identified that scent.

The other four attacked as Adrian and Jazlyn changed into a red
male wolf and a golden female wolf.

Scarlett yelled at Gan, "Break loose from the panthers so I can
help."

He ignored her.

If he didn't engage both animals, one would get to her. He
would use his last breath to keep her and the baby safe.

His tiger agreed. *Kill all. Save mate.*

One panther leaped on the back of Gan's tiger, but his beast had
learned something from fighting Adrian's wolf. His tiger locked
his jaws over the one in front of him and dragged that panther by
the head when he rolled all that weight over, crushing the cat on
his back. Screams, howls, and roars filled the air now thick with
the brutal smell of fresh blood.

His tiger hadn't killed either panther, but he'd slowed them
down. His jaws opened and closed again but with more force this
time, crunching hard to break neck bones in one crushing bite.
That cat whined and fell on its side.

The other panther got a second wind and attacked his tiger with paws slashing his shoulder like a fan on high speed.

Scarlett yelled, "Get me to the truck and I'll lead them away."

At hearing that, the two cats still fighting Adrian and Jazlyn broke free and started toward Scarlett.

Adrian's wolf slammed one predator.

Jazlyn's ravaged wolf made a wobbly hit at the other one that spun around and fought her.

Sharp teeth withdrew from Gan's tiger and turned for Scarlett, too, but his tiger tackled the black cat. They tangled into a vicious fight with the panther clawing gouges down his tiger's leg.

If more shifters showed up, Gan could not keep Scarlett and the baby safe. He wanted her out of here.

Gan told his tiger, *Scarlett and baby need truck. She can go. Be safe. We stay and help others.*

His animal shouted, *Stay with mate! Protect mate.*

No, Gan argued. *Do what is best for everyone.*

Adrian's voice came into Gan's mind. *Get Scarlett to the truck. Her female wolf friend is about to drop. I can't defend her while I fight. Stay with Scarlett so she has protection and draw some of these shifters away. Then I can get us to my truck.*

Gan argued, *I will not leave you to die.*

Every second you waste makes it harder for me to survive, cat. I've got this. Adrian broke off talking while he fought his way out from under a cougar bigger than Scarlett's, and with a darker coat.

Gan told his tiger, *Move to truck. Keep Scarlett on safe side.*

Scarlett caught on quickly and shadowed Gan in a fast trot to Vic's sport utility.

Gan had his tiger watch all around them as they kept a steady pace. He hated leaving Adrian with Jazlyn, who was damaged too much to continue fighting, but he would trust Adrian. The wolf had done this longer.

Gan herded Scarlett around the end of the house. When the truck came into view, Scarlett took off running.

A shifter in human form stepped out from behind the vehicle and ran at them. He changed into a jaguar, fresh and ready to fight.

Scarlett slowed.

Gan shot past her. His tiger screamed, *Save mate!*

They met the jaguar straight on in a barreling crash. Claws raked his shoulders and sharp fangs bit his head and back. The jaguar's teeth seemed to be everywhere at once.

The truck engine roared to life. Gan hadn't even considered where the keys were, but Scarlett tended to know these things. She probably planned ahead for a quick escape.

Smart woman.

He worried about losing this battle and told his tiger. *If we do not kill jaguar, he will get to Scarlett and baby.*

His tiger didn't reply.

Instead his tiger knocked the jaguar in the air and over on his back where his tiger could claw and rip the jaguar's soft underside.

"*Gan!*" Scarlett shouted.

He wanted to yell back to go, but he couldn't in animal form.

What was she waiting for?

As if she heard his thought, she yelled, "Not leaving without you."

The jaguar came up quick at the tiger and grabbed the loose skin of his throat. Another bite and the big vein Gan had seen cut on other animals would rip out. They would die.

He couldn't talk to Scarlett in this form. He ordered his tiger, *Finish. Kill.*

Slapping a paw on the jaguar's chest, his tiger locked his jaws on the jaguar's throat, ignoring claws tearing at his face, and ripped the cat's throat out with one vicious yank.

Gan said, *Change back. Must be human.*

His tiger sounded exhausted. *No.*

Scarlett snarled, "*Gan! Change!*"

He caught the sound of animals coming. One glance told him time was up. The cats had broken free of Adrian and Jazlyn … or killed them.

Gan forced energy hard through his body and into his next order for his tiger. *Change now.*

He had barely said that when he returned to human shape.

The cats were racing around the side of the house.

He roared at her, "*Go!*"

Scarlett had the truck turned to leave and his door open. "*Get. In. The. Fucking. Truck!*"

Gan set up and kicked the lead cat into the one right behind it.

He made a running jump into the truck as she hit the gas. Lunging for the open door, he dove in and slammed it shut.

She had the baby in one arm. "Take her."

Reaching over, he carefully pulled the baby from her.

Something heavy hit the top of the truck.

Scarlett swung the steering wheel back and forth. The cat held on and slammed a paw hard on the roof.

Gan grabbed a handle above his door with one hand and held the baby with his other arm. "Baby is safe. Knock off cat."

She didn't hesitate to wheel off the path and under a low limb that scraped the roof.

The cat screamed as it bounced all the way off the back. She wrenched the wheel hard, fighting ruts and dodging trees until the road came back into view. Not even slowing, she bounced her way back up on the road, fishtailing until she had control again.

She drove with surprising calm as the speeding vehicle slid around corners on the soft ground. Her knuckles were white with strain, but he had full trust in her ability.

"Put your seatbelt on, Gan," she ordered.

"Why?"

"Dammit. Do you have to question everything? Just do it." Taking a breath, she added, "Please. You're holding the baby. While you might not die in a crash, that doesn't mean a baby will survive."

"I will do." He moved the baby from arm to arm as he clicked the seatbelt latch in place.

She opened and closed her hands on the steering wheel. Claws shot out and retracted. "Sorry. I'm … stressed."

"I know. Baby is fine."

No one said a word as she fought her way to the paved road and made a sliding turn to a smoother ride. Gan considered asking where she was headed, but she'd just criticized him for asking questions.

The baby stirred and made a noise, but Gan shook the bundle gently like he'd seen done in the camps to calm babies. This little one gave a tiny sigh, moved its lips in a sucking motion, then turned toward his heat and remained asleep.

"How's she doing?" Scarlett asked, not taking her eyes from the road. Her gaze flicked to each side and the rearview mirror.

"Is girl?"

"Yes." Scarlett explained, "Lily is usually a female name."

"She is good. Sleeping. Happy."

Lifting an eyebrow at him with a bit of exhaustion and amusement. "How can you tell she's happy?"

"Is simple. If baby is not happy, it cries." He thought everyone knew that. He should point out she asked questions without him criticizing her, but Scarlett worried over Fayth and would not like being teased at this moment.

She turned on the ramp, taking them back on the interstate.

Leaving her alone while she drove, his mind returned to Adrian's words. Gan had never thought about trying to escape magic. He still had a hard time accepting that the Guardian had so much power he could call any Gallize shifter home.

How could he overcome an invisible chain? Adrian had made it sound as though Gan had no option if the Guardian called him.

He had no future.

Before now, he'd started thinking about finding a way to stay close to Scarlett, even if he had to give up snow.

He'd lost that choice.

As soon as the Guardian forced him to return, Gan would be sent back to Wyoming the minute he failed to prove he could control his tiger.

Because what little control he enjoyed now was due to his tiger being around Scarlett.

This time, ending up in Wyoming would be way worse.

His tiger believed Scarlett was their mate.

Gan would never want another as his mate.

I will not leave mate, his tiger declared.

Gan pushed his animal away from his mind for some peace. The tiger's voice dulled more and more until he could hardly hear the animal rumbling. He listened, waiting for the beast to react, but that never happened.

Was that what control felt like?

Why couldn't he figure out how to be a shifter all of the time? Not just when his beast was happy around Scarlett?

Gan still had two days with her.

He would not spend it wondering over what he could not do.

Two days of freedom with the woman he carried in his heart.

What about Adrian?

Had he and Jazlyn gotten away safely?

Why did Gan feel guilty about Adrian? That wolf had made his life difficult from the first minute they met. Adrian's wolf had bloodied Gan's tiger more than once in Wyoming.

Then Adrian showed up at the lake house, ruining the special night Gan had been enjoying with Scarlett.

On the other hand, Adrian had made it possible for Gan to get Scarlett and the baby to safety.

And the wolf had actually sounded as if he wanted to help Gan with the Guardian.

Now Adrian battled shifters over something that had nothing to do with him. He'd stood there, sending Gan to protect Scarlett instead of saving his own hide.

Gan had to be honest about Adrian.

His red wolf couldn't be trusted to turn a back on, but Gan respected the man. He only hoped Jazlyn managed to stay upright long enough to fight with Adrian and they both escaped.

They were probably gone by now.

Or were dead.

Gan couldn't believe he was going to ask Scarlett to contact the one person he had hoped to never see again. "Can you call Guardian? Tell him to send Adrian help?"

Sounding tired, Scarlett said, "I would have done that already, but I don't have a phone. Mine was upstairs in the bedroom. I normally carry it with me, but I ran to you the second my cougar said your tiger was in trouble."

Gan's guilt doubled.

How could he help Adrian and Jazlyn? He muttered, "Adrian made me go, to protect you. He said if you leave, cats follow and he would save Jazlyn. She was hurt bad. I am glad I did, but … did he give truth?"

"The panthers did follow," she said gently.

"Yes." That didn't ease his conscience. In the heat of the moment, he accepted Adrian's battle experience over his. Now that he thought back, he wondered if that had been the right decision.

Had he left Adrian and Jazlyn to die?

While he worked on that, something Scarlett said sank in. Her cougar told her his tiger was having trouble. That had to be when he struggled not to shift in front of Adrian.

How could her animal have known this?

What else did her cougar know?

Scarlett said, "We're pulling off at a rest stop in about a minute. Adrian's bag is still in the back and has extra warm ups. I'll find a place away from people where you can put on some clothes."

"Something wrong?"

"Sort of. Vic's ride has a tracking device. I'm going to find it and pull the wires out." She swallowed. "I have to get in touch with the Guardian to send help to the lake house. That won't happen until I find a place with a phone. Right now, I need to stop him from tracking us. I can't allow him to show up at the wrong time and interfere when I'm in the middle of getting Fayth back."

Gan thought about what he'd learned from Adrian. "You must leave me when you stop."

The look of disbelief she gave him hurt. "You want to go back?"

"No. I never want to go back. But when I see Adrian tonight, he tells me the Guardian can call me to him any time. Eagle shifter has strong … magic. He will be problem for you if I stay."

She slowed the car as they neared the exit into the rest area. "If you really want to stay with me, I'd like that, too. But keep in mind that I can't promise any of this will turn out well."

"Yes. I want to be with you. If I go back now it will be worse than before. My tiger will fight Wyoming. I promised tiger we would leave for somewhere cold. North. But Guardian will not let me. I want to stay long as possible."

In the quiet that followed, Gan sensed that she was sad. What had he said wrong?

Lifting her head high, she said, "If that is what you really want, let me worry about the Guardian. I have a few tricks up my sleeve. He will not be a problem for me and maybe not for you. Just tell me if you feel yourself being drawn away and … I might be able to stop it."

What could she do against a powerful eagle shifter?

He'd had one small moment of happiness.

Soon the Guardian would yank Gan away from … his mate. Scarlett was the mate of his heart.

He swallowed past the thick ball of misery.

He wanted more time with her, but in two days they would be ripped apart.

CHAPTER 23

—

L IGHTS BLURRED THROUGH HER VISION.
Scarlett shook off the exhaustion and blinked.

It had to be after four in the morning, because the last gas stop had been around three. She'd swung into a major truck stop right after leaving the rest area and asked a trucker to let her borrow his phone.

He thought she was calling her family to tell them she'd gotten lost and was running late.

When a male answered the Guardian's number, she didn't give him time to patch her to his boss. She told him the lake house address and to send help immediately, then hung up.

Before leaving, she used an electronic banking outlet to withdraw cash from a secret account no one could trace. Not without knowing the name it was registered to, which she'd set up a long time ago just for an emergency like this.

After that, she headed to Galax, Virginia, where she'd found an all-night super-store.

With no diapers, no baby food, nothing to care for an infant, she pulled into the parking lot with a mental shopping list. After a mad dash through the store while Gan watched the baby, Scarlet grabbed baby supplies, adult clothes, snacks, and a phone. She could win one of those grocery store races at the speed she'd filled a cart. Gan needed to change. Her brain saw him, but smelled Adrian's scent on his clothes.

Until she found a computer where she could tap her list of resources tucked away in virtual cloud storage, the phone would be of little use.

Not exactly useless.

She had to call the Guardian back and find out if Adrian and Jaz were okay, plus let him know Gan was safe. She couldn't put off this call when Gan said his boss had the ability to call him back to headquarters.

Could she use magic to block the eagle shifter?

She had her doubts.

He carried a load of magic.

Back in the car, Scarlett opened the phone and shoved in the charger. She wiped her eyes. "We're close to a motel. We need sleep."

"You are too tired." Gan ran his hand over her hair and rubbed her neck.

"Careful, Gan. If you relax me too much, I'll pass out." She smiled at him.

He smiled a moment, but it had been colored with worry.

Cranking the engine, she pushed on.

Gan checked Lily for the millionth time. Her tiger shifter had been a champ holding Fayth's baby girl the entire drive and cooing any time the child became restless.

She hoped that eagle shifter had good news or Gan would buckle under the guilt riding his face the whole drive.

Something along the lines of Adrian having survived and Jazlyn vanished into the night would be awesome.

Sure, that happened.

While she was having delusional fantasies, she'd wish up a national chain hotel happy to provide a room with a king-sized bed and full kitchen for the limited cash she had on hand.

No, a fantasy would be spending a week with Gan and lots of condoms.

Somewhere near a huge body of water or maybe a beach. Had Gan ever been to a beach? She doubted it from what he'd said. He'd never lived free.

The fact that she even thought about going somewhere with Gan after this nightmare pointed to a major loss of brain cells.

How could she think about tomorrow when today had so many question marks?

Look at her life right now. For all her freedom, she'd never exercised the right to just travel for pleasure. She hadn't stepped foot in salt water either.

There were so many things she'd like to share with someone. With him.

Her devil's advocate side argued that she would have even less time now that Fayth had been captured in spite of all Scarlett had done to keep her sister and baby safe.

That miserable Lincoln shouldn't have found Fayth. He wouldn't have if not for raiding small groups of shifters who only wanted to live in peace and off the grid. How had he managed to stay off the radar of SCIS?

She gave as much aid and time as possible to the shifter law enforcement organization, but to be honest, she shared some blame for Lincoln eluding the law.

She'd put as much distance as possible between the two of them after he'd tried to make her his mate against her will. If she had kept tabs on him through her resource network, she might have stopped him long before now.

The bigger question at the moment was how he'd teamed up with the Pagan Nomads to find Jaz.

He shouldn't have even known about her connection to Fayth.

Some piece was missing.

Something important she couldn't put her finger on.

Too many thoughts collided with each other. She needed to catch a nap and clear her head.

A bright yellow motel sign glared at her from a distance in the small town she drove through.

Single-level motels of the past rarely got a one-star rating, but a clean bed and functioning shower were all that mattered.

Turning in, she whispered, "I'll be right back with a key."

Gan eyed the small office. "Are you safe?"

She smiled at his sweet concern. "Yes. These are usually run by humans."

At the front door, a young guy watching a movie on a computer forced himself to get up and buzz the lock open. She passed through a small lobby with an old smell of having been visited many times over the years.

Because she'd technically arrived ahead of check-in for day one, she had to pay for two nights. She would not be checking out before noon.

Once she moved Vic's truck down to the unit with no vehicle

in front and parked, her muscles turned to jelly. She'd bought changes of clothes for her and Gan, plus shoes. She hoped his were large enough.

He got out and handed her the baby. "You go in. I bring everything."

"Thanks."

She forced her arms to hold the baby securely, ready to rip anyone to shreds who tried to take this child from her. She had placed the baby in Fayth's arms a minute after birth and she would put this child there again.

Inside the room, she scrunched her nose at the disinfectant smell, but everything appeared clean. Two full-size beds were covered in thin floral-patterned spreads. A squat wooden chair in the corner wore its age in scars.

One nightstand with a lamp.

No phone, but she'd paid for the two nights only after the kid confirmed the room had a microwave. She would not feed a baby a cold bottle. This one had to still be nursing. She hoped formula food would be suitable.

Gan dropped the bags in a corner. He took a look at her standing there with the baby and waited patiently as she did nothing.

She'd the point of exhaustion where she struggled to figure out her next move.

He pulled the covers back on one bed and piled pillows on each side of a gap. "Baby sleep there. Safe."

"Good idea. I've got to change her again then feed her."

"You change diaper. I make food."

"Do you know … how?" Scarlett asked, cringing when she realized how her words might have insulted him.

He pulled out a diaper, powder and baby oil, piling it on top of the baby. "Yes. Go."

She didn't have the energy to argue and turned to the corner of the bed with her back to Gan. He rummaged through the bags, muttering something to himself. She unwrapped the blanket and smiled at the sweet child. Her heart hurt to think about what Fayth had to be going through.

Gan kept up a string of noises that ended with him going into the bathroom to run water.

She called out softly, "What about the microwave?"

"Mamas in camps say never make baby food too hot. Burn baby. Machine worry me. This better."

Now that she thought about it, the package had said something about not microwaving. She doubted he could read all that. He paid attention to things he considered important.

She had to stop underestimating Gan.

Fayth's little girl tried to open her eyes, blinking twice, but whatever Fayth had given her kept the child half asleep. That meant Scarlett had to remain vigilant about feeding Lily until the baby was alert enough to let her know when hunger pains hit.

With the diaper changed and the baby wrapped in the brown blanket again, she lifted the small bundle to her shoulder and found Gan shaking drops from the bottle on his arm. That man continued to amaze her. He wiped his arm with a small towel, walked over and reached for the baby.

Scarlett pulled back. "I can feed her."

He didn't get angry, just looked at her with understanding. "I know this. You must make calls. I worry about Adrian and your friend. I feed this one." He waited another second and added, "She is safe with me."

What better protector could she ask for Fayth's child?

She'd rank him higher than herself at the moment.

Handing him the baby, she said, "I wasn't doubting you, but none of this is your responsibility. I feel bad enough about you being stuck in this mess without expecting you to care for a baby, too."

"Everyone must protect children and mamas. That is most important." That's all he said as he snagged the bottle on his way to the chair. The image of Gan holding Lily and smiling down as he fed her would stick with Scarlett the rest of her life.

Tears burned her eyes.

An unwelcome realization smacked her. Something she never expected to happen. Ever.

She'd met a man worthy of a woman's love, of her love.

A man she would trust with her life.

A man she could spend forever with.

A man she could never have.

Not if she wanted to keep him alive, and she did. Life had sucked since the moment she found out why she had abilities beyond being a shifter. She'd spent every waking minute looking over her shoulder after running from being captured. She'd grabbed Fayth and helped her find a life, then Scarlett had distanced herself to shield those she loved from evil.

She could have kept doing that and not regretting one moment of a lonely existence if she had never met Gan. She'd never find another one like him.

Even if she did, it wouldn't matter.

She only wanted this man.

He looked up and arched an eyebrow. "Phone?"

That snapped her out of daydreaming. "I'm on it. I'll step out to keep from disturbing her."

"Open window so I see you. Do not go far."

She huffed, about to remind him she didn't respond well to orders.

He had glanced away, then his gaze returned with a soft look in his tired eyes. He added, "Please."

A fast study, that one.

She swiped the drapes to each side of the window, then walked outside into the cool air, just feeling it now that she slowed down. After pulling the door quietly shut, she took a deep breath and punched keys, dreading the connection going through.

"Who's calling?" the male voice demanded on the Guardian's hotline.

"Scarlett. I'd like to—"

"Hold on."

Three seconds and the Guardian's smooth voice asked, "Where are my shifters, Scarlett?"

Well that didn't sound good. "Gan is with me. I had hoped you would have Adrian in hand by now. Did you not find him?"

"I had a team on the way by the time we got your message. My people had tracked him to a house on a lake near Johnson City, Tennessee. The team arrived to find a mix of cat, hyena, and wolf shifter bodies."

Her throat closed. "What about Adrian?" She couldn't ask about Jaz.

"He was gone. They found his scent, plus yours and Gan's."

The Guardian stopped, clearly waiting on her to fill him in on what he didn't know.

How much could she tell him? "You knew Gan was with me to help with my friend." She saw no reason to inform this eagle shifter that she had family involved. "We were on our way to find her when the cat shifters showed up."

"Lie." Mr. Polite had left the room.

She pulled the phone back after that sharp word. Even a shifter could not tell a lie through the phone.

Giving it another try, she said, "Not a lie, just not every detail. A female wolf shifter had been protecting my friend. She gave me the address of the house where your people found the bodies. She intended to come over once she knew for sure we were not followed. Her instincts proved true when Adrian showed up."

She waited this time, but the Guardian did not acknowledge sending Adrian. She continued, "Before we could meet, cat, hyena and wolf shifters found the two women first. They fought them off, but there were too many. They took one. Someone dear to me. The other female shifter broke free and came to warn us to leave, but more shifters from the attack group showed up right behind her."

"You and Gan left those two to fight a team of shifters alone?"

Time to make a decision to end the call or give him the truth. "They were after a baby that belonged to the woman they captured." Scarlett paused. When he said nothing, she continued, "The female who came to alert us managed to grab the baby and get it to me. I couldn't shift with a baby in hand so I told the others I'd get to the truck and take off to draw the predators away. Gan would have stayed, but Adrian told him to protect me if I was going to be the bait. Gan argued, but Adrian told him every second he wasted put all of them in more danger. Gan killed another shifter near the truck then jumped in and we left. Two panthers did follow. One landed on top of the truck, but we got rid of him." That's all this eagle shifter needed to know.

From the brittle silence following, the Guardian did not agree with leaving Adrian behind.

She hadn't been happy about abandoning Adrian and Jaz either, but she stuck to decisions made in the heat of battle and criticized no one.

"You disabled Vic's vehicle tracking," the eagle shifter accused.

"Yes. You told me I could return the truck with Gan, then you used the tracking to send Adrian to snoop on Gan, which is how Adrian ended up fighting those cats."

"I want my shifters back."

Did the Guardian think she could just snap her fingers and deliver Adrian? As for Gan, she had an issue with the way he'd been treated. She felt certain the Guardian had meant him no harm, but that didn't alter the fact that Gan hadn't been better informed or that he hated Wyoming and didn't want to be stuck there again.

She replied, "I want my friend back, too. I suggest we work together on a common goal."

"Gan isn't suited to being in the field like this with no oversight."

"Oversight? You mean sending Adrian to humiliate Gan? You don't know much about that tiger." She shouldn't have started a verbal war with the Guardian, but who else was going to stand up for Gan?

"I beg your pardon?" That was the eagle shifter's attempt at being polite in a chillingly cold voice.

"Gan has fought admirably. He shifts back between tiger and human form at will. He followed Adrian's direction. He … shit, he's just better than any of you realize. He deserves respect."

The Guardian made a sound she interpreted as cursing in a language she couldn't identify, because he was too well mannered to say it in English. She might as well unload everything off her chest now.

"Something good happened at that lake house as we were waiting for my friend to contact us. Just before Adrian showed up, Gan and I shifted to our cats and played in the lake. When he came out, he shifted back to human form. Adrian saw it. Gan said he had never been able to swim in a big body of water. He's a blasted tiger. They love water. Did you ever consider putting Gan somewhere he chose? He said you stuck him in Wyoming with Adrian's crazy wolf as soon as he shifted. Not the best role model. Gan has never been free. Never." She paused, trying to calm down. Her anger would get in the way.

When the Guardian responded, his words were no longer acidic. He sounded thoughtful. "Those are things I will discuss with Gan."

"Fine, but you told him three days. He has one and a half left.

He will never trust you again if you take that from him by calling him home."

She hoped that warning would prevent the Guardian from trying to make Gan return involuntarily. She had no idea if her special gift would prevent that from happening, but she wanted to keep Gan free as long as she could.

"Very well. Tell Gan I will discuss these things with him. In the meantime, how do you suggest we find Adrian and your friend … or is it friends?"

She'd hoped he would not pick up on that. "I don't know if the female wolf shifter who stayed to fight with Adrian survived."

"They identified a missing wolf shifter besides Adrian. We shall work under the assumption they were both captured."

She let out the breath she'd been holding. "Give me a little time to reach my people on the ground and see if I can turn up some intel. I'll let you know as soon as I know something."

"I will expect your call by sunset." Then he was gone.

Not even a goodbye.

She leaned back against the window for a moment.

Gan wanted to escape the Gallize permanently. That meant walking away from her, too, when the time came.

She'd accepted every loss in her life and moved on, but this one would leave a hole she'd never fill. The saying went that if you love someone to set them free. If they come back, they're yours.

If they don't, they never were.

He felt like hers, but she would not be selfish and stand in his way. If she had it in her power to free him of the Guardian's hold, she would kiss him goodbye and accept that she'd never see him again.

The Guardian would hound her for the rest of her days and she'd still be hiding.

Her life would remain the same, at least as viewed from the outside. Inside would be a train wreck she'd never be able to repair.

CHAPTER 24

—◆—

LINCOLN'S CLAWS HADN'T RETRACTED SINCE leaving that Power Baron. That bastard had humiliated him.

Did Robert think he was the only power player in this world? The only being with magic?

Every time Lincoln thought about how Robert had taken full control of his body sent tremors of cold chills rushing through him. His tiger wanted blood.

So did Lincoln, but he had to be smart about revenge.

If Robert wanted that woman, then someone else might want her just as much.

He swung around to his right-hand man. "You're sure it was a tiger you saw, Percy?"

"Yes, King." The young man who had stood out among his guards said, "A Siberian tiger. Huge mother."

"I want him. He had to be there for a reason. We use her to get him."

Percy hesitated then asked, "What about the Power Baron? Don't you have to—"

"I'll deal with him when I'm damned good and ready. He does not rule the Cat Clowder. I do."

Lincoln enjoyed the idea of Robert sitting in his mansion, waiting for Lincoln to contact him like a scrawny cat pleading for milk. That Power Baron would never get a second chance to catch Lincoln in a vulnerable position.

First he wanted the tiger.

Only one of Lincoln's spawn had survived birth and that one grew slowly. Each of the three female tiger shifters had been excited to be the one to birth the first male cub destined to be

Lincoln's next in line. After five stillbirths, the females looked at him as if they knew it could be his fault.

He'd tampered with the elements when he had his witch create a concoction to boost his tiger's power.

He'd caught a lion to test his strength against and trounced that shifter. Sure, his tiger had been a hundred pounds heavier than the lion, but the battle served his purpose.

No one following him would go up against Lincoln's beast.

He planned to give the Power Baron what he wanted, but only after Lincoln had this Siberian tiger in hand and under his control. When he met with the Power Baron, he'd have a monster tiger at his right hand and a powerful witch at his left. That should be enough to keep Robert out of his hair. Then Lincoln would breed that tiger around the clock to create a dynasty of tiger shifters.

If those babies did not survive, then neither would his harem of female breeders. He'd keep the Siberian caged until he had replacement females or if he needed an executioner in the meantime.

To insure Robert didn't turn the tables on him, Lincoln would have to set the stage perfectly. He ordered Percy, "Get the witch."

Percy's anxiety zinged to Lincoln, who looked up sharply. "Problem?"

"Not exactly, boss. It's just that the witch freaked out the last time we sent a cat shifter. That guard never shifted again. We had to put him down, which was not simple."

"Ah, yes. Johnson. That happens."

Percy's voice went up a notch with his obvious fear. "She also turned every wild animal along the southern border of our land crazy when something set her off. Birds wouldn't fly. Squirrels fought the raccoons for dead mice. Some of the animals just stopped moving and sat still for a predator to kill it."

That was exactly why Lincoln wanted her.

The Power Baron threatening him liked to control shifters.

Lincoln's witch once went up against a mage. When the man called forth fire to throw at her, the witch compelled him to toss the ball of fire into the air and try to catch it in his mouth like a peanut.

As the fireball came down, it widened to the size of a tire and lassoed him, consuming the body in flames.

He only screamed for a while.

Lincoln nodded. "Yes, she's peculiar, but the shifter we sent last time was not my second-in-command."

Percy winced.

"Be sure to announce yourself and that I have something special for her. Tell her I will gift her a shifter as payment. She has always wanted one."

Once she satisfied Lincoln's need to teach the Power Baron a lesson, he would give her the red wolf male shifter his men caught in the battle. She would have a fine specimen to use for her spells.

He still had the female wolf shifter they'd caught with the red wolf to give the witch if the male didn't suit her.

The one she didn't choose would be handed over to the Pagan Nomads as payment.

CHAPTER 25

———◆———

AT THE LIBRARY, SCARLETT TAPPED computer keys with preternatural speed. No human stood close enough to notice her fingers moving so quickly.

Humans had only learned eight years ago that shifters lived among them. Amidst the riots and chaos that erupted, the Power Barons made a move to form an alliance with human governments as the top of the preternatural food chain.

Scarlett put them at the bottom of the moral meter.

Humans feared all of them.

She'd just as soon slip in and out of this library without the elderly female librarian any the wiser. When she finished reading a reply to one email she'd sent, she glanced over to check on Gan. He sat in the children's area with little Lily, showing her a stuffed bear.

There sat a deadly apex predator caring for a baby as if he were the favored uncle.

He would make a great father.

Would he ever see that day? She wouldn't.

Sighing, she returned to her work.

She'd sent only three messages to the best of her network in this area, the ones she'd willingly pay their exorbitant fee if they could deliver on her time frame.

She made it clear to each one about competing with two more. Competition would drive the speed factor. Now, she had to wait. They had the number of her burner phone.

Lincoln wanted female cat shifters.

Fayth and Jazlyn were wolves.

If Scarlett could first establish a price for those two and make the trade, she could then find out where Lincoln kept Adrian.

If the wolf still lived.

She had yet to tell Gan they were less than a half hour from Lincoln's territory. He ran his businesses out of Roanoke, Virginia with his *clowder* living close to the national forest.

Rumors trickled out about haunted areas in the George Washington and Jefferson Forest not far from where his group resided. He had twenty-thousand-plus acres between what he owned in Roanoke and the national forest bordering his land on one side.

She'd always thought the rumors were to explain anything strange a human reported.

But whispers that he had a witch on his payroll who lived in those woods had been substantiated, according to a source called Zink. That weasel shifter had grown up here and had his finger on the preternatural pulse in this region. He'd been disappointed she offered the same deal to two others as she had to him, but she couldn't play favorites.

"Is all good?" Gan asked right next to her.

Scarlett jumped only because an hour of sleep was not enough to fully recover.

He put his hand on her shoulder, rubbing the muscles. "Too tired for this."

Lily made happy gurgles, drawing Scarlett's gaze around to the giant man and the tiny baby. "I'll sleep when we have her mama back."

"Spud is fine."

"Spud?"

"Yes." He looked at the little girl all wrapped up in the brown blanket again. "Like potato."

Not a nickname Fayth would support, but if it made Gan happy it was fine.

"What now?" He jiggled the baby, making her smile.

"Now we find a safe place for Lily while my contacts get me information on our missing people and hopefully set up a meeting."

Gan frowned. "I keep Spud safe."

"You've done a great job, but we need to have her out of harm's way the minute I find out if we can buy the freedom of our wolves.

If not, things could get dangerous and we both need to be able to shift."

Turning the baby to his shoulder and patting her back, he said, "I understand. Where is safe place?"

Scarlett's phone buzzed. She held up a finger and answered. "Naomi?"

"Why do you sound surprised? You called me," the cranky old woman said.

"I need a favor."

"I need a new pool boy."

Scratching her head, Scarlett said, "I wish I could help you with that, but I'm a little short on pool boys."

"Then why should I do you a favor?"

"Because Lincoln has my little sister, who I plan to take back from him. In the meantime, I need to leave her baby somewhere he can't get to this child."

"Bastard."

"That's putting it mildly," Scarlett agreed.

"Bring the child. We'll work out terms later."

"Thank you." After removing the history of everything she'd searched on the computer, Scarlett shut it down and stood. An electronic forensic expert could pull up that history, but the chances of that happening were slim with no reason to even be here.

If she freed the wolves and they all survived this, she'd return and perform better electronic cleansing.

Gan picked up the diaper bag on the floor at her feet and hooked the strap over his shoulder.

She couldn't get over how natural he acted with a baby in his arms.

Chica piped up, *Baby is fun.*

Scarlett silently shushed her cougar.

She could do with fewer voices in her head today.

Once everyone was loaded into Vic's ride, Scarlett backed away and drove north.

"Where is this woman?" Gan asked.

"In Roanoke."

"No! You said Lincoln live there," he growled.

The baby cried. He glared at Scarlett then smiled at Lily, cooing in that deep voice that soothed the child better than Scarlett had been able to do.

Being a future shifter, Lily picked up on things like tension probably streaming off Scarlett.

Once Gan had the baby quiet again, Scarlett said, "This home in Roanoke is a secure compound. It is the one place Lincoln will not go to at gunpoint or face the one woman he would not dare cross."

"Why? Who is she?" This time Gan's voice lost the edge, sounding curious.

"His mother."

CHAPTER 26

—◆—

GAN HAD HIS DOUBTS ABOUT taking Spud anywhere. He trusted Scarlett as much as his foster sister who had helped him survive so many times he had seizures at camp before they escaped.

But his sister had made bad decisions at times.

Everyone made mistakes.

Choosing a place for Spud had to be right.

Scarlett pulled into a drive between tall stone walls. Large black iron gates prevented going farther.

So did two men standing on the other side with weapons.

Scarlett lowered her window and gave her name to a man in a small building the size of a bathroom.

"Who's the other shifter?" the man dressed in black pants, white shirt, and a black jacket asked.

"Please tell Naomi he's my friend and the baby's guard." After saying that, Scarlett winked at Gan.

He would be whatever she asked of him if she winked again.

The guard waved at the two men with weapons. They backed to each side as the gates opened. Scarlett continued to the largest house Gan had ever seen. An entire camp could live there. So many people were busy outside.

Two tended flowers and mowed the grass.

Another cleaned windows.

The left side of the house had six large doors like the ones on the garage at the lake house. A man washed a shiny vehicle Gan had never seen before. "What is that?"

Scarlett glanced at the car. "It's called a Lamborghini."

"Too small."

"I've never heard that complaint about one of those."

"My head hit top. I have to bend over to ride. No room for Spud. This is better."

She parked and stared at him in the strangest way. "Where have you been all my life?"

"In camps."

"I know. I'm sorry about that." Her eyes softened then she shook off whatever was on her mind. "Let's get Spud in the house. Oh, hell. Now I'm calling her that. Fayth will strangle me if it sticks."

He laughed. "Good name always stick." Picking up Spud, he positioned the baby in one arm and carried the bag clutched in his other hand.

At the top of the wide stairway, one of two tall doors with the image of a tiger carved in mahogany wood opened. A young woman with dark red hair and a slim figure also dressed in black and white welcomed them in. He smelled wolf. She was a shifter. She led the way through the house then outside again where a large pool filled the first level of land that dropped down two steps and stretched out a long distance to more of the wall.

Gan took it all in, shaking his head. He'd never seen anything like this house that Scarlett had called a mansion when she explained how safe Spud would be. The polished floors appeared to be stone. A tall stairway curved up to another floor.

He liked the lake house better. It would fit in the big room they just walked through that had only paintings and narrow tables with flowers in vases.

And the stairway. Why have so much space just for that?

Outside the house, a far larger patio spread to the pool than what had been at the lake house.

He still liked the patio at the lake house better.

Beneath a white draped tent-like covering sat a very pretty woman in colorful underwear. Maybe that was a bathing suit. His sister had once shown him a picture of a woman dressed that way in a magazine. She sat at a tall table where she leaned an elbow. Her straight black hair slid over her shoulder when she turned toward another woman in matching black and white clothes who put a drink on the table.

"Naomi," Scarlett said softly, which clued Gan in that Naomi must be a shifter.

In fact, he smelled shifters everywhere.

When Naomi lowered her sunglasses, bright blue eyes stared at him, taking a long look of Gan from head to toe.

Did she think he had spoken to her?

"Oh, my, Scarlett. You do pay up quickly. I accept."

"What?" Scarlett looked between Gan and Naomi. "No, he is not your new pool boy."

"Please, dear. Don't play games with me. You knew I was serious."

"Yes, I did, but he is *not* payment."

Gan asked Scarlett, "Pay for what?"

Naomi gasped, clutching her throat. "That accent. He's an Adonis and I love that voice. I will give you so much for … him."

"No, no, and hell no," Scarlett said. "He's working with me to save Fayth."

"That dreadful Lincoln. He is why animals eat their young."

Gan took a step back, clutching Spud closer. "We are not leave Spud here. Need to go."

"No, Gan. You don't understand," Scarlett said with a hand on his arm.

"Tiger shifter eat baby," he argued. "No."

Scarlett cursed up a stream.

He covered Spud's ear not tucked against his chest. "Bad words for Spud."

Naomi made a spewing sound then burst into laughter.

Scarlett shot her a look of warning. "Give me a minute?" When Naomi quieted, Scarlett turned to Gan. "Naomi is always outrageous, but she would never hurt this child. We really need her help right now."

Gan had Spud clutched deep in his arms. He cut his gaze at the crazy tiger shifter. He spoke to Naomi. "Lincoln take baby's mama. How will you keep baby safe?"

"Don't question her like that," Scarlett hissed. "She's doing me a favor. I already told you I trust her."

"I must trust, too."

Naomi observed them quietly, then lifted a slender hand to stall Scarlett's next words. Lincoln's mother stood on bare feet and walked up to Gan, at eye-to-eye height. Tall woman.

He could feel power touch him.

The woman smiled sweetly, but her words contradicted any pleasant impression. "I am the worst nightmare of any male shifter who dares to threaten me or anyone under my protection. Did you notice all the shifters on your way in?"

"Yes." He didn't know they were *all* shifters, but he hadn't been around the people out front.

"They work for me because their families are also under my protection. If someone brought a shifter army and tried to fight their way through those gates, I have better weapons on hand than what protects government capitals. If my son dares to come near me, I would show him once again who is the most powerful. The last lesson I taught him required a month for him to heal only because I can't bear to kill him … unless he really pisses me off."

Gan did his best not to step back from the power swirling around her.

Scarlett asked Gan, "Do you trust me?"

"Yes." He didn't hesitate.

"Please give Spud to her."

Naomi looked appalled. "Not me." She snapped her fingers and two women ran out from the house. Both dressed in black dresses with white aprons. "Yes, Tiger Mum."

Naomi rattled off everything she wanted done in the next hour, which included baby furniture, food, clothes, and a healer on call.

When the orders ceased, one of the women turned to take the baby from Gan. He stood there, not making a move until he looked at Scarlett, who nodded.

He had to do this to save Spud's mother. Kissing her on the soft head, he whispered, "Be good baby. I come back for you."

Everyone seemed to expect Spud to cry, but she looked around more confused than anything. The woman must have her own children, because she started whispering to Spud as she walked off, holding the baby's attention. Just before the woman went inside, Spud made a noise and turned her little head.

His arms felt empty. He didn't want to leave her, but he smiled and she smiled back.

Naomi said, "It's fine. Go inside."

Scarlett waited until the servants ran to do Naomi's bidding to say very quietly, "The baby is a cougar shifter, so she shouldn't get sick."

Naomi had been in full control the entire time until that moment. Her mouth opened slightly, then her lips closed. "Are you telling me—"

"Please don't ask me, Naomi," Scarlett whispered, looking around again. "I'd like to just leave it at that. I can count on one hand the number of people who know this. I need it kept quiet. I'm afraid someone will tell Lincoln then he won't make a deal with me for Fayth. He sent a team after Fayth. The only reason they came for the baby was because the other female wolf shifter escaped with that child. His people were bringing in all female shifters and children. He wants cat shifters, but he can't have this baby no matter what."

"I will protect your secret."

Gan tried to make sense of Scarlett's comment. Her sister was a wolf, which had seemed odd, but maybe Fayth was a sister of her heart, like Siofra was to him, and not blood family. But had Fayth mated a cougar to birth a cougar shifter baby?

"Thank you. I will make good on this, but not with him." Scarlett angled her head toward Gan.

"What is payment? I will do," Gan offered.

"Be still my heart," Naomi muttered.

"No, she's fine." Scarlett grabbed Gan's hand and dragged him away. "Bye, Naomi."

"Goodbye, dear, but do bring him back when you return. I might accept a day of eye candy for partial payment."

"Not happening," Scarlett murmured.

Gan liked having her hand in his. He gave her fingers a squeeze. "What is candy she wants?"

"You. You're the eye candy." A tiny muscle jumped in Scarlett's jaw. She nodded politely at the workers as they exited the house.

Back in the truck, Scarlett cranked the engine and took off like she couldn't wait to get out of there.

"I am eye candy?" Gan asked, only because it clearly annoyed her. He might be wrong, but he sensed she was irritated by the attention Naomi gave him. "Explain. Please."

Scarlett growled and her eyes glowed for a few seconds. "Naomi likes to look at your body. She'd probably enjoy it even more if you were naked. That's eye candy."

"If that is payment, I can do," he said in a voice worthy of a martyr while trying not to laugh.

"No. No one is looking at you naked but me." Scarlett blurted that out as they passed back through the gate.

All three men laughed.

Shifter hearing.

"You like me naked?" he prodded, chuckling when pink painted her cheeks.

Her phone jingled before she answered his question.

She pulled off the road to the side and answered, "What?"

Gan had not appreciated his sensitive hearing as much until now.

A scratchy male voice said, "Zink here. Am I the first to get back to you?"

"Yes," Scarlett snapped, sounding more impatient with each single word.

"In that case, here's what I have. I confirmed that Lincoln has two female wolf shifters in his compound. I got word to him that someone was willing to buy the two female wolves. He sent back his terms. He wants some tiger shifter that killed his men or a baby. I sent back through my channels that I knew nothing about a tiger shifter or a baby. The last reply I received was 'ask the cougar shifter you're inquiring for' and tell her he will only make the trade with her. If that's you, Scarlett, I was not the one who told him your identity, but he also said if you try anything funny, the woman named Fayth would pay the price."

The phone case creaked in Scarlett's grip. She grimaced and her fingers relaxed. "What about the male wolf with them?"

"I did ask, but all I got back was that he would not be part of the trade."

A tight muscle in Gan's chest eased. That sounded as if Adrian was at least alive. He would find a way to rescue Adrian, too.

"What's Lincoln's deadline and meet point?" Her eyes brightened again, something Gan began to realize meant her animal pushed close to the surface.

He fisted his hands, wanting to pound this Lincoln. That tiger had hurt Scarlett once. Never again.

Zink said, "He said if you want to make the trade, to be at the entrance to his property at midnight tonight."

"Do you have any idea where the prisoners are being held on

his property?"

"Does a hobby horse have a wooden dick? Of course, I have that. I make a point of knowing as much as I can about everyone on my radar." He gave her a rundown of the property and where shifter cages were inside the compound.

She sat back holding her forehead. "Thanks, Zink. Give me a day to find a computer and I'll wire your money."

"Not worried about it. You've always been good for your word. Call me if I can deliver anything else."

Gan worked hard to hold his reaction in, hoping Scarlett would not realize he'd heard it all. He should have known better.

She rolled her head to the side, worry for the captives in her tired gaze. "We need a plan."

"Baby must be safe. I go."

"Oh, hell no, Gan." She sat up and slapped her hand on the console. "Do you really think I would hand you over to this maniac?"

"We talk, but baby needs mama. I go and free two women."

"No, no, and no. You are not sacrificing yourself to Lincoln."

He grumbled. "What is plan then?"

"I don't know yet, but we'll have one by tonight."

She'd tried to sound confident, but Gan surprised himself by picking up an emotion from her scent. Doubt. Scarlett did not believe they could save the women.

But this woman would not walk away and leave them to Lincoln any more than she would allow Gan to trade himself.

He could see what she had on her mind.

Scarlett would trade herself for the wolf shifters. She would convince Lincoln to give up two female wolves for one cougar.

Worry hit Gan's stomach heavy as a boulder.

His tiger growled, *Must protect mate.*

Gan replied, *Yes.* He'd agreed on two points. Scarlett had to be protected and confirmed to his cat that she was their mate.

By the time they reached the motel, he would have a plan of his own.

One that he could not share with Scarlett.

CHAPTER 27

———

CLOUDS BLOCKED THE MOON FROM shining through the sky that had gone pitch dark outside the motel. Time normally worked against her, ticking too fast.

At half past six, every second dragged along.

Scarlett paced the narrow walkway between the beds and dresser, explaining her idea to Gan. "I told the Guardian that Adrian had definitely been captured with my friend and I would inform him once I knew exactly where they held Adrian." That must have worked, because the eagle shifter hadn't called her a liar again.

Gan peppered her with questions on Lincoln's operation.

She explained what she'd known of him years before, stopping in front of Gan. "I don't think he's changed much. Probably just darker shades of the monster he'd been back then. He expects everyone to jump when he snaps his fingers, but he had little discipline when I knew him. I'm thinking that his operation might be just as lax, because he's so confident in his strength."

She had spoken to Zink again. The contact provided more specifics.

Gan must not have understood exactly what Zink had shared. "Where is his land? Where are prisoners?"

She began explaining the local geography.

Gan lifted a hand. "I know south, west, north, east."

"Okay, that makes it easier." She described the general direction of Lincoln's property, how it was west of Roanoke and butted up to a national forest.

He still frowned. "What is plan to save them?"

She had danced around that the best she could, because she

didn't want him to get his tiger worked up. Her idea had been to get him thinking about the rescue mission, not worst-case scenario where she'd have to trade herself if she couldn't save the wolves.

Lincoln would make that deal.

He wanted female cat shifters first and foremost, but he'd love to get his hands on her.

To avoid thinking about that, she launched into her plan.

"We have five hours to work out the details. Lincoln's guards run in twelve-hour shifts, starting at one in the morning. That means the ones on patrol should be most lax between eleven and midnight. Zink confirmed that word is Lincoln's security is loose. He still has no discipline. He just kills anyone who crosses him."

"Why hunt female shifters?" Gan sat in the same wooden chair he'd used to rock Spud. His body acted restless, fingers tapping, arms moving around, legs shifting position.

Was he missing the baby?

She could only imagine. Just like she kept thinking about the hell Fayth had to be going through, but Scarlett hoped Jazlyn had a chance to pass along that her baby was safe.

Gan remained quiet.

She kept pacing, feeling as agitated as if she were caged.

He waited for an answer.

"Lincoln has always wanted a dynasty of cat shifters. Tigers are his first choice and I heard he had three female tiger shifters, but my resources say only one cub has survived. That makes me think something might be wrong on his part of baby making."

"We make trade for all three," Gan suggested.

"Your heart is in the right place, Gan, but Lincoln won't do that. He'll trade the minimum to get what he wants. We have to go in and pull them out."

"Too many shifters to fight. Must call Guardian."

She'd paused her pacing and took in what had to be his game face. "I would love to have a team of apex predators going in with us, but there are problems. First, if we're successful, your boss would turn Jaz over to shifter law enforcement, where they'd shove her into an underground titanium box. He has a black and white way of looking at the world and can't make exceptions when it comes to supporting law enforcement for shifters with her criminal record or he undermines his authority."

"Why criminal?"

Scarlett frowned at the odd question, then translated it in her mind that he had asked about how Jaz had become a fugitive.

Nodding, she explained, "Shifters hate going to sanctuaries, which are just a large piece of land where they have to reside next to different species, some of which are prey to their animals. Most prefer to live alone or in a pack. Shifters are allowed to have a pack, clan, or whatever they call their group, if they have an alpha capable of enforcing the laws."

"What laws?" Gan had stopped fidgeting and focused on her every word.

"Shifter laws. Too many to list, but basically it's the alpha's job to put down an out-of-control member or someone who kills a human, or kills without reason. That sort of lethal ability. Jaz was part of a wolf pack ruled by a powerful alpha. She's accused of killing that alpha's first son."

"She is innocent?" he asked.

"She told me it was a justified kill. I did not smell a lie when she said that, but I also did not ask for details. She did a large favor for me and saved my life once, so I'm determined to help her."

"What favor?"

"Fayth needed help getting pregnant and Jaz had medical connections for shifters. She held a rare position as a shifter healer, trained by a human doctor."

After staring off at nothing in particular, Gan cocked his head at her. "Fayth is wolf. Why is Spud cougar?"

Ah, shit. She'd been surprised that he hadn't commented on that when she told Naomi. Gan had proven himself to her again and again. She could share this with him.

"My mother was a cougar shifter and I was her first child. She hated my father, who deserved that hate. So she hooked up with a wolf shifter and ended up pregnant. My father killed the wolf when she gave birth to Fayth. Remember I said how Lincoln might be the reason he only had one cub alive?"

Gan nodded.

"Fayth had physical problems, too, which is normally odd for a shifter, but we aren't perfect from birth. All she wanted was to have a family, because she had an awful childhood."

"You have same childhood." Gan made that statement as fact.

Scarlett shrugged. Fayth had suffered because Scarlett's father was a monster to beat all monsters. "I guess. Anyhow, Fayth and I left home together as teens. A little over a year later, she met a wolf and they mated. But she could not get pregnant no matter what they did. They lived with his wolf friends in a house up in Ohio, hidden deep in the woods."

Watching her every move as if he could see past her words, Gan sat back and crossed his arms. "Yes?"

She kept going. "I had Fayth call me on a regular basis to let me know she was okay. She cried more and more about just wanting a baby so I made a decision. I got in touch with Jaz who helped me get Fayth pregnant."

Gan's eyes widened. "How does woman make woman pregnant?"

She didn't think anything could lighten the mood, but at that she burst out laughing. Leaning against the old dresser, she smiled at him. "It's not what you're thinking. In modern medicine, they can remove an egg from a fertile woman and put it in another woman. That's what Jaz helped us do. She's a healer, not a killer."

He didn't look convinced.

She took a moment to explain how it all worked and assured him she had way more than one egg.

Gan finally sat back, still frowning. "Spud is … your baby?"

"Sort of, but not really. She is Fayth's child. Think of me as the godmother." Then she had to explain what a godmother was and how she would always be Lily's protector. Poor Gan kept getting a crash course on life outside a camp.

He had a thoughtful look. "I am godfather."

She laughed. That man oozed confidence. "I think Fayth might just agree with you."

He didn't laugh. "Family important. Mother and baby should be safe."

That pinged something she'd been meaning to ask him. "I understand that you and Siofra watched over each other in the camps, and that's why you are as close as brother and sister. But do you have any blood relatives?"

"No. Guardian tell me I am stolen as I am born. Jackal shifters kill mama and baby brother still inside her. Kill whole village. I never meet any family."

His voice held so much longing. He may not have met his people but he still hurt over the loss.

Gan cleared his throat. "Tell Guardian what Jazlyn tell you. He will smell truth."

Sometimes that man flipped subjects so fast Scarlett risked whiplash. He was determined to bring in the cavalry, but he didn't understand that life as a shifter was not so cut-and-dried. "SCIS alerted law enforcement that Jaz has the ability to trick shifters. She can pass a lie as truth. No one trusts her. The Guardian would smell the truth on me, but in the end he is not judge and jury. His people work with SCIS to police the shifters. It's a good thing they do, because we have plenty of bad shifters just as the humans have bad people."

Gan sat back in the chair. "You risk your life for someone who might not tell truth?"

Good question.

She shook her head. "It's hard to explain, but if you know her as well as I do, the lie may smell like the truth, but she has what you call little *tells*, things like facial movements that give her away. You have to know her really well to call her on a lie."

Scarlett wanted Gan to understand that she would not protect a criminal and definitely not a murderer. "I told you that Jaz has a medical background. Besides helping Fayth, Jaz has come to the aid of hundreds of shifters. That's one reason she has stayed free so long. She has a reputation as a healer who shares her gift freely with shifters who cause no harm."

While Gan took that in, she added, "Jazlyn would be turned over to SCIS. She won't last a day before her wolf goes mad. She told me she's innocent, but the alpha's daughter claims she saw Jaz kill her brother. Jazlyn won't speak about the incident even to me. She won't put me at risk for knowing the details. I would never betray her confidence, but I also can't swear I'll never be captured and have a drug used on me. She can't come forward until she has evidence to clear her name. By now, I'm worried Adrian has figured out who Jazlyn is and will give her up to his boss unless I can get her free first."

"Maybe not."

That brought her up short. "Why wouldn't he?"

"Adrian said his wolf made crazy in another country. He was put in Wyoming to heal. If not here when Jaz is criminal, he would not know."

Huh. There was some encouraging news. Even so, she had another concern. "I still have another just as important reason I don't want the Guardian here. I'm not letting him take you back to Wyoming. I will figure out a way to keep you free."

"I am good for Wyoming." A muscle in his jaw twitched.

She rolled her eyes and looked back at him. "That's a lie and clearly your tiger is not okay with it."

Arms crossed again, Gan's words carried conviction this time. "I will make tiger okay. We save three lives."

Scarlett admired Gan beyond words, but he had no idea he had no choice in this. "Thank you, but we can save them without your boss. I have …" She had not spoken these words since being a teen and that had kept Fayth safe. Maybe it was time to stop hiding everything from this man and step forward.

"Have what?" Gan's eyebrows dropped low over his eyes.

"I have powers that are more than a shifter."

Surprise lit his face. "What powers?"

Oh, boy. She couldn't back up now, but explaining was going to tick off Gan. "I can stop a shifter from moving in human or animal form."

Gan stilled, no longer restless. He had laser focus. "How?"

One word alerted her he might be figuring out what she'd done. "I was born with some magic in addition to shifting."

He angled his head. "Why did you not use power when cats attack?"

"I can't always isolate it. With everyone battling, I would have caused our friends to stop, too. I've never tried it in a large group. In fact, I've never been able to test my full capability. When I have used it to halt a shifter, it only lasts thirty seconds to a minute. If one of the predators had broken free before one of our people became mobile again, the predator would have ripped him or her to pieces."

He propped his elbows on his knees and his chin on his fists, staying like that for a long time. When he glanced at her again, suspicion led his tone. "You use power on me?"

She chewed on her lip, stalling until guilt shoved the words out. "Yes, but I was not trying to control you. When you first saw Adrian at the lake house and Chica told me your tiger was in trouble, I ran up behind you and did the only thing I could to stop you from shifting. It was clear that you fought against the change. I didn't know Adrian was there and I'm hoping he didn't see something."

"Why did I not stop like stone?"

She had wondered the same thing. "I don't know. That shocked the hell out of me. I've never had a partial failure. I was just glad you were able to stop changing, though."

"But I did not make happen. You did."

She heard the disappointment in his voice. "Gan, you can manage being a shifter. You blocked my magic somehow. That means you are a force of nature and just have to work things out with your tiger."

"He does not listen. Is arrogant."

She clamped her lips to keep from laughing and telling him his tiger was just like him. How strangely interesting. She and Chica were nothing alike. Other shifters had mentioned how their animals had their own personalities.

But it sounded as if Gan and his hardheaded tiger had a lot in common.

That reminded her about what Chica had said. "Gan, do you know what ghosts are?"

He had been staring down and lifted his face. "Yes. Dead people. No body. Spirits."

"Chica sees one with your tiger."

"What?" He looked down at himself as if he could find this ethereal being then back at her. "Do you see?"

"No, but my shifter is special, too. She picks up on things others don't, but it's usually from scent. She's never told me about a ghost before."

Chica rumbled softly inside Scarlett, a sound she'd come to understand as Chica stretching as she woke. Scarlett had heard other shifters say their animals never slept, but Chica enjoyed her beauty rest.

Scarlett asked her about the ghost.

Chica said, *Ask Gemelo.*

Shaking off the odd comment, Scarlett asked her animal, *Is that the tiger's name?*

I call him Gemelo.

Scarlett explained what her cougar said. "Can you ask your tiger about the ghost?"

Opening his hands wide, Gan said, "I will try." He dropped his hands to his hips and stared away from her as if concentrating. He grimaced once then spoke to her. "Tiger say he is alone. Only him. Now tiger is angry."

"Why?"

"He likes cougar only look at him."

The tiger was jealous of a ghost?

Switching gears, Scarlett started to suggest Gan try out the name Chica mentioned, but caught herself and said, "Tell your tiger that Chica has named him."

That shocked Gan. "When?"

"I just found out. She calls him Gemelo. See what he thinks of that."

Gan remained silent with no expression until his face relaxed and he started smiling. Glancing at her, he said, "Tiger very happy Chica named him. He is now Gemelo. He stop being loud. As if he relax."

One minute Scarlett was enjoying seeing Gan exhilarated about his tiger being at peace and the next he had launched himself at her. Gan had her in a bear hug and kissed her with so much happiness she felt it flood all around her.

He swung her away from the dresser and around in a circle, stopping with her back to the wall.

She wanted him more every time he came near her. She had no sense when he touched her. Cupping his face, she returned the kiss with plenty of heat.

He pulled in a deep breath. "You make me happy."

She had no way to tell him how being with him had given her happiness she'd never before experienced in her life.

But she could show him. She shoved a hand inside the new jeans she'd bought him and grinned when she gripped him.

He hadn't worn the boxer shorts she'd also bought.

Gan's body tightened and his hands gripped her on each side of her waist. In a strained voice, he said, "I will do anything."

Now was not the time to laugh at this powerhouse man who she held fully in her grasp. She snagged his lower lip between her teeth and pressed gently as she stroked him.

Eyes shut, he shuddered hard and muttered. "Too much. Too soon."

She ordered, "Put your hands on the wall."

His eyes flew open. He could defy her, but heat and need burned through those eyes. As instructed, he placed a hand on the wall to each side of her head and stared her down, challenging her.

Her skin missed him. Her breasts missed him. Her body begged for him.

Time for him to feel the same way.

Stroking his hard length again, she reached down with her other hand and massaged his balls. Muscles in his arms strained. His jaw flexed with the effort of holding back, because he was definitely trying not to let go "too soon," as he'd said.

She would show him that sometimes it should be all about him.

She kissed his lips and down his chin to his chest. She used her tongue to tease his nipples on that thick wall of muscle as she kept up a steady up and down stroke. His balls tightened.

Lifting her head, she said, "Look at me," just as he had made her do when the roles were reversed.

His eyes opened. The fierce gaze met hers.

Her fingers slid up and down again.

Shaking started in his legs and climbed his chest to his shoulders. He would not let go.

She paused and he made a sound of pain.

Then, very gently, she told him, "Show me you are happy."

With that, she stroked him quicker and clutched his sack, then bit his chest.

He came hard, calling her name and pounding the wall with his fists. She hoped he didn't smash it.

When she'd milked him dry, he dropped to his knees and put his head against her stomach. "You give me … like no other time."

She ran her hands through his hair, gentling him.

Yes, they had a mission tonight, but would not leave for hours. This could be the last moment like this. The last time she had a chance to show Gan what love felt like.

That word did not belong in her vocabulary when it came to men, but she could think of no other way to describe what she felt for him.

In a different life, he would be the man she would gladly mate.

This intimacy had been just for Gan.

She wanted him to remember her as nothing like those other women who'd used him in the past. She wanted him to remember her as the woman who had cared. She just could not tell him the truth, because he already returned that love without saying the words. Admitting her love would only make life more difficult for him when they parted, which would happen too soon.

She accepted that and would let him go when the time came.

What kind of twisted fate would let her live years convincing herself she could never have a mate then wave the one in front of her only to snatch him from her grasp?

When his labored breath slowed to normal, she shook off the melancholy moment. "Guess what I have, Gan?"

"Please say condom," he croaked out.

So much for surprising him. She laughed. "Yes."

For a man who had fallen to his knees, he came up fast, grabbing her and tossing her on the closest bed. Her back hit and she bounced in a fit of laughter.

———

Gan dove on top of Scarlett, but landed on his hands and knees so he didn't smash her.

A condom!

He would finally be inside her.

Of all the women who had come to him as their dirty plaything, Scarlett treated him as if he really were special.

She looked at him as a man.

Not some secret to keep in the dark.

He couldn't help the growl in his voice when he half asked and half begged, "Where is condom?"

Her eyes twinkled with amusement. She wanted to tease him.

Reaching between her legs, he gently teased her tender spot with a finger.

She arched. "My back pants pocket. Now."

In a second, he had her jeans unzipped and shucked off her

legs. He dug into both back pockets until he came up with his trophy, grinning like an idiot.

Both of her eyebrows lifted. "We doing this today?"

He bit the foil and ripped open the package, sheathing his now-hard-again dick. She had given him relief unlike anything he'd felt before. He should still be limp, but the thought of being inside her drove a new burst of energy through him.

With her jeans gone, she'd surprised him by wearing simple pink underwear she must have bought at the big store. He ran his hands up her legs until he could bite the elastic on her tiny panties and drag them down an inch.

Just enough to draw in a deep inhale of her.

He'd smelled her desire before, but never so strong and sweet as being right here when she wanted him.

And she did want him.

Leaving her panties in place, he ran his tongue up the crotch and her thighs squeezed him. He nosed her in the same spot and enjoyed smelling how much he affected her.

"No more condoms if you aren't going to use that one," she warned.

He laughed this time. He could easily tear off the panties, but he would not destroy something of hers.

Hooking his thumbs under each side of the silky material, he slowly slid them down to her knees then off her feet to drop behind him.

She sat up, reaching for him.

He moved to meet her, caught her wrists, and kissed her. Releasing her, he put his hands to good use and pulled her T-shirt off, breaking the kiss only long enough for the shirt to clear her head. Then he lowered her, kissing her the whole time until her head hit the pillow. She'd been running her hands all over his chest, driving him crazy with her touch.

He wrapped his fingers around her wrists again and pulled them slowly from his body. "Hold pillow."

"I can't. I have to touch you," she rasped.

"Hold. Pillow."

She muttered, "Dammit." Then grabbed a fist full of each end of the pillow. "Happy now?"

"No. Happy soon."

His hands were already on her breasts. He added his mouth to suck on her tits and tease them.

Her back arched off the bed. A ripping noise told him her claws had the pillows.

Leaving a hand on her breast, he used his tongue and lips to praise the smooth skin of her stomach and farther down, kissing the moist heat between her legs.

She made a sound of want.

His dick throbbed in response.

Their bodies knew each other as if they'd been this way for many years.

Keeping fingers on one hand busy teasing a breast and his mouth on the other one, he slid fingers through her heat, then dropped down to follow that path with his tongue.

She whimpered. He had never heard anything so wonderful. Her body tensed and shook.

He pushed a finger inside.

She cried out, pleading with him to keep going. To hurry up. To get done.

He smiled at every demand.

She could wait.

He moved his tongue faster, keeping in rhythm with his finger going in and out.

More sounds of cloth ripping. Her muscles tightened around his finger. Her body trembled.

With the next brush of his tongue and slide of his finger, she climaxed. He lapped up her sweet juice, pushing her release to go longer.

He had never lost track of time, but he did now.

When he had her limp, he laid his head on her chest to hear her heartbeat. He loved that sound. She drew deep breaths, lifting his head up and down slowly until her body calmed.

Leaning a little, he kissed her soft nipple and licked it with his tongue, then blew on it.

Both nipples hardened.

Her fingers drove into his hair and gripped, giving him a tug. Her voice deepened with desire. "Come here, wild man."

Swinging over the top of her, he lowered himself to kiss her softly.

She clutched his arms, holding him close as if she would keep him forever. He wished to hold her forever, too. She kissed him with soft lips, tasting, then her mouth demanded more.

Her knees slid forward as her legs bent. She moved until she stroked against his aching dick.

Enough. "Now is time," he said on ragged breath.

"Oh, yes, wild man." She reached down and guided him into her, moaning with pleasure when he took over and pushed deeper. She clawed his back.

Truly clawed it and he smiled.

He wanted only to please her, to make her feel the joy and power he did being inside her.

To see him as a mate.

She met his every move until he was pounding wildly into her.

Her body gripped him. She tensed, then called out, "Yes, oh yes."

With her satisfied, he gave into the sensation racking his body and let go. He could not feel his body without feeling hers. They were one right now.

Time moved slowly at first, then he floated on a happy cloud. Not anywhere. Just with her.

Too soon his mind woke him.

He rolled over, bringing her with him.

Never had he held a woman like this.

Never had he felt this ache in his chest whenever she was not close.

His heart hurt over what he had to do, but his needs were second to what he had to do for her. To keep her alive, he would find a way to hand himself over to Lincoln. He did not trust that tiger to allow Scarlett to walk free with the other women.

Gan swallowed the moment of pain.

His life had never been his own and never would be. He could be a prisoner anywhere.

He would trade himself to Lincoln to free the women and Adrian.

Once all of them and Scarlett were safe, Gan would turn his tiger, Gemelo, loose on the stupid tiger shifter who dared to harm Scarlett.

Lincoln had to die before the Guardian called Gan to headquarters.

CHAPTER 28

M AD RED CLAWED AT ADRIAN'S insides in a rabid push to break out.

No! Adrian powered that word to his animal through what was left of their telepathic link. They once had a much stronger one that allowed them to work as a perfect killing machine when the military needed it.

But now?

They used that line of communication to disparage each other.

You get us caught again. You hate us, his wolf snarled.

Did he hate both of them?

Adrian didn't think so when he had so much hate committed to himself. How could he blame his wolf when getting trapped in a titanium cage too small to allow shifting at all had broken their bond?

Adrian hadn't allowed the enemy to capture them on purpose, but the result ended up the same.

He'd been in his own mental hell while trapped. During that time all he heard were pained howls and crazy sounds from his wolf. Adrian's wolf had been called Red by his brothers in arms, who piled affection on his wolf that took the lead into any dangerous situation.

Adrian named him Mad Red in Wyoming when his wolf started talking to him again. Gone was his best friend, replaced by a demonic animal who despised him.

He accepted that as his due.

His job had been to watch his wolf's back just as his animal had watched Adrian's every day of their joined existence.

But some days, the pain of living so close to the result of his mistakes crushed his soul.

"Cut it out, wolf," a voice hissed nearby.

Adrian blinked to focus his gaze again. He had a habit of losing touch with the world. Bad habit for someone carrying a dangerous beast inside him.

Turning toward the sound, he realized where he was again. In a cage again, but he could stand if he wanted to and open his arms wide without touching the bars on each side.

Had this been built for a lion shifter?

No. Probably for a tiger shifter, based on the comments he'd heard while being brought here. Their alpha hunted strong female shifters, especially female tigers. That bastard's cats had overwhelmed him and the female wolf shifter when they'd fought at the lake house.

Now he recognized the voice speaking to him as the female who'd fought beside him.

He didn't even know her name.

She looked like hell with blood and mud covering her face. It had been battered looking when he first saw her. The bruises had begun healing.

That made sense.

She'd said the capsule in her back had stopped her from shifting. Her hair needed a bucket of water dumped on it to wash out the blood that had dried there.

Streaks ran down her face.

Speaking of water, he felt a drizzle falling on his skin and looked up at the rain. He should have noticed that sooner, too.

He would never be able to return to full duty again. Not with his corrupted senses. He'd put his men in danger.

"What is wrong with you?" she asked in sharp whisper.

Former instincts sometimes kicked in, like now. He sat up, alert and scanning the area. Two more cages were farther away. One held a woman, wolf shifter by the smell, curled on her side, looking asleep.

Not sleeping. She sobbed quietly.

Could that be the woman everyone had been trying to save? Fayth?

The last cage sat empty.

No guards nearby.

No obvious electronic equipment, but now that the fog in his brain cleared, he recalled taking in all he could as they dragged him to the tiger shifter.

"Are you mute? I recall you snapping orders before." She hadn't said that as a compliment.

Sitting back against the cage, he moved closer to the side nearest her, just as she had done in her cage. That limited how loud they had to talk.

"Not mute."

"Then what's wrong with you?" She shifted her position as if she'd been sitting that way a while and gotten stiff. Did she have injuries?

Why did he care?

The part of his soul that struggled to keep him sane said, *Because protecting others had been most important to you and still is.*

He could not accept he was still that man, but caring cost him nothing at the moment. She kept asking what was wrong with him.

Should he give her some answer that would shut her up?

One look at that determined face said he'd be wasting his voice. She'd call bullshit.

"We're fucked up." He always included Mad Red so the wolf wouldn't feel left out.

In return, Mad Red slashed his insides. Adrian grunted. Fucker.

"I knew that," she said the same way someone would say "duh." "I asked what was wrong with you specifically. Your wolf was fighting strategically, which I thought you might have had something to do with until you shifted and fought them in your human form."

"I did?"

"You don't know? Shit, I can't believe I stayed with a berserker. Scarlett's going to get an earful for your crazy ass. Where'd she find you two?"

What the hell? She thought she could criticize him after he knocked shifters off to save her ass?

He remembered that, just not shifting to human to fight. Mad Red might have done that because Adrian did something dangerous like criticizing him during the fight.

Still, her words pissed him off when he thought he'd fought well.

Since she opened the door to honesty, he pointed out, "Why don't you use the rain and wash that crap off your face and hair. I've never known a shifter to stay nasty when she could clean up."

Her eyes had been sharp and aggressive, but they widened.

Had he hurt her feelings?

Shit fire. He should not talk to anyone. Ever. He offended everyone around him, even strangers.

Truth, his wolf muttered.

Shut up, asshole, Adrian shot back. He had enough to do just trying to make conversation with this female.

Mad Red. Not asshole.

Adrian sighed and gave up.

He pushed his attention back to the female and sucked up his bruised pride. Not much left of that anyhow. "Hey, uh, whatever your name is. Sorry. That was not nice. I said I was fucked up. I shouldn't talk."

She pfft at him. "As if I care what you think?"

Good. He was off the hook.

Lifting her chin, she said, "Just to be clear, I wear this mud and blood on purpose. I do whatever I have to when fighting to stay alive. This protects me from predators."

Those words resonated with him.

Hadn't he said to all of his men, human or shifters, to do whatever it took to stay alive?

"Who hunts you?" he asked.

"The fewer I share that with, the longer I stay alive."

Fair enough. He understood the only way to keep a secret was to tell no one.

She returned to her earlier questioning. "Why can't you control your wolf?"

"How …?" He caught himself before he agreed with her. He'd only admitted to being screwed up. He had not said he couldn't control his wolf. "Why would you say that?"

"I can smell that attempt at lying by evasion all the way over here."

That was not easy to do when she had to scent past the rank smell of dried blood and needing a bath.

His soul warned him to keep that thought to himself.

He sat there, unwilling to toss out words that would backfire on him.

Making a big ordeal of sighing, clearly for his benefit, she said, "When we fought Lincoln's shifters, we had it down to two that were losing after the others chased Gan and Scarlett's truck. Do you even remember when I shifted and told you we needed to run before I shifted back … because you turned human and jumped back into the fray?"

No, he didn't. He stared away from her, unwilling to admit so much loss of memory while he tried to rebuild what he could of his mind.

He ran through the fight mentally. He told Gan with telepathy to get Scarlett and leave when it was clear the cats would follow her and the baby. Those two fought their way to a sport utility … he wasn't sure what happened then, if they made it out.

This woman would know.

He was loath to ask her anything.

Forcing his brain to work harder, he had flashes of the battle and … ah. There it was. The image of a naked female shouting at him to run.

If he had any luck left in his miserable life, he'd never lose *that* memory.

He'd been busy fighting a panther shifter.

In his mind, he'd shouted at her to run while he held his panther in place. The other cat had started regaining consciousness after he'd been slammed to the ground.

She hadn't run after yelling at him to cut loose and go.

Instead, she'd shifted back to her wolf, which had been a really stupid move, because he now recalled how clearly exhausted she'd been. He'd had to knock his panther aside and tackle a hyena going for her.

Swinging his head to face this woman again, he said, "You should have run. I couldn't say the words while I was a wolf, but I was fighting the panther to give you time to escape. When I changed to human … think I lost touch with reality."

Her lips parted. Surprise swept through her gaze. She had no comeback.

He asked, "Why did you change back to wolf again? It was

slow. I'm not criticizing, but you had to know you couldn't make a fast shift that soon and all banged up." How could she have wasted that opportunity?

Grabbing a bar and pushing her face between two of them, she replied, "I shifted to stay and fight, because I know how Lincoln operates. He would send a second wave. They showed up as soon as my wolf took form."

Shit fire.

He could see it now. Adrian clutched his head with both hands, struggling to piece it all together.

One thing came through crystal clear.

She'd stayed to save him.

"Shut up, you two," shouted from seventy feet away, where a pair of guards paused beneath a dim light hanging off a pole.

The still nameless female shifter swung around until she leaned back against the bars.

Adrian settled against his, too.

She had stayed to fight by his side.

What had he done?

Insulted her hygiene.

He should be thankful they were in separate cages where she couldn't claw him. He'd deserve that.

He had no business being around a female, but he still had to find one in particular. The sister of his friend who had sent a letter to his last military post overseas. That was the letter the Guardian delivered to Wyoming.

The only thing keeping him standing and not turning his throat to the Guardian to end this hell was a debt to a fellow brother in arms.

Once he found the man's sister and paid that debt, Adrian was done.

The sooner the better, Mad Red told him.

That was new.

He and his wolf normally never agreed on anything.

CHAPTER 29

WHILE SCARLETT SHOWERED, GAN PICKED up her phone and stepped outside. She said they had an hour until time to leave so they could reach Lincoln's place before midnight.

Gan had been watching her use the phone and found the last call she received on the way back to the motel.

He hit call back number. When a man answered, Gan said, "You are Zink. I am Gan, Scarlett's mate. Lincoln tried to kill her. I need your help."

No one on the other end spoke.

Gan pulled the phone away and looked at the bright display. Had he done this wrong?

"Let me talk to Scarlett," Zink finally said.

"No. She is sleeping to heal. Was hurt bad. Lincoln's men come for her. We barely escape. I must meet Lincoln."

Zink cursed. "This is not the way it works, dude."

"You said you trust Scarlett to pay."

"She told you that?"

Gan lied, but didn't think Zink would know, since most of what he'd said to this point had been a lie. She was his mate even if he never told her. "Yes. She explain all you said. I need your help to protect her."

"Man, you're putting me in a bad spot. I am always straight with Scarlett. Can you send me a picture of her healing?"

Gan gripped the phone, frustrated, then forced himself to stay calm or this had no chance of working. "No. This is burner." Isn't that what she called the phone?

"Shit. She's been a great client. First, what do you need?"

"Take me close to Lincoln, then I go alone."

"What if I just give you the address?"

Gan shook his head at so many questions. "I have address. Do not want to leave truck or anyone know I go there. I will pay twice."

"You're *doubling* what she's paying me?"

"Yes." If this worked out and Scarlett lived, she would be able to pay. That was not too much to ask for keeping her safe.

"Okay, look. I'll get you within a mile. That's as close as I want to be to Lincoln's property."

Relieved that money swayed this man, Gan told Zink he'd meet him at the super-store in five minutes, because he did not want anyone to know where Scarlett rested. To delay at all would mean he couldn't slip away from the motel in time. He hated to take Scarlett's phone, but he had to slow her down more than slicing a tire on Vic's vehicle would do.

He ran maybe two miles to the big store in a light drizzle that ended by the time he got there. He shook water off his head and wiped his face.

Zink had said he'd be in a red Subaru, whatever that was, parked close to the road. When Gan reached the parking lot, he spotted a red car immediately since the other vehicles were all closer to the store entrance.

He slowed to a walk until he stood in front of the car with headlights turned off.

A tall, slender man with a thin mustache, glasses, and balding head got out. "Gan?"

"Zink?"

They nodded at each other.

Gan walked to the passenger side and folded himself into the seat. He groaned at being in the tight space.

Zink frowned at his wet clothes, but asked, "Why didn't you take her truck and just park it somewhere for when you're ready to go back?"

There would be no coming back for Gan.

He brushed off the question with a simple answer. "Has tire problem. Fix in morning."

"Okay, I guess," Zink muttered as he took off, driving at a steady speed.

The trip seemed to take a long time, but that was likely due to Gan being balled up inside a small car. According to the phone he still carried, which showed the time, the drive had taken only twenty minutes.

Almost the same time as the journey to Naomi's house.

Zink let him out near the first stretch of wooded area they reached that had no houses close by. "I sure hope Scarlett is good with this. I hate to lose a client like her."

Gan dropped his head to look inside before closing the door. "This is only way you keep client. Thank you for help."

Zink smiled weakly and left.

Humans could not smell lies.

He struck out, using the directions Zink had given him on the drive over. Zink knew a lot about Lincoln's compound and how everything worked there. A few things Gan felt sure Zink had not shared with Scarlett, which meant Zink had held back information to sell later. He probably gave Gan more, in case Scarlett wasn't happy he helped Gan without her approval.

When Gan reached a property with large gates protected by two men with weapons, all of which fit Zink's description, he stayed downwind to scout around the outside. The wall surrounding this land was tall, but different than the black iron one around Naomi's house. This barrier had thick support structures of cement four feet wide, with ten-foot-high chain-link fence running between the solid wall sections.

The air smelled heavily of cat shifters.

Male, his tiger said.

Gan asked, *You can tell male and female?*

Yes.

Gan took in another breath. He picked up a faint scent of wolf and turned to his left.

His tiger said, *Wrong way.*

That stopped Gan in his tracks. *How do you know?*

When his tiger didn't reply, Gan tried his new name. *Gemelo?*

Thinking, tiger answered. *Go to right. I know this, but not why.*

He had no reason to think he knew better than his tiger on this, so he changed direction to the right. Once he was far enough from the gates, he moved over to a beaten-down path that ran along the outside of the wall. When the wolf scent grew stronger, he told his tiger, *I smell more wolf now. You are right.*

His animal said, *Of course.*

Gan smiled at the overconfident beast.

But he'd like to figure out what was going on right now. His tiger never talked to him.

Not like this.

With the rain having passed and moon peeking between clouds, he made out a large house deep inside the property and behind two walls shoulder high and maybe twenty or thirty feet long. Moonlight glinted off large metal tiger statues standing on top of each wall section flaring out from the driveway to the house. He couldn't make out more about the house as bushes and trees on the inside of the fence blocked his view.

While keeping an eye out for any threat and his nose tuned to new scents, he still wanted to find out what had changed between him and his tiger. *I am glad to talk, Gemelo. But why now and not before?*

Before, I claim mate. Now you claim her.

Was Gemelo talking about when Gan called Scarlett his mate when he spoke to Zink? When he'd said those words, he had felt it to be true in his heart. Is that what it had taken to find peace with his animal?

His tiger added, *Mate claim us.*

Gan stumbled a couple steps, paused to listen for anyone moving toward him, then started out again.

He pushed his tiger for more. *When did mate claim me?*

Us, tiger corrected with loud snarl.

Gan covered one ear with his hand, which did nothing to lower the tiger's volume.

When did she claim us? he amended.

When she stop change. She use love to help us.

Gan had been torn when Scarlett admitted taking charge to stop his shift in front of Adrian. He'd been disappointed to find out he had not been in control, but he hadn't been angry with her.

Just as the tiger said, she'd done it because she cared.

No, his animal had used the word *love.*

His heart thumped at a crazy pace. Had he found love? He thought about all that she meant to him and realized that must be love. She had been ready to put her life on the line for him and he was here doing the same for her.

Happiness he'd never known rushed through him along with despair that hit him in the gut.

He would never get to experience love with Scarlett for the rest of his life. That life would end soon, but he hoped the love stayed with him when he was gone.

If he survived fighting Lincoln, the mating curse he'd heard about would kill him.

He would never look at another woman the way he saw Scarlett.

A stronger whiff of wolf yanked Gan's head up.

Will you change when I ask? he put to the tiger to find out what the two of them could do.

Maybe.

Clearly, choosing a mate had not solved all their problems, but Gan would take what his animal gave and hope for the best.

When he saw a sectioned-off area inside the fence, he moved slowly toward the strongest wolf smell.

Large cages came into view that landscape hid from anyone entering by the gates.

His eyes adjusted to the poor lighting near the opening between the cage area and the rest of the compound leading up to the house.

He located a cage holding Adrian, who sat with his chin dropped. The Gallize wolf was still alive.

If those enclosures had held humans, they would be too far away to hear Gan speak in a normal tone, which he couldn't risk. Getting as close as he could, he whispered, "Wolf man."

Adrian's head came up slowly then he turned glowing silver eyes to Gan.

Without making any sudden move, Adrian asked in a low voice. "Are you alone?"

"Yes."

"Then go call the Guardian."

"No. Will not make Scarlett happy."

Adrian dropped his head back, murmuring something toward the sky that sounded angry. He turned to Gan again. "You're gonna get captured, Psycho Cat."

"Yes. I am here to trade me. You three leave."

Adrian's eyes dimmed back to his normal dark gaze. He seemed at a loss for words. "I thought you wanted to escape. Live up north."

"Yes, but will not be. Guardian can call me any time. I am captured no matter where I go."

"Shit fire, Gan. Don't do this."

"Why not? You and women can be free. Is good."

Adrian's head swung away from him. He stretched his neck, looking toward the gate then turned back. "Get out of here. Guards are coming."

"I look for them. I only want to know you are here."

Gan walked off with Adrian trying to send him away.

When he reached one of the cement fence supports he'd passed, Gan backed up and ran then leaped to get a hand on the top. He pulled himself up and over, landing softly inside the wall.

There was just one guard and he had entered the gate to the cage area by the time Gan dropped inside the compound.

Gan crossed his arms and waited. When the guard closed the small gate, he must have scented Gan. His head snapped around quickly. He lifted his rifle, aiming for Gan's chest. "Put your hands on your head and get on the ground."

Shaking his head, he told the cat shifter, "Lincoln will not be happy if you kill tiger he wants. Tell him I have deal."

The rifle lowered an inch. Speaking into a headset similar to the one Vic had given Gan when they hiked into the farm, the guard told someone a cat shifter claiming to be a tiger had snuck in.

After a moment, the guard said, "Walk ahead of me."

Gan told him, "No. I have no weapon. You walk first or I leave."

They were back to a standoff while the guard spoke to his invisible person again. Whatever he heard must have startled him. He nodded then turned to Gan. "Follow me."

Gan shrugged. Walking behind the guard, Gan noted how thick shrubs walled off the cage area and were cut to form walls leading to the house.

That meant Adrian and the women would be brought to Lincoln through those passageways if Gan convinced the tiger to make this swap.

The wall of hedges ended at the solid cement walls supporting the tiger sculptures.

As the guard passed through that entrance to Lincoln's home,

Gan stopped in the center of the wide paved driveway that continued inside, circling a large fountain with a metal sculpture of a woman with a fish tail. Enough room for twenty vehicles to park around the entrance to the house.

Scarlett might call this one a mansion, too.

He swallowed, hoping she did not hate him for changing her plans.

From this point, the house resembled Naomi's but not as large or expensive looking.

Cat shifters swarmed the interior area of the yard and fountain leading up to the house.

He'd remained in the middle of the drive to wait.

Scarlett had been right. Lincoln's people were not disciplined. That cat shifter guard had no idea Gan had not followed. Gan glanced behind him to find six shifters, but they were all over a hundred feet away at the gate where a vehicle would enter. Lincoln must have plenty of guards close to the house for those six to stay at their original duty.

He took in the mix of cat shifters. Some ran into the circular drive half-dressed as if pulled from bed. Others were in the process of changing into their cats.

An imposing man with jet-black hair falling loose around his face rushed out the front door of the two-story home. He had Naomi's beauty in a male face and a tall body, too, but muscles had grown so large on his arms and chest he looked unnatural even for a shifter.

His scowl diminished his too-pretty face. He barged through his men. They parted and reformed behind him in scraggly order.

Gan held up a hand to stop the man when they were fifty feet apart. "You are Lincoln?"

"Yes. Who are you?"

"Gan. I am tiger you want."

He turned to his men. "Who was at the lake house raid that can identify this shifter?"

A hand shot up. The man did not step into view, but said, "It's him. I followed and leaped on the truck as they were leaving after he shifted back."

That must be the panther Scarlett shook off the roof of their vehicle.

Satisfied with that answer, Lincoln turned to face Gan again. "Where is Scarlett?"

"Not here."

"That's obvious," Lincoln snapped. "She set the terms through her contact. She has to be here to make the trade."

Gan had been pulling in scents as he stood there. He couldn't be sure, but he believed Lincoln smelled desperate. That tiger shifter would never touch her again.

Opening his arms in a gesture of this is all to expect, Gan said, "You want tiger shifter or not? I am Siberian tiger. Very powerful. I am yours for three wolves."

"Three? I said the two female wolf shifters."

Crossing his arms, Gan said, "Never mind. I will go." He took a step back and all the cats moved forward.

Lincoln called out, "You do realize my men could just take you or kill you."

Gan had considered that and hoped Scarlett was right about Lincoln building a dynasty. "True, but you lose tiger to breed and many guards. Why lose so many when trade keeps cat shifters alive?" He waited for an answer. When a tense moment had passed, Gan added, "I am here to make deal. You lose much if you do not trade now."

Gan gave that truth and shrugged, trying to convince Lincoln he was bored, when in truth he worried this would not work. He hoped Lincoln was desperate enough to make this deal before Scarlett showed up and ruined his plans.

Lincoln turned to a shifter on his right and ordered, "Get the two female wolves."

"But, boss. What about—"

"Don't ever question me. Get. Them."

Gan said, "All three."

Having dispatched his mouthy guard, Lincoln smiled at Gan. "You would leave those women and disappoint Scarlett? She'll come back on her own and make a new deal."

Gan had no answer for that, which told Lincoln all he needed to know.

When the guards brought out two ragged-looking women, Gan recognized the tall one as Jazlyn, who continued to look worse every time he saw her. The other woman's head drooped forward with hair covering her face. She made awful sobbing sounds.

That had to be Fayth.

"I am not releasing them until you are closer, Gan," Lincoln told him from where he stood inside the entrance with arms crossed.

Gan walked forward to stand between the large rectangular pedestals rising above his shoulders and displaying a ten-foot-long bronze tiger facing toward anyone who passed through.

Stopping next to the sculpture on the right, Gan said, "Is close enough. Send them."

Lincoln bled excitement through his grin and his scent. The guard who had resisted bringing the women, pushed the two wolf shifters toward Gan, but remained behind as the women reached him.

Holding Fayth up by her arm, Jazlyn slowed next to Gan. "What are you doing acting like some hero?"

"Not hero. I am tiger."

She rolled her eyes. "Scarlett will kill you for this."

All joking gone, Gan told her, "Take Fayth. Do not let Scarlett come. I do this to keep her safe. Lincoln will hurt her. That cannot happen."

Jazlyn gave him a look of wonder. "You really are protecting her."

Why did she have such a difficult time understanding? "Yes. Go. Sooner you leave, less chance Scarlett comes."

She took a breath. "I will. Thanks."

"Welcome."

Jazlyn kept hobbling along with Fayth, who had not even lifted her head. No mama should be treated that way. He would make everyone here pay once he freed Adrian.

Lincoln said, "Well?"

Gan held up a hand. "I will come when they are gone." He made everyone stand that way until the women passed through the gates at the street. A minute later, he heard the howl of two wolves.

They'd shifted, which he hoped meant they were on their way. That was the best he could do.

Gan said, "I will not fight guards. I want to see male wolf shifter."

"You are done giving orders," Lincoln shouted. Then he called out, "*Azalina!*"

"Move," a feminine voice boomed from somewhere behind the cat shifters.

Those in human form and cats scattered as if afraid to be touched.

Lincoln smiled at someone Gan might have called pretty, before meeting Scarlett.

Her red hair glowed with half of it bound up on her head and the rest falling to her waist. She had porcelain skin, so smooth and white it didn't appear to be real. Long lashes and deep-red lips. The shimmering silvery gown seemed odd for a young woman in today's world, but she walked as if she wore a crown.

Gan had been caught up in her odd attractiveness until she turned black eyes, empty as a pit of death, to him.

He stepped back.

She noticed his reaction and smiled, then spoke to Lincoln. "Yes, Tiger King?"

Indicating Gan with a wave of his hand, Lincoln said, "This is my tiger shifter. I want you to use *the* spell and compel him."

Her smile turned sour. "I am still working on the spell. I told you I would have it by two this morning."

Gan took that to mean midnight had passed. No Scarlett. Good sign.

"I want it now," Lincoln ordered.

"It will only work for a short time if you use it too early. Once it has been placed on someone, the spell will always work the same way. Do you want minimal obedience from your new pet or a permanent leash?"

Gan's stomach turned at what he heard. He had expected to be used in some way, but not to give up control of his life to a witch. He told his tiger, *I am sorry, Gemelo. I try to find place to live free. I thought this would not be worse than camps, but I am wrong. This was not plan.*

His tiger asked, *Was plan to protect mate?*

Yes.

This is plan. We will escape.

Gan wished he could believe in his tiger's words, but he argued, *You have not met witch before now. I saw witch in other country. They have power. This one speaks of spell to control us. We will be puppet used to do bad things.*

It took a few seconds, but his tiger finally understood and started beating his insides. *Free me. I kill them all now.*

Gan clenched his muscles against the upset tiger.

He had run out of ideas. The women were free. Now that Jazlyn was gone, he would call in the Guardian if he knew how, but he didn't know if Gallize could call the eagle shifter to them the same way their boss called them.

Probably not. Eagle shifter was powerful.

He couldn't help Adrian if Lincoln took control of Gan's free will. Adrian had been right when he told Gan he needed field training.

That wolf shifter would have done this differently.

While Lincoln and his witch continued to argue, Gan swept a quick head count of the cat shifters gathered behind their leader. Maybe twenty.

He could not take down twenty, especially if Lincoln shifted into a tiger and joined the battle.

But he would not deny his animal.

Gan told his tiger, *You want to fight? We fight. Now is time to turn into monster we can be for any chance to escape.*

The change flowed over him fast, sucking the air from his lungs as his body twisted into a new shape. His tiger burst out, full of energy and ready. Just to give him more reason to do his best, Gan said, *We fight to keep Lincoln from hurting our mate, Gemelo.*

The witch started chanting.

Lincoln appeared shocked that anyone would challenge him.

His guards still in human form, fell to the ground, fighting out of clothes to change.

But the four already shifted charged Gan's tiger.

CHAPTER 30

—◆—

GAN'S TIGER BATTLED PANTHERS, MOUNTAIN lions, jaguars … until his back legs buckled from the weight of being piled on and blood seeped from his body. Teeth and claws tore into his coat. He gave as much as he got.

Lincoln's voice roared, *"Get off my tiger!"*

His power washed across Gan's animal as it reached all of Lincoln's men.

In the next instant, jaws unlocked from his body and legs. The weight on his tiger's back lightened, then all of them were gone.

The only reason his tiger had not suffered a ripped throat or worse had to be due to Lincoln's men knowing he would kill them for destroying his tiger shifter.

Gan's tiger moaned, *No. No stopping.*

He understood and supported his crazy animal, but said, *Lincoln stop them. He wants us alive. The witch still close. Stay down and heal, if we can.*

Must kill all. Stop bad tiger.

Gan kept talking to his animal, trying to keep the animal still while their body mended itself. He explained, *If you rise now, bleeding and broken, Lincoln will have witch compel us. If you stay quiet, he will wait to see if we are dying.*

The thick smell of blood filled each breath. His tiger had killed six shifters.

Lincoln would likely punish them in some way for that loss.

"What have ya done, Lincoln?" a smooth male voice asked in an odd accent.

Gan's tiger lifted his head to see who had spoken.

A man with searing green eyes sat on the back of one tiger

sculpture with his legs dangling and dressed in a black suit, but not like the Guardian's. This one had a high collar and shined as if it picked up light when he moved. He leaned forward with his hands on his knees, staring calmly at the bloody scene.

"What are you doing here, Robert?" Lincoln sounded angry.

Gan's tiger sniffed the air and said, *Bad tiger scared.*

Lincoln feared this stranger? That was interesting.

"Where is she?" Robert asked in a quiet voice that carried a deadly threat.

"I don't have her. If I did, I would have called."

Robert looked over at Gan's tiger. "Who do ya have here?"

"No one. A tiger I just acquired."

Robert studied Gan's tiger, the dead shifters, then he pushed his gaze to Lincoln again. "Ya be hiding somethin' from me, Lincoln. Did ya learn nothin' in our last meetin'? I suggest you begin tellin' the truth."

Gan smelled what his tiger had pointed out a moment ago. Lincoln feared Robert and that fear jumped another level to terror.

Lincoln shook his head. "No. We have a deal. I will make good on it. I just need … time."

Robert made a tch-tch sound. "Have yar tiger shift back to human."

"Why?"

When Robert spoke this time, his voice turned deep and rang with power. "Do as I tell ya or we end our deal here and now. I promise ya will not be likin' that much if ya force me to show ya who be in charge."

Lincoln ordered Gan, "Shift back!"

When power rolled over him and continued past, Gan tried to decide if shifting was a good idea or not. He asked his tiger, *What do you think? Do we shift or not?*

His tiger replied, *You ask me?*

Yes. We must figure out together.

Lincoln shouted the order again.

Another shot of power buffeted his animal's body. His tiger asked, *What is best?*

As if Gan knew? Then he realized he did know. *Let me have human body. I can talk. Maybe find out if man on wall is better place to go. Someone we can escape.*

Just like that, Gan shifted to his human body. Unwilling to lay on the ground in his human form, he stood, though wobbly. His tiger had healed much of the damage as they'd stayed down, but he still had wounds and cracked bones to heal. But this speed of healing was an improvement over their days in Wyoming. Maybe getting along had also improved their healing.

"Who are ya?" Robert asked him.

Before Lincoln could interfere, Gan said, "I am Gan."

"Do ya know Isleen?"

"No." Gan shrugged. He had no idea who the man talked about.

Lincoln jumped in, sounding anxious to please Robert. "He does know her, but as Scarlett. I sent word to meet with her tonight so I could capture her, but he showed up instead. He wouldn't be here if he didn't know her."

Gan stared at Lincoln, confused over the words he spoke. Scarlett was called Isleen? Two names?

Why had she not told him?

Why did this Robert search for her?

Not slowing down, Lincoln told Robert, "I'll have my men hold the tiger shifter while you torture him to find Scar … er, Isleen. That way, my part of the bargain is fulfilled."

Gan told Lincoln, "You will die for your words and if you touch Scarlett."

Gemelo made a growl of agreement.

Robert had been studying Gan while he spoke and now gave him an order. "Turn around, tiger."

With no reason to deny the man, he turned a complete circle.

Robert snapped his fingers. "He carries a claw mark on his shoulder. 'Tis her doin'. I want him."

Everyone looked at Gan.

He couldn't see the back of his shoulder.

Scarlett had marked him?

That made Gan ridiculously happy. He had to be important to her to mark him.

Robert dropped to the ground as if he floated. He brushed off the arms of his jacket, but nothing had soiled the fine material. "This tiger shifter be goin' with me now. I shall find her. 'Tis fortunate for ya, Lincoln, that I be callin' our agreement settled."

"No. Not the tiger, you Scottish dick," Lincoln argued. "You said one woman. Isleen. That was all."

"For this tiger to be standin' here, ya lost Isleen. I won't be makin' that mistake."

Lincoln yelled, "*Azalina!*"

The witch came forward much quicker this time, cast an ogling eye over Gan's naked form and declared, "I'm still not ready, but I can start on him."

"Not yet with the tiger. This Power Baron thinks to steal what is mine."

Giving a casual sigh, Robert said, "Do ya really think a forest witch is any match for me?"

"You arrogant excuse for a mage," she shoved back at him.

Before another word was said, she lifted her arms and called up a black cloud that surrounded all of them, spinning as it gained size.

Gan's skin crawled.

His tiger banged back and forth, panicked and trying to get out. *We run*, Gemelo shouted at him.

If Gan thought his tiger could fight their way out and escape, he would do just that. He told Gemelo, *Wait. Too many shifters to escape. Watch this man. See what happens.*

Robert stood calmly with his arms crossed, a picture of confidence in the face of black smoky shapes that began forming from the cloud. One form stepped forward, growing into a ten-foot-tall hideous dragon-like beast, but unlike anything Gan had ever seen. This thing had jaws wide enough to cut the man in half.

Additional odd creations surrounded Lincoln.

Gan backed up slowly while the witch distracted everyone.

As he did, he caught the fleeting movement of a wolf leaping over the thick walls of dense bush out to the right of him. The streak of golden wolf vanished just as quickly, headed in the direction of the cages.

Had Jazlyn come back to free Adrian?

He hoped they both got away while this was going on.

Screaming a gut-wrenching noise, the repulsive dark smoke creature swung its head down to chomp Robert in half.

Before that could happen, the Power Baron, whatever that was, opened his hands, palms out flat, and blasted out words Gan had never heard in a voice that did not sound human.

The witch's creation stopped as if caught in a huge fist.

Black scales formed over the smoky body.

In fact, scales covered all of her creatures.

With more strange words, Robert turned the creatures around toward Lincoln whose face lost all color. He started shifting into his tiger.

The magic beasts attacked him partially shifted. A misshaped leg went flying with blood spilling from it. The witch yelled demands. Her words were lost in the sound of Lincoln's animal screaming horrible noises until everything fell silent at the same moment.

The Power Baron's counterattack was over in less than a minute.

The shifters lifted their mouths and howled together.

Gan had heard jackal shifter guards from the same pack cry out that way when they lost one of theirs.

His tiger had calmed down, watching.

Azalina turned crazed black eyes to Robert. Her hair erupted into fire and her mouth filled with needle-sharp teeth. She spewed a string of words and lifted bony fingers with curved claws sprouting from the tips.

Was she a witch, shifter, or both?

Robert already had his hands up, shouting her down.

Flames erupted at spots on his jacket.

He ignored them. His lips moving nonstop with a constant blast of strange words he directed at her. His voice gained power until he stabbed a finger at her and slashed downward.

Her body split in half from neck to hips, then her organs spilled out. Black eyes rolled up, leaving white sockets. She fell back, crashing to the ground.

Grass shriveled and died anywhere it touched her skin.

The flames on Robert's jacket disappeared, though scorched spots were left behind.

Still wild-eyed furious, Robert ordered the shocked shifters, "Kneel now, beasts!"

Every shifter dropped to his knees, even those who fought the action. The Power Baron had forced them down against their will. They all bowed their heads.

Gan still stood.

Robert gave him an odd look. "Did ya no hear me? Perhaps ya need a personal order."

Gan cast a glance at the shifters and said, "Kneel to a weak man and you will never stand again."

Half the shifters lifted their heads, eyeing him with disbelief.

Robert unleashed the full force of his earlier order. "Gan the tiger shifter, ya will kneel now and do as I say from here forth!"

Gan struggled against the power that wrapped him, determined not to lose this battle. His muscles ached and his bones felt driven into the ground, but only for thirty seconds.

Then the power slid away.

The fact that Gan remained standing had Robert more perplexed than angry now.

He had made a major power move and failed, but Gan saw what the man could do if he intended to kill someone. If Robert had not wanted to keep Gan alive to find Scarlett or use Gan to trick her into showing up, he would be dead.

Without hesitation, Robert pointed at two cat shifters and ordered, "You two. Change into yar animals and attack this tiger shifter!"

Gan turned in time to face a jaguar and a panther coming at him. His tiger shouted for him to shift.

There was not enough time.

The cats would maul him in mid-shift.

Two wolves hit the cats before they reached Gan.

Instead of fighting the wolves tearing into them, the cats tried to break loose and continue going for Gan. They couldn't disobey Robert's order even to save their lives.

The wolves took advantage of the compelled cats, ripping them apart.

As the cats fell to the ground where blood flowed freely, Robert focused on the golden wolf Gan knew as Jazlyn. Gan shook his head at her and cocked it to the side in a *get out of here* motion.

She ignored him and snarled at Robert.

Adrian's big red wolf hadn't stopped making demonic guttural sounds. This probably looked like playtime for that messed-up animal.

While he had those two watching his back and keeping Robert busy, Gan called forth his tiger that had been waiting at the edge.

It hadn't been as fast as before, but not slow either. Now standing on four legs, he and Gemelo had more killing power than he'd had as a human.

Yes, his tiger agreed. *This is how we win.*

Hearing his tiger say "we" stunned Gan.

Gemelo said, *We fight together to protect mate.*

Yes, Gan confirmed, reinforcing that they would work as a team.

They might just survive if Robert didn't hit them with magic they couldn't handle. Gan didn't know how he'd refused Robert's orders, but he had a feeling it might be connected to the mark Scarlett had given him.

At the moment, Robert seemed to struggle with his thoughts.

But not for long.

He pointed at the group of cats still kneeling. "You first six cat shifters, stand and attack these wolves and the tiger."

This time, Robert didn't give specific targets. That provided the cat shifters a better chance to win the battle because of not being directed at only one target.

Three of them jumped his tiger.

Howls and snarling mixed with claws and fangs, ripping through fur and muscle.

Gemelo knocked the first one down and hammered a paw at the cat's head over and over until it cracked open.

Jazlyn fought her mountain lion to the ground and turned on one of two jaguars attacking Red Wolf.

Adrian's wolf spun and twisted to knock a jaguar off that had been clawing his back. He pinned the animal and ripped the throat open.

Cats screeched in agony.

Gan's tiger clashed with a cheetah that moved like a strike of lightning. That cheetah kept up the fast strikes and jumping back out of Gemelo's strike zone when his tiger slashed a big paw full of claws at it. He could feel his tiger tiring from all the shifts and battling.

Adrian's wolf jumped around and banged into Jazlyn who had just torn a leg off the jaguar she'd been fighting. The beaten cat lay in a heap taking its last breaths.

Adrian and Jazlyn's wolves turned on the panther clawing Gan's tiger's hind legs.

With the panther distracted trying to survive two wolves, Gemelo caught the cheetah on his next strike, lunging as the smaller cat leaped away. Gemelo slammed the cheetah's smaller body to the ground. His tiger used his mighty weight to crush the cat's chest as his jaws ripped out the throat.

His tiger's back legs burned and his back felt no better, but he praised his animal. *You are best tiger in world.*

No words came back, but he sensed how proud and happy that made Gemelo.

With half-dead cats scattered across the ground amidst pieces of the ones no longer breathing, Gan called to Adrian telepathically. *You must leave. Take Jazlyn with you. That man is something called Power Baron. You saw. He can control your body.*

Adrian sent back, *Are you fucking kidding me? A Power Baron. That's like the worst enemy of our kind in the world.*

I do not joke, Gan shouted. *Hurry. Leave before worst enemy puts spell on you.*

I'm not leaving you, Gan.

You will not stop him, wolf. Find Guardian.

Adrian said, *Damn. I hate to abandon you, but you're right. We need the Guardian to deal with this guy.*

Before Adrian took a step to move, Robert lifted his hands and shouted, "Wolves return to human form."

His power worked on Adrian and Jazlyn, who both made painful noises as their bodies changed so quickly.

Now in human form, Adrian sent Gan a worried glance that said he was convinced.

Too late.

Smiling now that he had control again, Robert asked Jazlyn, "What's your name?"

She stood up. "Bite. Me. Capital B. Capital M."

Robert ordered, "Kneel, bitch."

Her knees hit the ground. She snarled and wrenched, trying to free herself.

Adrian took one look and must have figured he would be next. That meant he had no chance of escaping. He rushed Robert, shifting as he went.

The minute his wolf appeared fully formed in mid-leap, the Power Baron ordered, "Sit."

Having gone airborne, Adrian dropped in mid-flight and landed hard. He struggled to sit up. His wolf whined.

Gan had never heard that sound from the red wolf.

He told his tiger, *I know will hurt and sorry to ask. I need human body to help friends.*

Gemelo only groaned, but allowed Gan to make the change and stand on two feet again. The pain of shifting so often had taken a toll. He did not know if he could do this again any time soon.

"*I'm here! Stop!*"

Gan looked over in horror as Scarlett came running into all of this. He bellowed, "*No! Leave!*"

She slowed, catching her breath. When she looked up, her eyes held an apology. "Did you think I would not come for you?"

"Go. Please," Gan begged. "He is bad."

"I know." Shifting her gaze to the Power Baron, she said, "Hello, Father."

CHAPTER 31

———

"HELLO, ISLEEN," THE POWER BARON replied. That bastard gloated.

Hearing his voice ran chills up Scarlett's spine. She still couldn't believe she'd allowed this to happen. She had guessed at what Gan had done when her phone went missing. The minute she borrowed a phone from the motel manager and Zink confirmed he'd dropped Gan near Lincoln's property, she hung up, racing to find her tiger shifter.

She could feel Gan and Adrian's eyes on her back and picked up emotions from both men.

She'd stunned Gan, but Adrian's fury boiled off him.

Jazlyn knew of Scarlett's heritage, but even Jazlyn had not known her real name.

The sickening scent of fresh blood and dying animals nauseated her. She should expect no less from her father and Lincoln. Speaking of which, where was that miserable tiger shifter?

It didn't matter.

She needed to get Gan and her friends out of here. Even the angry red wolf who no doubt saw her as nothing more than the spawn of a Power Baron.

She lifted her voice. "Let them go and I will stay."

"*No!*" Gan shouted.

She took one look and knew he could not hold his tiger even though he'd just shifted, which should slow down making another change so quickly. His claws broke through his fingers. His jaw widened.

She pleaded, "Don't shift, please, Gan."

"Leave or tiger will not stop." He visibly struggled to hold his human form.

"Do shut up," Robert said to no one in particular.

Chica spoke in a trembling voice. *He is bad. Scent is sick. You promised we never see him again.*

Scarlett hated to drag her cougar into this, but Chica had been just as determined to save their mate. *I'm sorry, Chica. I wish you were not with me.*

I would not leave you now if I could. You need me.

Scarlett swallowed a lump of emotion. *You're right. I have always needed you. I will protect you from him as much as I can.*

Her father started negotiating. "I need more than words spoken in haste, Isleen. I need your vow. You up and ran before ya could be fully bound with our family. Our word to each other is bindin'."

She hated hearing that Scottish burr. "You're surprised I ran?" Scarlett realized she had one chance to let Gan know that she was not like her father. That she'd kept her identity and background a secret to avoid what was happening right now.

She didn't want him to think she had played him.

Raising her voice, she said the words she'd yelled at her father silently for years.

"I may share your blood, but you were never my father. Not a real father. For that, I thank you, because otherwise I might not have realized just how hideous you were until I was about to turn eighteen. You told my mother her part was done, that it was time to take possession of what you'd created. I had been nothing more than a biological experiment."

"Enough, Isleen. Time to give me yar word and we can leave."

"No. You want my vow? Then I want the truth known."

"Who be carin'?" Robert asked with amusement.

She looked to Gan. "I care. I have carried this secret my entire life to protect those I love."

A tear ran down Gan's proud cheek. He shook his head, still begging her not to give in to Robert.

"I will indulge ya this one time, Isleen, then ya will no speak these words again." One of the cat shifters snarled. Robert snapped his fingers. "Silence ya disgustin' animal while my daughter is speakin'."

She hated to be called his daughter, but Gan deserved the truth, all of it. She held his gaze. "My mother came clean and told me the truth and that Robert would return to take me, because he could not compel me until I came into my powers. He needed that connection to first bind me to his blood. Fayth had the good fortune to not carry his blood. I always thought my mother was a doormat, always cowering to Robert, never taking a new boyfriend who could be our father. I didn't realize yet that he had killed Fayth's father and placed spells around the house to prevent anyone visiting. I thought other people sensed we were odd and avoided us."

While she talked, Scarlett took slow steps as if needing the motion to get her thoughts out when in truth, she had a destination.

Poor Fayth had grown up so reclusive and afraid of her own shadow. When she ran with Scarlett then found a man she fell in love with, Scarlett had been glad to see her sister live with a small group of wolves in a remote area. All Fayth had ever wanted was a family, but she couldn't get pregnant.

If her father ever found out about Fayth's baby being a cougar shifter, a child of Scarlett's blood, he'd take the child.

Scarlett would die to stop him from ever touching that baby.

She continued to move three steps one way, turn, and four steps the other way as she spoke. She might appear to go in no particular direction, but she gradually angled closer to Gan. "After Robert killed the wolf who got my mother pregnant with Fayth, she feared he would take Fayth, too, just to control me. That's when our mother told us to run."

Her father quirked an eyebrow, questioning her words. "She could no do that."

"It's true. Her tongue thickened and she struggled to breathe, but got the words out. Evidently a mother's love is stronger than whatever spell you placed on her many years back." She smiled at his consternation. "I knew when I first met you at twelve that you were evil. I just did not know why. I took the head start she gave us and ran with Fayth. I never wanted to be a monster like you."

He scoffed. "Doona be tellin' me ya havena used those powers, daughter. Ya couldna have gone all this time without tappin' 'em. 'Tis in our blood to harness our power, and it only grows stronger by wieldin' the energy. So doona sound so high and mighty. Fayth woulda been better off with me, too."

Scarlett's erratic pacing brought her to stand in front of Gan.

He whispered, "Do not do this. I have no freedom. Do not give up yours."

She squeezed her eyes shut to stem the tears. She would not give her father that satisfaction.

Power boiled inside her. She struggled to not lash out. The energy she'd kept hidden for so long behaved much like Chica, churning to tear out of her and attack Robert.

That might be due to Chica.

Her power from Robert and her shifter gifts could have joined over all this time.

The minute she gave her vow, she would never be free of her father. If she didn't, Fayth would always be on the run.

She only hoped Adrian heard her truth and that the Guardian had listened to her words so he would not send Gan to live alone in Wyoming.

"I will make you wish you had never done this, Teàrlach," she said, using his real name. She might never get a chance to do that again.

"I will make ya regret having spoken so foolishly, daughter," Robert warned in a quiet voice that promised retribution.

He could try to drag her away, but he had no idea of her power until he bound her. He would not make a move that important and risk failure.

Her mother had said to never speak his name or he would find her. She also said using his true name would boost anything said against him.

Scarlett wanted to fist pump over that strike, but didn't. "Once I had Fayth in a safe place, I returned for mother, but you showed up sooner than she expected. I felt a punch of pain in my gut a quarter mile out. The smell of her death hit me a block from the house."

"I find that arrivin' early allows me to catch people tryin' to betray me," he quipped.

"You didn't have to kill her!"

"Ah, Isleen, that's past history. I didna come here to celebrate old times, but to plan for the future. I've indulged ya to have yar say. 'Tis time to leave this disgustin' mess. Be ya ready to speak yar vow or … will I be needin' to inspire ya to make the right decision?"

He threatened harming Gan to get her compliance.

Gan whispered, "Use magic on him. Run."

She wouldn't take that risk and have him lash out at everyone here.

If Robert had been sure his magic would work on her, he'd have used it by now, but wielding power unsuccessfully in the world of preternaturals would be a mistake.

She hoped she would be able to hold her own around him once she entered his world. If she thought about what she was about to do too much, she'd lose her nerve. He terrified her.

It wasn't as if she hadn't known what to expect by coming here, but all she'd thought about was getting to Gan before something bad happened to him.

Something worse than getting involved with a woman who had deceived him.

He'd called her his mate.

She claimed him as hers.

Now was the time to stand up and protect her tiger shifter, to prove to him she had kept the truth from him only to shield the man who held her heart from harm.

Taking a deep breath, she accepted her only choice, but she had to get the words right.

She spoke clearly. "If you, Teàrlach, allow the two wolf shifters and this tiger shifter present to leave safely, and agree to never harm any of them in the future, plus agree to never harm, contact, or hunt for Fayth or her family in any way in the future, and agree that all the other shifters present will be unbound upon your leaving, you have my word I will go with you voluntarily. Do you agree?"

Gan grabbed her shoulders. "No. No. No."

She put a hand over his and felt his love pour through her. She whispered, "I'm sorry for all of this."

Robert scratched his chin. "I really wanted that tiger shifter, but ya are the prize. I, Teàrlach, agree to yar terms."

Gan made a painful sound followed by his body distorting and changing. He groaned, "No," but it was lost in his transformation to tiger.

She stepped aside and would do more harm by trying to stop Gan's shift. But she had to wrap this up while she had the Power

Baron ready to contain his deadly hands. She could feel his power rolling around him in a protective veil, pushing out against her.

Reality smacked her between the eyes.

After spending a lifetime hiding from this man, she had just consigned her soul to the devil.

She would do it again to keep Gan safe.

His tiger roared and snarled.

Lifting a hand, she implored, "Please don't, Gemelo. Keep Gan safe for me. I love you both more than you'll ever know. Chica loves you, too."

Fury raged in the tiger's eyes.

He growled and slapped a big paw on the ground.

Teàrlach called out, "'Tis time to start yar trainin' now, Isleen. You shall learn the penalty for defyin' me."

She turned in shock. "What?"

As Teàrlach raised a finger to point at her, Gan's tiger blasted past her and leaped at him.

That dangerous finger moved to the tiger. Teàrlach called out a command.

Gan's tiger kept going.

Teàrlach repeated his command, but added more umph this time.

Gan's tiger slowed and stopped in midair right in front of Teàrlach who reached up and grabbed the animal's throat. "You shall obey me now!"

Scarlett moved the second Gan's tiger blew past her. She jumped on his back, gripped each side of his massive shoulders, and pushed energy into the animal's body.

Her hands heated when her power pulsed, joining with his.

His tiger screamed, unable to get away from Teàrlach.

Scarlett called up Chica to help the tiger. Chica's energy wound up in a frantic rush and flowed through Scarlett's fingers in a wave of soothing magic.

She'd always known her cougar had her own gifts.

In the next seconds, Gan's tiger dropped to the ground, standing on all fours. He shook his head as if trying to get his bearings.

She slid off his back, but kept fingers gripped in his coat, allowing her energy to surge to him and take what he sent back.

Teàrlach sidestepped away.

His eyes turned amphibian with dark elongated irises in pools of yellow. "Ya dare defy me?"

"Stop hurting my tiger and I won't defy you. You gave your word and broke it." Scarlett relaxed her hand in the thick coat, feeling the warmth. Gan's tiger angled in front of her and began forcing her back a step at a time, nudging her away from her father.

"I did no break my word. He attacked me and he still lives," Teàrlach complained. "Ya broke yar word … but you still stand."

"You didn't include attacking you first in the fine print." She felt the tug when Gan drew energy from her again.

He shifted quickly, but she could tell he was not as strong. Too many shifts and attacks had weakened him.

Still, Gan pushed to his feet. He shouted at Teàrlach, but his words were for Scarlett. "He can*not* have you. You are my mate."

That got Teàrlach's attention. "Mate? Have ya no respect for the power? Ah, Isleen, ya have made a grave error."

She hated that name. Her mother had told her that Robert would bind her to him with what he considered Scarlett's true name. To never use it and risk him tracking her that way.

But Scarlett had given her word to this mad man.

Smiling through tears, she said, "I can't change what I've said, Gan."

"I will stop him."

She whispered, "He will kill you now that he has me if I do not keep my word."

His words were a mere whisper and filled with love. "Then run when I fight. Please live."

Gan didn't understand every word sometimes. He didn't realize she held more than his life in her hand. She would keep her vow if she bargained only for him, but she held all the lives present, and Fayth's, in her hands as well.

Her father would make them suffer slowly in front of her.

Teàrlach shook his head and made a disgusted sound. "Yar no worth the effort of givin' my precious seed for. I'm glad yar no the only one I bred."

Her stomach dropped. There were more like her that he could use?

Teàrlach now sounded as if he would intentionally break their deal. Wouldn't that have a backlash on him?

She'd made a grave mistake all right. She'd failed to gain his word not to kill her.

She should have realized negotiating with the monster she called father meant he'd have a trick card up his sleeve to protect him from a broken agreement.

"So now you're not proud of your creation?" she taunted, but only to buy time for some way to stop him. "Did you expect me to be spineless? To just stand by as you hurt someone I love?"

"Love?" Teàrlach laughed with gusto. "I had no idea ya would turn out so damaged. Our kind doesna love. We rule. Yar not worthy of my blood." Casting a look across everyone, he declared, "No one who observed this will live to tell about it."

Oh, shit.

Chica said, *He fears you. Your power is stronger.*

Scarlett said, *I can't bet everyone's life on attacking him.*

Teàrlach shouted, "You have poisoned blood, daughter. You have joined with a lowly animal. For that, you forfeit all you protect and your life." He lifted his hands in Gan and Scarlett's direction.

She dove in front of Gan, who grabbed her in his arms and swung her around.

He dropped her when Teàrlach's magic struck his back.

In one second, the powerful hit lit up Gan's body in a blue glow as if he had been hit by a live power line. His teeth chattered. His muscles expanded. Veins stuck out at his throat and along his arms. His eyes rolled up.

She screamed and grabbed for Gan. Power flooded her. Chica yelled to save them. Scarlett forced her energy to him, unsure if she could actually do it again.

He groaned.

Her heart thundered. He'd live.

She eased him to the ground then swung around to find her father studying Gan as if shocked his strike had not killed at least one of them.

"You monster!" She took a step toward him.

Robert's gaze jerked to her. He snarled out words full of power and slapped a hand at her.

The hit knocked her off her feet and had her seeing her life race before her eyes. She sucked in a gulp of air and made a hoarse sound of agony.

She would not stop.

He would not stop her.

He hit her again.

She screamed. Energy crackled close to her ear and sizzled across her scalp. She struggled to her feet.

The demented Power Baron lowered his hands, looking a little spent as if he'd emptied the majority of his accessible power, or his manna, on them.

Standing once more, she narrowed her gaze and flexed her hands where claws shot out.

Behind her, Gan scuffled around, hissing in pain. Then his arms came around her. He latched his big hands on her arms and said, "We fight as one. With our animals."

Energy sizzled through her, shooting down her arms and into her hands that glowed blue.

If they were going to die, they would die together.

With Gan's solid weight behind her, she lifted her arms so loaded with energy they hurt. Before starting forward, she told Gan, "Time to kick ass and take names."

Teàrlach stared with a slack jaw. "Ya should be dead."

"Is that a problem?" Scarlett balled energy in her hands and sent it barreling at Teàrlach.

He stumbled back, throwing a hand to the ground to keep from falling flat on his ass, then stood up.

She'd expected a little more damage.

Eyes now black orbs, Teàrlach spewed a new verbal attack. "All shifters, stand up and kill Gan and Isleen."

Gan's heart thumped wildly at her back. He hugged her hard. "You are my love. Gemelo and I protect you."

Her heart cried out to save him. "We fight together to the end." She caught her breath. "I love you more than you'll ever know."

Chica sounded worried. *Too many … but we are strong.*

Scarlett prepared to stand with her mate and their animals.

Shifters howled and screamed, bursting into action as their bodies were freed.

CHAPTER 32

—

TIME SLOWED UNTIL EVERY SOUND of Gan's impending
death came to Scarlett in vivid clarity.

The wind high above her whistled in a strange way. Gan's
heartbeats thumped like war drums. The rabid sounds of shifters
scrambling to attack her and Gan.

Through it all, Gan held her surrounded in his love, determined
to protect her to the end.

Energy like she'd never felt began building. She opened herself
up wide, calling for more, and the power answered. Gan clutched
her to him, trying to surround her with his body and his power
surged.

As the world spun back into focus and the thunder of animals
headed their way, she felt an ocean of energy flood her.

Robert would laugh his last laugh.

A dark brown missile shot down from the sky and slammed
Teàrlach against the wall.

A mega-burst of power swept out across the chaos.

Scarlett and Gan were blasted off their feet.

He hit the ground and rolled, holding her tight. Energy burst
from her, zapping the grass and popping trees.

A blade of silence slashed through the frantic sounds.

She heard a mechanical whumping noise for just a second then
it disappeared.

She pushed up, wheezing breath after breath.

All around them shifters were frozen in different positions, but
every set of claws and fangs were pointed at the spot where Gan
and Scarlett had been standing.

Even Jaz and Adrian had been about to jump them.

The massive eagle blistered through the opening, made a hard bank, and returned, landing between them and her father.

Pushing hair off her face, she said, "Great time for air support, even if your boss sounds like a helicopter." She took in the mass attack put on pause. "Did Teàrlach do that to the shifters?"

Gan got up and brought her with him. "No. Guardian is reason shifters stuck. They are safe." He grimaced with each move. His back, still covered with claw marks, had not healed completely.

"Good." Scarlett had one thing on her mind. "I'm ending this." She had just lived through the most terrifying moment of her life and was done enduring years in constant fear of being found.

Teàrlach had found her and she would finish him.

She saw only one way to destroy the deal she'd agreed to and ensure that Power Baron would never harm anyone again. The job fell to her alone.

Standing, she started for Teàrlach who had crumpled by the wall, still shaking off the hit he'd taken.

She lifted her hands, calling up her energy. She'd burned a lot of manna with that explosion, but he'd burned more with his last hit. Forcing steel into her voice, she informed him, "You will not hurt anyone I love again, Teàrlach the Scottish Terror."

Gan caught her around the waist, holding her in place. "I want to kill, too, but this is not good. The Guardian will not understand."

In a flush of energy, the eagle changed into a striking male who appeared to be in his forties with a dash of silver at his temples. She had never seen him in anything but suits. He wore a deep-blue one with a white shirt today.

He always had clothes on when she'd witness his shifting into human form, another testament to the extraordinary power of the Gallize Guardian.

She'd seen those eagle eyes in his human face, so they no longer disturbed her.

She struggled against Gan. "Let me go."

The Guardian's robust voice softened. "Do not kill him and stain your soul, Scarlett."

"No." She slapped at Gan's arms. "Put me down. He is mine to destroy. I have to stop him." She shook with the need to kill.

"Please, Scarlett," Gan begged. "Let Guardian help."

"He can't. Teàrlach holds too many lives in his hands. He will never stop coming for me and the people I love. He's weak now. I can do this."

The eagle shifter said, "He will harm no one again. I give you my word."

Teàrlach lifted a cocky eyebrow at that and chuckled. "Fools." His smug gaze went to Scarlett. "Ya think to kill me, daughter? Strike me now and ya shall learn yar last lesson."

She stilled, realizing her vow remained intact. "I made a deal that I'm bound by, Guardian."

"Maybe not."

The Guardian didn't understand. He had not been present when she made a pact. "I gave my word. The word of our blood is binding." She would not say the word of her family. That monster had never been family.

The eagle shifter listened with a thoughtful expression. "Have you gone through the ceremony of being brought inside his power circle and bonded to his blood?"

"Don't listen to that eagle shifter," Teàrlach warned, but her father was not backing his words with actions.

Was he bluffing?

Gan pulled her around in his arms. "Please trust Guardian's word. Power Baron does not have honor."

She saw all she'd ever wanted in those blue eyes. Her heart had climbed into her throat. "If he doesn't die, none of us will be free."

"Wait for Guardian to talk."

Gan's boss tilted his head at the tiger shifter for the comment of support, then the fierce gaze she'd seen before in those deadly eagle eyes when his shifters were in danger returned.

Robert curled up his lip and snarled. "I be done with all of ya." He raised his hands and pushed out power.

She twisted out of Gan's arms and raised her hands to block his strike with her power. When it came, she hardly felt his energy.

The Guardian didn't so much as twitch in reaction.

She'd been right about Teàrlach's power waning.

Lifting her hands, she stared at them.

If not for Gan and his boss, she would have destroyed her soul for this mad man. She'd carried fear and hate because of Teàrlach for so long she'd been ready to sacrifice the woman she'd become just to wipe him out of her life.

Her hands trembled at that realization.

To have killed her father when he could not defend himself would have been murder, putting her in the same category with him, a place she never wanted to be. She would have lost the woman she'd created to prove her genetics wrong.

Exhaling relief, she gripped Gan's forearm that wrapped her waist, letting him know she was so thankful he'd had her back. But where did she go from here with Teàrlach still in power?

The eagle shifter commented, "It appears you have used all your manna for the moment, Teàrlach. You shall no longer terrify this woman."

Scarlett wished it could be as simple as Gan's boss making a declaration. "I do trust you, Guardian, but I still fear him going after those I love unless you can make him change our deal."

Gan spoke up, urging his boss, "Yes, change deal. I go with him if he frees Scarlett and her people."

"No, Gan." She grabbed his face. "You have no idea what he would do with you."

"If you are safe, I accept."

"I'm not giving up Gan," she made clear to him and every set of ears listening.

"Stop ya blatherin'. Changing our deal is no gonna happen," Teàrlach said defiantly. "It stands as is. You leave with me now and I will let them live."

"Actually, it will not be necessary to alter any previous agreement," the Guardian countered.

Gan hugged her and started to speak again, but the Guardian said, "Silence please."

She turned in Gan's arms to face his boss in a show of respect for the eagle shifter.

Sighing as if needing a rest after all his hard work, Teàrlach ordered, "Come now, Isleen. Ya shall regret wastin' my time."

"I am not Isleen. I am Scarlett." That name settled into her bones. Speaking it out loud made it so. She no longer felt fragmented by her past. She. Was. Scarlett.

Addressing Teàrlach, the Guardian said, "You and I would not have met had you stayed away from what is mine."

Scarlett wasn't covered by that statement meant for Gan and

Adrian, but she'd take any residual help.

"Isleen is mine," her father bellowed. "Yar makin' a deadly mistake to be interferin'. My power regenerates as I stand here. I will no allow this circus to happen again."

"There will be no next time, Teàrlach."

"Oh, eagle eyes? Who is gonna be stoppin' me? No a shifter."

The Guardian didn't acknowledge or deny that his power could take down Teàrlach. Instead he said, "You are not my responsibility. Your actions are answerable to the Power Council."

All signs of cockiness vanished. "I warn you against threatenin' me with involvin' them." Teàrlach's demeanor changed again, exposing just what an egomaniac he was when he began talking to himself. "What am I sayin'? The council will no listen' to you. No Power Baron is foolish enough to draw my ire. Many know I hold more magic than any of that bunch. Soon, I shall rule the Power Council."

"Your warning to not reach out to them is too late," the Guardian said.

Three male images shimmered into view around Teàrlach. They took corporal form and energy pulsed out from them as if in warning. Each stood at least seven feet tall and wore long gray robes, but they all had white hair and beards, looking older than dirt. The more Scarlett thought about it, the men had appeared as if an invisible cloaking had dropped rather than being teleported. She also sensed this was not their real identities, but the way they'd expect others to see them.

Gan whispered, "Who are they?"

In reply, the Guardian announced, "My appreciation to the elders of the Power Council for their prompt attention to this flagrant disregard for the laws of this land and mistreatment of preternatural beings. I stand witness to the crimes Teàrlach has committed as well as the threat of treason against his own council."

Teàrlach stood perfectly still as if those words had sucked the life from him, then he started rambling. "Liar. These be shifters, lowest of humanity. Ya canna believe them, Seamus. Their word does no stand in our court."

All three Power Barons representing the council had long white beards, but this one spoke slowly in a deep tone. "The three of us were witness to your treasonous words."

Scarlett's heart leaped at the oh-shit look in Teàrlach's face. It sounded as if Seamus and his elder buddies would hold Teàrlach accountable for a transgression against the council they considered worse than any crime against a shifter or human.

But of course, Power Barons were more important than mere shifters.

Whatever. She just hoped he paid a penalty that would send him away and stop him from continuing to threaten her.

"Ya canna do this," Teàrlach shouted. "Ya shouldna even be speakin' to me this way before others. Ya—"

All three elders lifted a single hand and pointed at Teàrlach who saw the move and jerked up his weaponized digits to attack.

His fingers curled into his hands and melded together into two clubs of flesh at the ends of his arms. His lips clamped shut and blended until he had no mouth.

Panic rocked his eyes. His arms pinned to his sides.

In the next moment, he slowly vanished as did the three elders.

Gan asked, "Where did they go?"

The Guardian turned to him. "The Power Barons are rarely seen in public. They prefer anonymity and the elders may have all appeared ancient, but those were not their real faces. They have taken Teàrlach with them to face consequences for his actions."

A whump, whump, whump sounded in the distance, interrupting conversation.

The Guardian explained, "That would be a helicopter also cloaked from view."

"What will happen?" Gan asked. "Will bad baron escape?"

"From them? No." The Guardian left zero doubt. "While that council will ignore smaller infractions, they will never tolerate any threat to their power. I feel confident we shall not see him again, because they punish their own for eternity."

Forever? Scarlett's shoulders relaxed with the release of so much weight she'd carried for years.

Gan glanced past the Guardian. "Adrian not happy stuck in air."

Putting a hand on his forehead, the Guardian muttered, "I forgot the shifters were behind us with the greater threat in front." Without turning around, he waved a hand over his shoulder.

Every shifter finished leaping or running a few steps then

stopped and looked around.

When the Guardian spoke, his words reached out in all directions. "You may shift back to your human shape or leave in your animal form, but you will not attack any shifter present."

Scarlett pulled his attention back to her. "Thank you for coming after I called. I know you aren't happy with me—"

Gan broke in. "Was not her fault. I stole phone and left. She came to save everyone." He moved his shoulder closer to hers.

She noticed he had a T-shirt and jeans on. That's right. The Guardian clothed his shifters when they were naked after shifting. What kind of power did it take to do that?

Gan's boss said, "I had hoped to locate you two before we received the alert of Gan and Adrian being in danger. We were very close. While we do not have your ground resources, Scarlett, we can locate a person or vehicle eventually if I put everyone in one region on a single search."

Scarlett cringed a little. Hunting her and Gan had shut down the Gallize operations probably across six to eight states.

Eagle man quieted for a few moments as he studied her. He crossed his arms and propped an elbow then rested his chin on his fist. "I have felt a great deal of power from you, Scarlett, since our first meeting."

He had? She said, "Okay, but I haven't used it to hurt anyone."

Sticking his head forward, Gan said, "She use power to help me."

She wanted to smack him. "Wrong move, Gan. Now he's going to think I'm trying to control you."

Adrian strode up, also dressed. "You mean what you did at the lake house?"

"You saw that?" Scarlett said before she realized it was a duh moment. Of course Adrian witnessed her use of power.

"What did you do?" the Guardian asked.

Gan would not shut up. "She see me struggle and give me little push to stay human. She did this for good reason. But I am changing better now. I talk to tiger. He talks to me."

Eyebrows raised on both the Guardian and Adrian.

Scarlett said, "Really? That's great. You two are going to be awesome."

"Yes. He is happy with name Chica give him."

The Guardian's gaze bounced from Gan to Scarlett, back and forth.

"Ahh, Chica was so happy when I told her," Scarlett said.

Adrian pushed in. "Wait. Who is Chica?"

"My cougar."

"She likes Gan's tiger?"

Gan frowned at Adrian. "Yes. Chica is nice to Gemelo. He is nice to her. If they could talk without us sharing words, he would listen to her."

"If you two bond, your animals *can* talk to each other," Adrian pointed out.

"Really?" Scarlett said.

Gan grinned. "Yes. Is good."

The Guardian asked, "Do you believe you can bond, Gan?"

He put his arm around Scarlett again. "Yes. She is mate. Our mate."

Scarlett waited for the eagle man to inform Gan he could not be with someone who carried Power Baron blood. Whatever these Gallize were, they came from better stock than hers.

"Have you accepted an offer as his mate?" Adrian asked Scarlett.

"No."

Gan's face fell.

She laughed at him. "I picked you first. You didn't ask."

"No, I pick first," Gan boasted.

"I don't think so, wild man."

Holding up a hand for silence, the Guardian told Gan, "You must be careful in selecting a mate—"

Gan must have thought his boss was dissing her. "She is good mate. She is best mate. She is only mate I want."

Adrian said, "Just so you know, boss, the cat shifters have left so we can speak freely."

Sighing, the Guardian said, "I hope to one day instill manners in my shifters. When that happens I might be able to finish a thought."

Adrian gave Gan a zipped mouth motion.

Gan frowned, appearing perplexed.

Scarlett hooked an arm around his waist and he smiled again.

"As I was saying," eagle man continued, "our shifters are

powerful and must be careful not to bond with someone who might be harmed by their power. Scarlett has proven she is quite capable of accepting the level of energy generated during bonding." He asked her, "Do you have an older sibling, because Gallize females with great power are always the second born?"

He gave her an opening to be considered one of them, but she would not lie even if she could pull it off. "Nope. I'm the first child. My power is from that jerk they dragged away. If that's a deal breaker, I can't fix it."

Nodding, the Guardian continued. "That is not a deal breaker, as you put it. Your integrity does not come from who fathered you, but from inside."

She made a small gasp. Was he saying she would be acceptable as a mate for Gan? Her skin tingled at the hope of keeping Gan.

His boss explained, "There is one important question, though. Do you and Gan both understand what bonding with a Gallize means?"

Gan opened his mouth then shut it.

She had no idea what to say.

Adrian must have taken pity on them. He said, "You both have to accept your responsibility as a Gallize, because every decision you make affects all of us and our mates." He muttered, "For those who have mates."

Facing the Guardian, Gan said, "I can do only if tiger is free. Not in Wyoming."

When Gan finished, the Guardian turned to Scarlett. "As you heard from Adrian, we are one large family. Everyone in our circle watches over the others. They will watch over you and yours. You would have to be willing to become more than a friend of the Gallize."

Her heart raced at how close she stood to true happiness, but she needed more. "I didn't hear a reply to Gan's wish to be free. If we do mate, I will be there for Gan to develop his relationship with his tiger, but I will expect everyone to give him some leeway to learn."

"Good grief, Scarlett. That's what we do," Adrian groused.

Gan smacked his arm. "Talk nice to mate."

She laughed. Evidently in Gan's mind they were mated regardless of whatever Gallize ceremony happened. The Guardian's smile seemed to echo her thoughts. She had one more concern.

"If I do this, you said you and yours would be safe. I need my little sister Fayth and her baby to be included."

"Yes." Gan nodded. "Need place for her and Spud."

Adrian murmured, "Spud?"

"The baby," Scarlett answered.

The Guardian gave them both a curious look. "Am I correct in assuming you have not asked each other to be a mate? Because I would have felt your joined power if you had bonded, plus your animals are not communicating directly yet, correct?"

"Right," Scarlett said.

Gan pointed out, "We have both power when fighting."

The Guardian said, "That's encouraging, Gan, but once you ask her to mate, and she accepts, your Gallize power and her energy will join forever so that you are both stronger individually."

Taking Scarlett's hand, Gan asked, "Do you want to—"

"Wait!" eagle man and Adrian shouted.

"Why? Too much talk," Gan grumbled. "Want to be with mate."

The Guardian glared him into silence. "I wish for Scarlett to speak with the other mates prior to making this important decision. She deserves to get honest input."

"How many?" Gan asked holding a hand to his head. "Are mates everywhere?"

His Guardian chuckled. "Yes, we have them in other countries, but I'm only talking about the ones in the Spartanburg area. She knows Tess, but Tess has only shared what is allowed, to those outside our circle. Now Scarlett can ask any question, plus she should meet Eli and Siofra."

"Yes. I will go with her."

"She hasn't agreed to anything yet, Gan," Adrian offered, but his attention had shifted past Gan.

Scarlett followed his gaze in time to see a golden wolf slide into the shadows. She didn't want Adrian following her friend. She rushed to keep the conversation about her and Gan going. "Yes, I have, Adrian. I officially want to meet these mates and be considered as Gan's mate."

"What?" Adrian said in a distracted voice. "Okay. That's good. Uhm, boss, I'll be back in a few."

The Guardian waved him off then finished with Gan and

Scarlett. "Please do not bond until you return to headquarters and after Scarlett speaks with the other mates." He lifted a hand. "I have no objection to her as your mate, Gan. I am very pleased about the union and even more pleased about you and your tiger bonding."

Scarlett said, "Thank you. I'm sure I won't change my mind, but we will wait. I need to check on Fayth."

"And Spud," Gan added.

"Absolutely. We'll go together to give her the good news." She raked a hand over her hair that felt atrocious. "That reminds me, I've got to find out where my friend left my truck."

"We located your truck," the Guardian explained. "We found that right before you called. My people are cleaning up the mess on that property as well as the one where scents for you, Gan, and Adrian were found as well as … a female wolf. Her scent was in your truck as well. Do you know her?"

First test as Gan's mate. She knew better than to lie. "Yes."

After a few seconds, his boss said, "But you're not volunteering it?"

"Do I have to?"

"No."

She smiled.

He added, "Not unless we have cause to find her."

Did that eagle man know about Jazlyn?

Maybe, maybe not. He could just be clueing Scarlett in to the fact that she could no longer run like a lone wolf.

Chica said, *Lone cougar. Not wolf.*

Scarlett smiled at her cat.

At the sound of trucks coming down the drive, Scarlett recognized the Hummer she'd seen a Gallize shifter named Justin driving when they saved Gan and his sister.

When the two vehicles parked, Tess's mate, Cole, climbed out of one and Vic stepped down from the driver's side of the other Hummer with one more shifter that smelled like wolf.

The eagle shifter gave them directions to begin cleanup and locating any cat shifters still around to process through the placement system.

She wondered what exactly the process would be, but that was not her job today.

"I shall return to headquarters," the Guardian announced.

She told Gan, "We're going to have to use our legs. I don't have a vehicle."

Vic said, "If you let me get a handle on this, I'll get you to your motel. I can have a truck pick you up from there."

Evidently happy with that, the Guardian gave Gan and Scarlett a stern look. "I shall expect you in headquarters in two days."

Gan nodded. "Yes."

Scarlett bumped Gan with her elbow. "Yes, *sir*."

"I say yes." He lifted his shoulders in an irritated move.

Shaking his head but with a wry smile, the Guardian shifted into his magnificent eagle and took flight.

Scarlett muttered, "I want to be him when I grow up."

Gan said, "Eagle? No. Gemelo want cougar. I want you." He wrapped her up in his arms and kissed her.

When the Gallize men drifted into the background, the sounds melded into a buzz of background noise easily ignored.

Scarlett soaked up the feel of Gan wrapped around her, happy to have him safe and a chance at a life with him. When he started nipping kisses to tease her, she laughed and pulled back, staring into crystal-blue eyes that saw into her heart.

She had to come clean. "I'm sorry."

"Why?"

"I didn't tell you about having that monster as my father. I didn't tell you why I had to get to Fayth or her child. I feel like I deceived you, but I really didn't mean to in a harmful way. I thought we would only have these few days together, then I'd never see you again. The less you knew about me, the safer you would be. I didn't want to lose anyone else to that Power Baron."

Gan brushed his hand over her face and let his gaze roam softly until his eyes met hers. "I forgive but no forgive needed. You did for family. I would do for mine."

"I'm sorry you lost everyone at birth, Gan."

"You are mate. We do what Guardian want, but you *are* my mate. I will always protect mate and baby. My life for family." He looked away with a pained expression. "I owe truth, too. I want go with you at first to escape Gallize. I feel tiger never stop killing. I had plan. Take him to cold country, live alone." He shrugged. "All before I know you are special. Before you are mate, but I did not tell truth either."

She understood what he said. He had only wanted freedom when they first met and he pushed her to take him with her.

"What about now, Gan? If the Guardian said it was okay by him, would you want to go live somewhere else in this country and roam free?"

It took all she could to ask that without panicking. She couldn't lose him now, but neither would she stop him from having all he wanted.

The smile he gifted her with took her breath. "I am free with you. Happy with you. My tiger and I understand love is you and Chica."

Her legs threatened to fold at that declaration. "I think the same thing. You are my love and so is Gemelo."

"We want to stay with you and Chica," Gan admitted. "One day, you drive us to snow country and cats play."

"That sounds like a great mating honeymoon, tiger."

Chica said, *Can I talk to Gemelo?*

Scarlett told her, *Soon. I think that will happen when we bond. Human, tiger, and human bond?*

Gan asked, "Why frown?"

"I just told Chica that she could talk to Gemelo when we bond. She asked if the shadow person or ghost that stays with Gemelo would bond with us. We should figure out who that person is."

"Ask more."

Didn't he think Chica would have said if she knew who it was, but Scarlett figured out what he said. Gan wanted Chica to explain what this person looked like.

When she questioned her cat again, Chica said, *Like human.*

Now Scarlett had to translate Chica talk, too? She pressed her cat for more detail, *What human?*

Gemelo. Her cougar paused and added. *Gemelo human.*

Scarlett studied on Gemelo for a moment. She hadn't picked up the Spanish language except for bits and pieces when she'd been with the family where Chica had been named.

Scarlett asked, *What does the name Gemelo mean?*

Two humans.

Do you mean ... twins that look alike?

Yes.

Gemelo's shadow looks like Gan? Scarlett shouted telepathically.

Yesss. Chica could have a sassy mouth when she wanted.

Gan asked, "Chica say what ghost look like?"

Scarlett took a few seconds to arrange her thoughts. "Chica said the ghost looks like you."

He frowned and scratched his head.

She thought back over all he'd told her about losing his family. "You said your family was all killed and you lost a brother in the womb."

"Yes."

"But you also said you were captured right after birth. The baby that hadn't been born would be your twin."

"Yes. Guardian say they kill brother."

She gave him a watery smile. "That could be the ghost. Your tiger might have your brother's spirit."

Gan put his hand on his chest. "Brother?"

"Maybe. Once we mate, we'll let our cats talk. They might be able to tell us more." Her heart filled with so much love it might burst. She'd spent her entire life on the run and alone. Gan had been just as alone.

"I have you, Chica, Fayth, Spud, and Gemelo … brother." His voice was thick.

Tears streamed down her face, but she didn't care.

He smiled the biggest smiled she'd ever seen. He caught her as she leaped up to hook her arms around his neck, kissing him with fire burning in her soul.

This was life.

This was love.

This was true happiness.

He wouldn't free her lips once he had them, kissing her with so much more than passion. With all his heart had to give.

When she smiled around the kiss, he pulled back, glancing around. "Too many people. Always too many."

She cupped his neck and leaned close to his ear to whisper, "Guess what, wild man?"

"I guess. What?"

"I'm out of condoms."

He lifted her away until they were nose to nose. His blue eyes lit with mischief. "Spud need cousin."

Three words and her womb came to life. "You will be the best father."

Tears pooled in the corners of his eyes. "A family," he said in a hushed voice. "I have … family."

Then he lifted her high in the air and swung her around. He let out a tiger roar for all the world to hear and yelled, "I am free. I have *family*!"

Her heart might just burst after all.

The Gallize paused, staring at them, then started clapping and cheering. Gan had her and his Gallize family.

He pulled her back to him and kissed her gently. "I. Love. *You.* Always."

That was a vow she'd hold in her heart the rest of her life. "I love you, wild man. Forever."

CHAPTER 33

ADRIAN STRETCHED OUT IN THE Spartanburg hotel after a long hot shower and finishing off two heavy meals he'd had room service deliver. His wolf couldn't be trusted around humans who might drop a tray of glasses and set the maniac off.

He'd have caught up to that female wolf if Mad Red hadn't fought him for control. Gan told him Scarlett called the golden wolf Jaz, short for Jazlyn. What could she have done to be running from the law?

If he hadn't been in Wyoming the entire time since returning from Iraq, he might know what was going on these days. He could have mentioned her to the Guardian and gotten anything the Gallize had on her, but … she'd fought beside him.

She'd stayed at the lake house when she could have run.

He wanted to find his own answers, plus Gan had asked him not to get her in trouble because she was a friend of Scarlett's.

Adrian's code of duty came before anything, but he wouldn't add to Jazlyn's troubles for no reason. He wished he could get that sexy body and those fierce amber eyes out of his mind, too. Tough to be objective when he wanted her.

For now, she'd have to sleep on the back burner in his head.

His boss had given him a couple days downtime to allow him to find his friend.

He opened the letter and read the scrawled writing again.

Adrian

You don't know me, but I'm Tanza, Leonard's younger sister. He always talked about his days in the special Army shifter unit with you. He said if something happened to him and I ever needed someone that I could trust you.

Dropping the letter to his side, Adrian pinched his eyes, seeing Leonard's laughing face. The guy loved to prank everyone. Anything was worth a laugh. He kept the unit's spirits up and had Adrian's back more than once.

In fact, Leonard had died covering Adrian's six.

His death had been hard on the entire unit, but Adrian couldn't say to this day if Leonard had died because of a mistake. Adrian's mistake.

Too many things had been lost when he ended up captured and his wolf went insane.

Lifting the note, he kept reading until he reached the part again about her other brother, Kaiser, being murdered and the wolf that killed him escaping.

His sister spilled grief all over the pages, but he understood the need to get it out. She would never heal until the killer was brought to justice.

He and his wolf had managed over the past week helping Gan, even showing glimpses of sanity. Mad Red had his moments, but the animal couldn't be fully trusted. He would turn on Adrian in a flash, yanking control away.

Adrian read the letter again and thought through what it would take to do this mission. He asked his wolf, *Will you work with me to help me find the shifter who killed Leonard's brother?*

His wolf said, *Wolf died in battle.*

No, this was that wolf's younger brother left at home. His name was Kaiser. Someone killed him. I want to do this for Leonard. His wolf was good to us.

Yes.

One thing about Mad Red, when he made a decision, good or bad, it was final.

That was as much as Adrian could ask for.

He scanned the letter to the end where Tanza had left her phone number.

She answered on the first ring. "Yes?"

"It's Adrian."

"You got my letter." She sounded as if that fact brought her to tears. "No one will help me. The pack is a mess, because our

SCENT OF A MATE

father is shut down. He's going to lose control of the pack if we don't find who murdered Kaiser."

"I'll find the killer."

"You will?"

"Yes. Give me all the information you can."

She sniffled, then seemed to gather herself. "Thank you. This means a lot. I can give you her description."

He sat up. "Her?"

"Yes. She's got a reputation as the Golden Kodiak wolf and has a scar running down her face in human form."

Adrian's breathing stuttered.

He had a memory of a scar that appeared when rain washed off the mud and blood. He confirmed, "On the right side of her face."

"Yes. *Yes!* When you see her shift, she turns into a big golden wolf with a white star on her forehead."

He'd never forget the face of the wolf he'd fought beside.

Shit fire.

Jazlyn had killed Kaiser.

THANK YOU FOR READING MY new League of Gallize Shifters series. I hope you enjoyed this story and would appreciate a review wherever you shop for books.

If you'd like to join my Private Reader Community, visit the CONNECT page (https://authordiannalove.com/connect) on my website and join my newsletter list. I'll only send messages about new releases and special offers just for my readers, plus events. Also, I *do not* share anyone's information. I hate to have mine shared.

Also, you can order any of my books signed/personalized here: *www.DiannaLoveSignedBooks.com*

You can also preorder the next book (when it is posted) and get it shipped 2+ weeks early, signed and personalized.

ALSO BY...

New York Times **bestseller Dianna Love** delivers an all-night read with her new League of Gallize Shifter series.

Wild Wolf Mate is the next shifter romance in this series.

WILD WOLF MATE

Mad Red isn't just a nickname for Adrian's wolf, it's the truth. His teammates want to save him, but his wolf is deranged and it's Adrian's fault. While on a rescue mission overseas, he successfully extracted captives only to end up getting captured and locked in a titanium cage too small for shifting. His Gallize brothers rescued him, but nothing can save his wolf. Now, he just needs to stay alive long enough to answer the call for help from the family of a fallen soldier who Adrian also considered a brother. But to bring the shifter who killed the soldier to justice, he'll have to hunt down a woman who saved his life and put her in prison.

"The League of Gallize Shifters is definitely original in many areas ... a ground-breaking paranormal romance." ~~**Always Reviewing**

"There are shifters and then there are Gallize shifters."
~~ **In My Humble Opinion**

———◆———

More stand-alone Gallize shifter stories coming soon.

LEAGUE OF GALLIZE SHIFTERS
Book 1: Gray Wolf Mate
Book 2: Mating A Grizzly

Book 3: Stalking His Mate
Book 4: Scent Of A Mate
Book 5: Wild Wolf Mate

———

To contact Dianna –
email her assistant @ *authordiannalove.com*
Websites: AuthorDiannaLove.com
Facebook – "Dianna Love Fan Page"
"Dianna Love Reader Community" Facebook group page

RAVES ABOUT DIANNA'S OTHER SERIES:

BELADOR URBAN FANTASY:

"When it comes to urban fantasy, Dianna Love is a master." ~Always Reviewing.

"There is so much action in this book I feel like I've burned calories just reading it." ~D Antonio

"There are SO many things in this series that I want to learn more about; there's no way I could list them all." ~Lily, Romance Junkies Reviews

---

SLYE TEMP ROMANTIC THRILLERS:

*"...suspense, thrills, excitement, danger and a super romantic couple...**Dianna Love** writes romance suspense so well, as I consider her one of the best at creating believability and hooking us in from the start all the way to the exciting climax."* ~ Barb, The Reading Café

"Dianna never disappoints! ... would have give it a 10 if they would let!!! Very enjoyable read, can't wait for the next one :-)." ~~ Amy, Goodreads

---

DIANNA WRITES THE ***BELADOR URBAN FANTASY SERIES*** and the Slye Temp romantic thriller series (completed for those who want to binge read!). Keep watch for more Belador books and her new League of Gallize Shifters coming out soon.

Book 1: Blood Trinity
Book 2: Alterant
Book 3: The Curse
Book 4: Rise Of The Gryphon
Book 5: Demon Storm
Book 6: Witchlock
Book 7: Rogue Belador
Book 8: Dragon King Of Treoir
Book 9: Belador Cosaint
Book 10: Treoir Dragon Hoard (2018)
Tristan's Escape: A Belador Novella
Order SIGNED Print Books at **DiannaLoveSignedBooks.com**

*To keep up with all of Dianna's releases: sign up for her newsletter on her website.

The complete Slye Temp romantic suspense series
Prequel: Last Chance To Run (free for limited time)
Book 1: Nowhere Safe
Book 2: Honeymoon To Die For
Book 3: Kiss The Enemy
Book 4: Deceptive Treasures
Book 5: Stolen Vengeance
Book 6: Fatal Promise

For Young Adult Fans – the explosive sci-fi/fantasy Red Moon trilogy by *USA Today* bestseller Micah Caida (collaboration of *New York Times* Bestseller Dianna Love and *USA Today* bestseller Mary Buckham).

Book 1: Time Trap (ebook free for limited time)
Book 2: Time Return
Book 3: Time Lock

To buy books and read more excerpts, go to
http://www.MicahCaida.com

AUTHOR BIO

New York Times **Bestseller Dianna Love** once dangled over a hundred feet in the air to create unusual marketing projects for Fortune 500 companies. She now writes high-octane romantic thrillers, young adult and urban fantasy. Fans of the bestselling *Belador* urban fantasy series will be thrilled to know more books are coming after soon with the new *Treoir Dragon Chronicles.* Dianna's Slye Temp sexy romantic thriller series wrapped up with Gage and Sabrina's book–Fatal Promise–perfect for bingers! She also has the new *League of Gallize Shifters* paranormal romance series. Look for her books in print, e-book and audio.

On the rare occasions Dianna is out of her writing cave, she tours the country on her BMW motorcycle searching for new story locations. Dianna lives in the Atlanta, GA area with her husband, who is a motorcycle instructor, and a tank full of unruly saltwater critters.

———◆———

Visit her website at *www.AuthorDiannaLove.com* or *www. DiannaLoveSignedBooks.com*

A WORD FROM DIANNA...

THANK YOU FOR READING SCENT OF A MATE and to all the readers who have written wonderful notes about my new League of Gallize Shifters series. I appreciate your feedback so much! And, yes, I do have more books planned.

As always, thank you to my husband, Karl, who makes it possible for me to write my stories.

A special thank you to Judy Carney, who gets better with every book she goes through, and Stacey Krug, who jumps in super early to read pages before they're totally clean. Also, I appreciate Jennifer Cazares and Sherry Arnold for being terrific early beta readers, who catch a number of small things missed by all of us even after multiple editing passes.

I want to send a huge thank you to my Super Read-and-Review Team peeps who read early versions for review – you rock!!

Sending a shout out to Candi Fox and Leiha Mann, who work hard to support me in so many ways. Thanks to Joyce Ann McLaughlin, Kimber Mirabella and Sharon Livingston, too.

As always, the amazing Kim Killion creates all of my covers and Jennifer Litteken saves my butt time and again with great formatting just when I need it. Much appreciation to both of you.

Hugs and love to Karen Marie Moning, a wonderful and talented woman I think of as more than a friend.

Thank you to my peeps on the Dianna Love Reader Group on Facebook. I love coming out to visit with you.